"I apprecia_____ feel better. I ... sorry I woke you."

Laura shivered.

Sean caught that and said slowly, "Why don't you snuggle down and get some rest? I'll stay until you fall asleep."

Laura marveled at how easily he'd read her mind, that she dreaded being alone after a nightmare. Scooting down inside the covers, she let him arrange her pillows more comfortably. "Thank you," she whispered, and closed her eyes.

Sean lay gazing at her in the dim glow of the night-light. She was every bit as lovely as he'd said she was. And she was going through a bad time. She needed someone to help her through it. And as he settled in with his arms around her, he thought that maybe *he* was that someone.

There was that protective urge again. He hadn't felt that way in a very long time.

Maybe it was a good sign.

Dear Reader,

During the warm days of July, what better way to kick back and enjoy the best of summer reading than with six stellar stories from Special Edition as we continue to celebrate Silhouette's 20th Anniversary all year long!

With *The Pint-Sized Secret*, Sherryl Woods continues to delight her readers with another winning installment of her popular miniseries AND BABY MAKES THREE: THE DELACOURTS OF TEXAS. Reader favorite Lindsay McKenna starts her new miniseries, MORGAN'S MERCENARIES: MAVERICK HEARTS, with *Man of Passion,* her fiftieth book. A stolen identity leads to true love in Patricia Thayer's compelling *Whose Baby Is This?* And a marriage of convenience proves to be anything but in rising star Allison Leigh's *Married to a Stranger* in her MEN OF THE DOUBLE-C RANCH miniseries. Rounding off the month is celebrated author Pat Warren's *Doctor and the Debutante,* where the healthy dose of romance is just what the physician ordered, while for the heroine in Beth Henderson's *Maternal Instincts*, a baby-sitting assignment turns into a practice run for motherhood—and marriage.

Hope you enjoy this book and the other unforgettable stories Special Edition is happy to bring you this month!

All the best,

Karen Taylor Richman,
Senior Editor

Please address questions and book requests to:
Silhouette Reader Service
U.S.: 3010 Walden Ave., P.O. Box 1325, Buffalo, NY 14269
Canadian: P.O. Box 609, Fort Erie, Ont. L2A 5X3

PAT WARREN

DOCTOR AND THE DEBUTANTE

Published by Silhouette Books
America's Publisher of Contemporary Romance

This book is dedicated to Brooks Rector,
a dear friend of my husband's for years,
and now mine, too.
Happy reading!

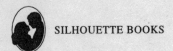 SILHOUETTE BOOKS

ISBN 0-373-24337-5

DOCTOR AND THE DEBUTANTE

Copyright © 2000 by Pat Warren

This edition published by arrangement with Harlequin Books S.A.

® and TM are trademarks of Harlequin Books S.A., used under license.
Trademarks indicated with ® are registered in the United States Patent
and Trademark Office, the Canadian Trade Marks Office and in other
countries.

Visit Silhouette at www.eHarlequin.com

Printed in U.S.A.

Books by Pat Warren

Silhouette Special Edition

With This Ring #375
Final Verdict #410
Look Homeward, Love #442
Summer Shadows #458
The Evolution of Adam #480
Build Me a Dream #514
The Long Road Home #548
The Lyon and the Lamb #582
My First Love, My Last #610
Winter Wishes #632
Till I Loved You #659
An Uncommon Love #678
Under Sunny Skies #731
That Hathaway Woman #758
Simply Unforgettable #797
This I Ask of You #815
On Her Own #841
A Bride for Hunter #893
Nobody's Child #974
*A Home for Hannah #1048
*Keeping Kate #1060
Daddy's Home #1157
Stranded on the Ranch #1199
Daddy by Surprise #1301
Doctor and the Debutante #1337

*Reunion

Silhouette Romance

Season of the Heart #553

Silhouette Intimate Moments

Perfect Strangers #288
Only the Lonely #605
*Michael's House #737
Stand-In Father #855

Silhouette Books

Montana Mavericks
Outlaw Lovers #6

PAT WARREN,

mother of four, lives in Arizona with her travel agent husband and a lazy white cat. She's a former newspaper columnist whose lifetime dream was to become a novelist. A strong romantic streak, a sense of humor and a keen interest in developing relationships led her to try romance novels, with which she feels very much at home.

Chapter One

The snow had been coming down for at least three hours, lightly at first, then more heavily. Hands in the back pockets of his corduroy slacks, Sean Reagan stood looking out the front window of his cabin in the Gray Mountains of Arizona, a frown on his face as he watched the wind hurl a mound of snow onto the porch. The temperature had undoubtedly dropped since he'd taken a walk several hours ago. It never ceased to amaze him how quickly the weather could change in winter this far north.

Then again, what difference did the weather make? Sean thought as he crossed the big open room and bent to throw another log into the fireplace. He was inside, warm and safe. And alone, at least for this second week in February, a ritual he'd begun four years ago. Fortunately Dr. Jonah Evans, his partner in their busy

OB-GYN medical practice, understood Sean's need to get away at this particular time and covered for him.

It wasn't a vacation, not really. The thing was Sean hadn't much use for people who constantly felt sorry for themselves or grieved in public. So each year, he set aside this one week where he could weep in private if that's how he felt, or rail at the fates for changing his life so radically. Alone up here, he could chop wood, take long walks, read a book and hopefully heal. Then he could go back and get on with his life. Or so the theory went.

Sean had built the cabin himself and knew it was rock solid. Some would call it rustic and remote, sitting as it was in the midst of evergreens and rocks large enough to be called boulders. There was a stream that ran along the back perimeter with water so pure and clean you could count every pebble. The evenings and early mornings he'd sat on his covered porch and listened to the birds and small wildlife scurrying about in the tall grass had been some of the happiest of his life.

But that had been then and this was now.

He'd learned the hard way that not everyone shared his pleasure in seclusion and solitude, in the simple life, in hard work and patiently moving toward a goal.

Straightening, he dusted off his hands and decided to warm some soup. But a loud crashing sound from outside had him stopping in his tracks and cocking his head to listen more closely. Was it just the wind and the storm escalating? Or could a tree limb have broken loose and fallen onto his attached garage where his Mercedes was parked? Moving to the window again, he tried to see out, but the snow was coming down thick and heavy. Reluctantly, he decided he'd better go check.

He tugged on his boots, then his sheepskin jacket, zipping it up against the swirling snow as he ventured out, pulling on his leather gloves before closing the door. The wind howled past, the snow blowing every which way. Stepping off the porch, he sank into a drift almost to his knees, making walking difficult. Squinting as he looked up along the roofline, he could see no damage to the garage. Still, something had made that noise. There were trees all around—pine and cottonwood and paloverdes—but he couldn't spot any fallen limbs.

Only late afternoon and yet it was growing dark rapidly with no sign the snow would let up anytime soon. Already he could barely make out his driveway leading to the one-lane road two miles in from the highway. Trudging out aways, trying to spot anything amiss, Sean felt a clump of cold white stuff fall beneath his collar, causing him to shiver. Suddenly he noticed some wide tracks veering off the driveway that seemed to be fresh. That was odd.

As he gazed off to the left, he saw lights glinting off something silvery coming from the hillside below. Curiosity had Sean stepping gingerly along the incline toward the light. Closer now, he could see more tracks in the snow that were definitely recent, wide tire tracks.

Through the snow-covered branches, he peered down and was able to make out a large vehicle stuck between two trees near the bottom of the gully. Smoky steam was spiraling up from beneath a crushed hood. Getting closer, he saw that it was a late model silver Bronco that had probably hit a tree, then done a complete 180, swiveling about in the slippery snow, its back end wedged in tightly, its nose pointing upward.

Hurrying over, Sean peeked in through the closest window. A woman was slumped over on her side in the front seat, her thick hair hiding her face. A fat tree limb had broken through the windshield, probably on first impact, stopping mere centimeters from her very still form. He could see no one else in the vehicle.

Medical instincts on alert, Sean knew he had to see if she was alive, to check out her injuries. He tried to open the driver's door, but it was too close to a large fir. Moving as fast as humanly possible in the deep snow, he went around to the other side where there was a little more room between the passenger side and a tall pine. But the door was locked.

Worried about the woman trapped inside, that she might be bleeding to death while he figured out how to rescue her, he looked around for any fallen branches large enough to break the side window. He could see none.

Cursing under his breath, he retraced his steps to the cabin. He'd need some tools to break a window or pry open a door. But the overhead door of the garage was blocked by mounds of windblown snow. Rushing, he entered his house and all but ran through to the connecting door to the garage. Grabbing a hammer and crowbar, he made his painstaking way back to the Bronco.

The woman hadn't moved.

It took two swings to break the passenger side window enough so he could reach in and unlock the door. Wedging the door open as far as the pine tree would allow and propping it in place with the crowbar, Sean leaned into the front seat and yanked off one glove. He brushed her hair aside and placed two fingers on her throat, searching for a pulse. At last, he felt her heartbeat, thready but definitely there. He let out a relieved breath.

If she'd been driving a smaller car, she probably wouldn't be breathing. The heavy Bronco had saved her life.

Decision time. To remove her might make any internal

injuries worse, yet he couldn't leave her there with the blowing snow and the temperature well below freezing. The chances of getting an EMS unit here quickly in this storm were slim to none. He'd have to do his best to get her inside his cabin and tend to her injuries.

As if to remind him to quit stalling, the merciless wind sent a rush of snow right at him, powdering his face and hair. The storm was building in intensity. Sean knew from past experience that residents up here could be marooned for days before help could arrive to dig them out. He was the woman's only hope. And he was a doctor, dedicated to saving lives.

There'd never really been any other choice.

Carefully, he leaned back in, reached over and unbuckled her seat belt. Slowly, he eased the woman's upper torso away from the protruding branch and the steering wheel, maneuvering her toward himself. As her head fell back, he saw blood from a wound on her forehead, but he'd known she'd probably have some lacerations from the flying glass of the windshield, if not from the impact itself. With no small effort in the cramped space, he finally got her shoulders through the door, but he couldn't reach back in for her legs.

Praying that he wasn't adding to her injuries, he dragged her through the confined space until she was totally free of the vehicle. Bracing his booted feet in the slippery snow, he bent at the knees and managed to hoist her up into his arms. Thankfully, she was a small woman. Her head angled toward his shoulder, and she mumbled something he couldn't quite make out. Something that sounded like Max or Mex.

Had he missed someone, perhaps a child? As best he could with the woman in his arms, he squinted into the back seat, searching for a tiny form, a movement, a sound. No, there was only a leather handbag on the floor next to a somewhat tattered blanket.

It seemed a mile to the cabin door as he carried his dead-weight burden in nearly knee-deep snow up the incline and across the unshoveled driveway. At six-one and a healthy thirty-one years old, Sean was in good shape, yet he still found the going rough. Boosting her up for a better hold, he climbed the porch steps and almost dropped her legs as he struggled to open the door.

At last inside, he carried her to the couch in front of the fireplace and placed her on it as gently as he was able. Letting out a deep breath, he shook the snow off his hair, then went back to close the door, remove his gloves and toe off his boots. Unzipping his coat as he hurried back to her, he saw that blood streaked her face and she was quite wet from the snow that had fallen in on her through the broken windshield and the walk to the cabin. The crash he'd heard in the cabin had undoubtedly been the Bronco which meant she hadn't lain out there too long.

Still, hypothermia can set in quickly when an injured person's blood pressure drops, Sean knew. Quickly, he whipped off his jacket and went to his bedroom, returning with his medical bag and a towel. Shifting her into a better position on the oversize couch, he again checked her pulse, pleased to find it even stronger than before. She looked to be somewhere in her twenties, which would definitely be in her favor.

Gently he pushed up first one eyelid, then the other. Pupils okay, a good sign. Her eyes were large and deep blue. Probably one of her best assets, Sean thought absently.

Dampening a sterile gauze pad with alcohol, he brushed back her long black hair and cleaned the wound on her forehead. Quite deep but still just a superficial cut. He put antibiotic ointment on a clean gauze pad, placed it on the wound, then taped it in place. Next he eased off her leather jacket. As he lifted her, she moaned out loud, her face contorting as if in pain. He tossed the jacket aside. Underneath, she had on a blue sweater with designer jeans and leather flats on her sockless feet.

Her clothes weren't off the usual racks, Sean noticed. They were expensive and in good taste. She had a gold chain around her neck that was heavy and very real. On her right hand, she wore an amethyst ring in a simple gold setting that didn't come cheap.

Moving his hands very carefully, he trailed them over her body from her head to her toes, letting her groans tell him as much as his fingers learned. He was more doctor than man now, his experienced touch trying to ascertain the extent of her injuries. Finishing, he leaned back, studying her face.

Probably a concussion if she'd hit her head hard enough to sustain that cut, hopefully not too severe. There were some bruises forming on her face, and she might wake up to a couple of black eyes, but no other cuts visible. Her right shoulder was dislocated, her arm hanging limply at her side. Her left ankle was swollen, but didn't appear to be broken.

Nothing too serious if the concussion wasn't bad. He'd fixed many a dislocated shoulder in his residency days and ER rotation—painful but not life threatening.

Gently, he pulled up her sweater and saw red marks on her stomach that would surely darken into some pretty nasty bruises from where the steering wheel had slammed into her. The seat belt had kept her upper body in place, yet her right shoulder had still dislocated. Without the belt, she'd have been tossed onto the floor like a rag doll, sustaining far more serious injuries. Or her head might have smashed into that jutting tree limb.

All in all, she appeared to be one lucky lady, Sean concluded.

She didn't look comfortable, so he settled her into the soft folds of the corduroy couch, adjusting pillows around her. Again she moaned, mumbling, and this time he could make out a word. Max. There'd been no one else in the Bronco, of that he was certain. Was Max her husband? She wore no wedding ring, but that didn't necessarily mean she wasn't married. Many of the nurses he worked with chose not to wear their rings, for whatever reason.

Gazing at the woman as a man and not just a doctor, Sean saw that she was beautiful with all that lush black hair, high cheekbones and thick lashes dark against her pale skin. He couldn't help but wonder where she'd been headed in such a storm, where she was from and who if anyone was waiting for her arrival. Maybe Max? If not a husband, was he perhaps a lover she was rushing to meet?

None of his business, he decided, frowning.

He reached for the towel and gently patted her face dry, then used it to dry her hair. As he shifted her, she shivered and began shaking, probably from shock. He set his medicine bag on the floor, then went to get an afghan his mother had made. Laying the cover over her, he tucked the ends around her feet after removing her shoes.

She should wake up soon, he thought, unless he'd missed something in his somewhat hasty exam.

Returning to tend the fire, Sean put two more logs on, then hunched down and poked at the wood, working up a strong blaze. His pant legs were almost dry, but his socks were wet from padding around the cabin in the snow tracks made by his wet boots.

With one last look at his unexpected guest, he went to his bedroom for a pair of dry socks.

Pain intruded into her consciousness and made itself known. It seemed everywhere—her head, her shoulder, her ankle, her stomach. Sharp, throbbing, intense. She tried to move, but the pain stopped her. She tried to sink back into the black oblivion of sleep, but the pain pushed her awake.

Slowly, she opened her eyes. Hazy vision. Blinking, she tried to clear it. When finally she did, she recognized nothing.

She was in a large room on a couch, covered with a blue-and-white afghan. There was an oak coffee table nearby, a braided oval rug over plank flooring, dancing flames in a huge fireplace. The heat felt good for she was cold, shivering.

Where was she?

She heard a door open, footsteps. Who? Though the pain sliced through her, she sank deeper into the couch, fear causing her heart to race. Then he came into view.

She sized him up in seconds: tall, over six feet, broad shoulders, sandy hair cut short, a lean, tan unsmiling face. He wore a black turtleneck sweater over gray cords and leather moccasins. He stopped by the couch, looking down at her with blue-gray eyes filled with questions. Unable to hide the fear in her eyes, she clutched the afghan in trembling fists and stared back at him.

"Glad you're finally awake," he said, pulling a footstool over to the couch and sitting down.

She withdrew deeper into the cushions surrounding her. "Who are you?" she managed, her voice raspy. Her gaze did a quick circle of the cabin. "Where am I?"

"You're in the Gray Mountains. I'm Sean Reagan and

this is my cabin on Hollow Oak Road. You had an accident. Your Bronco swerved off the road and hit a couple of trees.'' He watched her take that in, digest it.

''Yes, the Gray Mountains. I remember I was on my way to my family's place on Ridgeway Road.''

He nodded, recognizing the street. ''You turned about a mile too soon. Ridgeway's just north of me.''

''It was snowing hard and I couldn't recognize anything familiar.'' Fear hadn't left her altogether. ''You…you live here alone?'' *Please let there be a wife, a mother, somebody.*

Sean was well aware what was bothering her. He softened his expression, trying to relieve her mind. ''Actually, I live in Scottsdale. I built this cabin for times when I want to get away from the city. I'm a doctor, an obstetrician.'' He pointed to his bag on the floor next to the couch. ''Quite legit. My office is on Scottsdale Road.''

He watched her face as she assessed that information. ''I could show you my hospital I.D.'' He finally smiled. ''Honest, I'm not an ax murderer.''

The smile made him look less menacing, but she didn't return it as she glanced down at the gray bag, still wary. ''I thought all doctors had little black bags.''

''Not really. They come in all colors.'' He shifted closer. ''I'd like to examine you again, now that you're awake.''

The startled look was back on her face. ''How do you mean? You…examined me?'' She had trouble thinking of this very attractive, very masculine man as a medical person.

''Please relax. I'm a doctor. And I didn't undress you, if that's what you're thinking.''

Without waiting for her permission, he forced her eyes wider to check her pupils then took out his stethoscope and listened to her heart and lungs. Her breathing was a bit fast as was her heartbeat, probably because she was still nervous about him.

With careful fingers, he touched her shoulder and she cried out. "This is your worst injury, a dislocated shoulder. Fixable but with some discomfort." His hand went to her ankle, examining the tender swollen flesh. "Just a sprain but you'd best stay off it for awhile." He indicated the gauze on her forehead. "That's a cut I've already cleaned and bandaged." He tapped lightly on her stomach through the sweater. "You've got some bruising here, from the steering wheel. Not serious, but painful."

Sean watched her hand snake under her sweater as she realized he must have looked her over quite thoroughly. *He's a doctor,* she reminded herself. She raised a hand to check out the forehead bandage, then let her fingers drift into her hair. "My head really hurts."

He nodded. "You undoubtedly have a concussion, but not a serious one. I'll give you something for the pain."

So many questions whirling around in her brain. "How'd I get in here? You say you found me?"

"I heard the crash and went out to check. I got you out and carried you here." He could see concern and lingering pain in those midnight blue eyes, and wondered how they'd look when she laughed, when she was happy.

"I...thank you." It was the least she could say.

Pausing, he studied her face. Her color was better, her complexion not so pale. "What in the world were you doing out in such a storm? Were you rushing to meet someone at the Ridgeway cabin? Because, up here, when it storms like this, the phones generally go out for days at a time. Is someone waiting for you—a parent, a husband, a boyfriend?"

She frowned. Her father was generally too busy to

wonder where she was, her husband was now an ex and she hadn't had a boyfriend in…well, a very long time.

She was honestly trying to remember, but everything was oddly hazy. "I'm pretty sure I wasn't going to meet anyone. I often go to the cabin alone. I love it there, like a secure haven. It was raining in Scottsdale when I left but I never dreamed I'd drive into a snowstorm." She closed her eyes, willing the memory to return. "I remember I was in a hurry. That much seems clear. I had this urgency to get away, from something or someone. But I'm not sure who or why." Her eyes opened and met his, filled with distress. "It's really odd. I can't seem to remember any more."

"Not so odd. Can you think of anyone you're afraid of?"

She just looked more confused. "I don't know."

No use pushing right now. She'd remember in time. Sean studied her huge blue eyes, the kind that could make a strong man weak. Then there was that cloud of jet-black hair and her lovely face without so much as a blemish, not even a freckle. To say nothing of her very feminine curves beneath the bulky sweater, her chest rising and falling with her nervous breathing.

He scooted the stool back a bit. "You haven't told me your name," he reminded her. Did she even remember it?

Good manners had been drilled into her from childhood. They had her setting aside her fear and responding to him. After all, he was a doctor, a caregiver. She had no reasonable reason to be afraid of him. The fear she felt was lingering from…from whatever it was she'd left behind.

"I'm sorry. Laura Marshall. I have an interior design

studio in Old Scottsdale. My father's Owen Marshall. He's…''

''I've heard of him. He's a Realtor.'' Not just any Realtor, but one who owned half a dozen or so residential offices plus a large commercial division. He should have guessed from her clothes. Her family had pots of money. And yet, here she was, running from something. Or someone.

''Yes, that's right. I decorate the company's model homes, but I have a private clientele, as well.''

''Do you live with your father?'' Sean had never met Owen Marshall, but he'd read that the man was widowed and lived in a large sprawling home on Camelback Mountain.

Something flickered in her eyes, a quick distaste, then was gone so quickly he wasn't certain he'd seen it at all. ''No, not since I left for college. I have a town house in Scottsdale in Old Town.''

''I'm not far from you. I have an older house on Mockingbird Lane that I've been renovating. Near Judson School in Paradise Valley.''

Finally, she believed him. ''I know exactly where that is.'' But a frown creased her forehead. ''Why is it I can remember personal details, but not why I was in such a hurry to leave town?''

''It's called traumatic amnesia. Someone who's been traumatized by something fearful can't recall the hurtful details but remembers common facts about her life. The rest will come back to you in time. Maybe gradually, or perhaps all at once. It's the mind's way of protecting you from an event too painful to recall. Something will trigger the memory when you're ready to remember.''

Laura stared at his face, thinking he looked sincere and

concerned. "You really are a doctor, aren't you? I'm sorry I doubted you, but..."

"You don't have to apologize. You had a frightful experience, then a bad accident and you woke up in a stranger's house with injuries. Anyone would be skeptical."

"My Bronco. Is it in bad shape?"

He shrugged. "Depends what you mean by bad. You must have veered off the road and down this incline, hit a small tree, then the Bronco spun around and wound up with its back end wedged between two trees. I think it can be repaired. If you'd have been driving a smaller car, you might not be here talking with me."

She shuddered at the close call. "I just bought the Bronco about six months ago. I used to drive a BMW two-seater. But I have to carry around all these samples—carpeting, drapery, paint swatches, wood panels. I guess it was a good decision to switch."

"Amen to that."

Laura shifted on the couch, attempting to sit up, but a sharp pain shot through her shoulder. "Oh!"

"I think we'd better get your shoulder back in place," Sean told her, getting to his feet. "I take it you've never had this type of injury before?"

Her face registered discomfort and reluctance. "No. How exactly do we get it back in place?" Laura had a feeling she wasn't going to like whatever he was about to suggest.

"You're going to have to trust me." He bent to help her stand, moving gently, aware of her many sources of pain and that her ankle might prevent her from standing without help. "Put your good arm around my shoulder and hold on." When she did, he lifted her into his arms.

Laura bit her lip so she wouldn't cry out with the pain

that stabbed like a knife through her shoulder. Her arm felt limp and useless. Despite that, as he carried her across the room, she couldn't help but be aware of how strong he was, holding her as easily as if she were a child. His hands were large and powerful. She could scarcely imagine this big man delivering tiny babies. She'd always pictured obstetricians as middle-aged, comfortably solid, inviting confidence not speculation. Sort of neuter, sexless, harmless.

Sean Reagan was anything but. With his ruddy complexion, windblown sandy hair and athletic build, he looked more like a man who worked outdoors chopping down trees rather than bringing new lives into the world. Unbidden, her gaze settled on his mouth. Full lips, a small dimple in one corner, thoroughly tempting.

Lord, what was wrong with her, thinking sexy thoughts about a man she'd just met? That bonk on the head must have rattled her more than she'd thought. But there was a dormant sexuality about him that, even in her bruised and battered state, made her very keenly aware that she was a woman.

She didn't need the reminder just now.

At the paneled wall, Sean stopped to explain. "I'm going to set you on your feet and brace you with my body up against the wall since I know your one ankle won't hold your weight. I need you to hold very still, and I'm going to tell you now, this will hurt. But only for a few seconds."

Eyes wide, Laura stared at him. "What are you going to do?" Laura remembered vaguely reading a story where someone had fixed a dislocated shoulder for a patient. It hadn't been a pretty scene.

"The ball of your shoulder has slipped out of the socket. The only way to fix it is to yank really hard on your arm and allow the ball to jump back into place. Can you handle that?''

She wasn't sure. ''What if you yank and it doesn't go in?''

He almost smiled. ''It will. I've done this many times.''

''Ever lose anyone doing it?''

Now he did smile. ''Keep that sense of humor.'' Carefully, he stood her up and held on while she settled most of her weight on the uninjured foot. Only she was wobbly, perhaps even a little dizzy, and her knees kept buckling.

''I've got you. Don't worry.'' He aligned their bodies so that he was very close up against her, keeping her from sliding down by pressing himself into her as she stood with her back to the wall. The top of her head came to just under his chin. The warm womanly scent of her drifted to him as her hair nuzzled against his nose. Sean swallowed hard and dipped his head back. He'd better hurry before he embarrassed himself. ''Ready?''

She felt light-headed, whether from her combined injuries, her painful arm or the reaction of being all but glued to this very male stranger, her breasts flattened against his chest, her ear pressed to his pounding heart, she couldn't have said. ''Let's get this over with, please.'' Praying she wouldn't faint on him, Laura mentally braced herself.

Sean eased his upper body slightly away from her, placed one arm diagonally across her chest to keep her upright and took hold of her right arm with his left hand. Counting to three, he yanked hard and heard the pop as the ball slipped back into her shoulder socket. It was almost drowned out by Laura's sharp cry.

Disliking having to hurt her any more than she was

already hurting, he scooped her up into his arms and held her close, letting her absorb some of his strength. He'd always been a sucker for a woman in pain. Her face was again very pale and pinched, her eyes closed. She cradled her arm against her chest. "Are you all right?"

Just then, all the lamps went out, the furnace clicked off and the only light came from the soft glow of the fireplace clear across the room, the only sound that of their labored breathing.

Chapter Two

"Oh, no," Laura muttered. What a time for a power outage.

"Just wait a minute," Sean said, holding on to her. In seconds, there was a shuddering sound, then a large click. The lights blinked back on, and the furnace made a whooshing noise before resuming. "The generator kicked in," he explained. "I have it as a backup since these winter storms often knock out our power." He carried her back to the couch, easing her down carefully. "I'm sorry I had to hurt you."

Laura held her injured arm close to her body, hugging it. "Had to be done." She licked her lips, struggling with a sudden wave of nausea. Swallowing hard, she looked up at him, beginning to panic. "Where's your bathroom? I think I'm going to be sick."

She did look a little greenish. "Not far. Let me help you." He slipped an arm around her and half-carried, half-supported her to a door off the kitchen. ''I'll be right outside the door if you need me,'' he said, directing her inside, leaving the door slightly ajar so he could hear. He didn't want her passing out on him.

Poor kid, Sean thought, walking away, giving her some privacy. Shock often brought on nausea. The jolt of repositioning her shoulder had likely been the last straw for her battered system. He wandered over to the front window. It was still coming down just as hard as ever. At this rate, her Bronco would be all but hidden by morning.

Sean walked over to the phone, picked it up to check. Sure enough, it was out, and would be for God only knew how long. Hands in his pockets, he slowly paced the perimeter of the large room, reluctantly admitting that he was stuck with his uninvited guest for quite some time.

Lousy timing. He wasn't an uncharitable person, and it wasn't that he didn't want to help someone hurt and stranded. But he'd had a purpose in coming to the cabin at this particular time, and her arrival messed up his plans. Maybe it was for the best, he thought with a shrug. His partner had repeatedly told Sean what he thought of his annual pilgrimages, that they did more harm than good, and perhaps Jonah was right. Yet each year, as the fifteenth of February approached, Sean would feel compelled to return.

Glancing toward the bathroom door, he wondered how she was doing in there. And how she'd handle being marooned in a strange place with a melancholy man.

Laura splashed cold water on her face, then grabbed a hand towel to dry off. Standing with most of her weight on one foot, she leaned into the sink and stared at her image in the wall mirror. Oh, Lord, was that a black eye? Just what she needed. Hair a mess, face pale, eyes reflecting fatigue and remnants of fear. She wasn't a beauty to begin with, and now this.

What on earth was she doing here in the house of a sexy stranger who, although he'd been kind, looked as if he wished she'd stayed home? Laura wished she had, too, except for a lingering uneasiness about the home she'd left behind so hastily. How had her life turned into such a chaotic mess in such a short time?

She finger-combed her hair back off her face, realizing that her head hurt too much just now to try to figure things out. She checked the medicine chest and found no new toothbrushes. Mostly shaving stuff, toothpaste, a bottle of aspirin and mouthwash. And a packet of birth control pills. Now that was odd for a man living alone.

Then again, maybe he didn't live alone some of the time.

She used the mouthwash and felt fresher, but she wished she didn't have to go out and face Sean. How embarrassing, to get sick like that. She reminded herself he was a doctor, but the reminder didn't help. He simply didn't *look* like anyone's idea of a doctor. She would never choose a doctor so young and handsome, let him poke and prod her with her wearing only a skimpy gown.

Grimacing, she hobbled to the door and opened it.

He was standing at the window watching the snow and probably wishing he hadn't gone out and found her. Yet when he turned to look at her, his face registered what seemed to be genuine concern as he walked over to her.

"Are you feeling better?" Sean asked, noticing the bruised look about her huge blue eyes. The right eye was definitely turning black.

Involuntarily, her face flushed. "Yes. I'm so sorry. I never get sick like that, but…"

"Don't apologize," he said, slipping a supportive arm

around her before she lost her balance. "Shock does that to people. How's your shoulder?"

"Sore," she answered, allowing him to help her back to the couch where she sat down gratefully. She'd give anything if he'd go about his business and just let her lie here. A short nap and she was sure she'd feel all right again.

"Can I get you something to eat?"

The mere mention had her stomach churning. "Thanks, but I'm not hungry." She hated this feeling of helplessness, of not being able to remember, of needing assistance. Her ankle was throbbing, but she wouldn't let on. Doctor or not, the man would soon tire of her aches and pains, her complaints, if he hadn't already.

Sean ignored her polite refusal of food. She needed something in her stomach if he was to give her a pain pill or she might get sick again. "I'd been about to warm some soup before I heard the crash and went out. I could make a sandwich. There's tuna salad and…"

"Tuna? Oh, heavens!" Laura's voice was agitated.

"What is it?" he asked. How could the mention of tuna upset her?

"Max, my cat. He was in the Bronco with me."

Sean frowned. "Are you sure? I looked into the back seat and I didn't see anything but a large handbag and an old blanket on the floor."

"That's Max's blanket. He was probably hiding under it." Panic colored her voice. "What if he's hurt? Or if he got out? He'll freeze to death in this storm."

"I'll go look." Reluctant resignation tinged every word. A cat. She would have a cat.

"I…I hate to ask you, but he's ten years old. He's not used to fending for himself and…"

"Don't worry." Sean was already pulling on his boots.

"If he's out there, I'll find him." Macho man, taking on the world. Was he nuts, making such a promise? He shouldered into his jacket. "You're absolutely certain he was in the Bronco with you?" After all, her memory was spotty at best.

"Yes, positively." She remembered grabbing her purse and scooping Max into her arms, then hurrying to the Bronco, her need to get away uppermost in her mind. She'd been afraid of…of what? Damn, why couldn't she remember the rest? "You're awfully nice to go back out there."

That he was, a truly nice guy. Wordlessly, Sean zipped up and went out. He didn't even like cats. Dogs were more his thing. One day, he'd get a dog, when he could be home more. He didn't feel it was fair to coop up an animal all day, not with the hours Sean worked. Head bent against the wind and blowing snow, he made his way toward the incline.

From the couch, Laura twisted about, gazing out the window across the room. The snowflakes were so thick she could scarcely make out anything. She couldn't blame Sean for being annoyed at going back out in that. But they couldn't let Max die, which he surely would if he wasn't found soon.

With no small effort, she shifted painfully until she was lying down on the couch, then pulled the afghan over herself. She ached so much she couldn't even define where it hurt most. To distract herself, Laura gazed around the room.

It was big with large, comfortable furniture, the couch she was on and two deep chairs facing the bricked hearth and the crackling fire. For the first time, she noticed a framed drawing hanging above the fieldstone fireplace. Laura's studio in Scottsdale was next to an art gallery, and she recognized that this drawing had been done in pastel chalks.

A young boy no more than three years old was standing alongside a gnarled tree. His hair was blond and his smile mischievous. From one small hand dangled a bedraggled brown bunny with one ear missing. An old-fashioned red wagon sat off to the side. She was no expert, but the picture was well done, seemingly drawn by someone who loved the boy. Laura wondered if the subject was Sean as a child.

Her gaze swept to the far left where a serviceable kitchen was set off by a counter with two high-backed stools and, off to the side, a maple table with four captain's chairs. There were three closed doors off the kitchen, the middle one the bathroom she'd used, the other two probably leading to bedrooms. A nice compact cabin, the walnut-paneled walls lending a cozy warmth. It lacked a woman's touch, though, with no curtains on the windows, no photos on the end tables, no cloth on the sturdy oak table. The half dozen pillows on the couch were the only hint of softness.

Definitely a man's retreat, Laura decided, struggling with a yawn. Leaning back, she spotted an easel facing away from her in front of an overstuffed bookcase off to the right. Was Sean the artist or perhaps someone who visited him? None of her business, she decided, closing her eyes.

What was keeping Sean?

Darkness had settled in, but the whiteness of the snow allowed Sean to see. The drifts were thigh high, however, which made the going very slow. And treacherous, he thought as he slid down the embankment and stopped just short of the almost buried Bronco.

Cursing under his breath, he scrambled to his feet, feeling cold, impatient and annoyed. He didn't even want to think about what he'd do if Max wasn't in the vehicle. If the animal had gotten out, his paw prints would have been covered over by now. The thought of tramping about in this storm looking for some old cat that could be anywhere didn't thrill him.

With gloved hands, he scraped accumulated snow from the passenger door and managed to wedge it open again. Ducking inside, he knelt on the front seat and looked around. He picked up the large leather shoulder bag thinking Laura might need it. No luggage anywhere, but then she'd said she'd left in a hurry. On the floor he noticed a box of assorted tiles. On the back seat were material remnants and three large books of wallpaper samples. Sean remembered what she'd said about the blanket and gingerly picked up one end, whipping it to the side.

He heard a hissing sound, then a paw lashed out at him, the claws digging into his leather gloves. Yellow eyes peered up at him, looking unfriendly and combative. Max was shorthaired, yellow and beige, kind of skinny and obviously frightened. "Okay, shhh. You're okay," he said, trying to sound reassuring. The cat hissed again, louder.

"Look, Max, I'm a friend, honest." Feeling foolish trying to pacify a stubborn cat in a tangled wreck of a vehicle in a raging snowstorm, Sean leaned forward and grabbed Max under his front legs, maneuvering him into a body hug, sharp claws pointed away from him. Pushing back, he ignored the cat's protests as he backed out of the Bronco and shoved the door shut with his hip. The strap of Laura's shoulder bag dangled from one arm.

Max struggled as cold snow enveloped them both, but

Sean held on. He'd have put him inside his jacket, but he knew the cat would start clawing him. So he trudged back up the incline, realizing that he now had two guests he hadn't been prepared for. "Listen, if you stop fighting me, I'll give you a dish of tuna for dinner. How's that?" Max told him what he could do with his offer in no uncertain hissy terms.

"Okay, chum," Sean said, high-stepping through the snow. "Your loss."

By the time he stomped some of the snow from his boots and propelled his way into the cabin, Sean was soaking wet from the waist down, and the silly cat was still hissing at him. He wished he could say that seeing Laura's relieved face was worth his effort, but Sean didn't think so.

"Here you go," he said, thrusting Max into her lap and laying her bag on the floor.

"Oh, thank you, thank you." Mindful of her sore shoulder, she hugged the frightened animal and cooed to him. "Max, Max, I'm so sorry. You'll be fine, baby." The cat allowed her to soothe him, but he shot Sean a look that seemed to say this was all his fault.

Grumbling under his breath about the inequities of life where a mangy cat gets hugged and he, the rescuer, gets wet pants, Sean brushed snow from his hair and went to his room to change for the second time in a matter of hours. He took his time drying off, then pulled on a pair of gray sweatpants and thick socks. Towel-drying his hair and face, he heard his stomach growl. The invasion of Laura and Max had caused him to miss dinner. Maybe she wasn't hungry, but he was.

Sean came out and saw that Laura had her eyes closed, the cat cuddled up against her, purring away. In the kitchen, he paused, considering dinner. "How about that soup now?" he suggested.

"I honestly couldn't, but thanks."

All right, he'd let her have it her way. He filled a glass with cold water before bending to his medical bag and pulling out a vial of pills. "I think you'll feel better if you take one of these," he told her.

Laura opened her eyes. "I don't like taking pills." Especially when she didn't know what they were.

"Look, isn't it time you started trusting me? I'm a doctor, remember? There's a time to be brave and a time when it's plain silly to insist you're not hurting when I know you are." He held out the water and medication. "This will help you rest."

Laura swallowed the pill, then burrowed back into the nest of pillows, closing her eyes and hoping the medicine would put her to sleep until the pain passed. "Thanks. Please, go back to whatever you were doing. I don't want to inconvenience you any further. I'll just lie here for a bit, if you don't mind, and then I'll call someone." But who? she wondered, frowning. Her father was never around, it seemed. She couldn't ask her friend Molly to drive up all this way when the roads were undoubtedly worse than before. She'd sure picked a rotten night to have an accident.

Sean sat down on the stool, noticing the cat's yellow eyes watching his every move. "I'm afraid the phone's out. Has been since before I found you. It could come back on any minute, or not for a couple days. Hard to tell."

"Oh. Well, maybe I can make it over to our cabin on Ridgeway. The snow's bound to stop soon and..."

"Not likely. It's coming down heavier than before. Have you ever been up this way in the winter?"

"Not since I was a child."

He'd thought as much. "The snow probably won't let up until tomorrow sometime, the wind blowing drifts as high as the roofline." He tucked the afghan around her legs. "And you're in no condition to go anywhere. You're bruised all over, your ankle's probably aching like the devil and your shoulder will be sore for several days."

His assessment was right on the money. Still, she hated to impose, to be a problem for anyone. She was used to being on her own, fending for herself. And although a doctor, he was a total stranger. "I'm so sorry I stumbled onto your property and messed up your plans. I'll bet you could throttle me."

She looked genuinely regretful, erasing Sean's resentment at being inconvenienced. She should have looked bedraggled, dissipated, cranky even. Instead she look intriguing with those wounded eyes and that haunted air about her that made her seem vulnerable and very appealing. "Not a problem, really. I have a spare room with a bed that's a lot more comfortable than this couch."

Laura thought she'd be just fine on the couch if he'd just go off and leave her be. But she'd have more privacy in another room where she could close the door and be alone with her cat. "All right, if it's not too much trouble." She moved to sit up, the pain somewhat dulled by the medicine beginning to kick in.

He reached over to pick her up, but she stopped him. "I can walk, I think."

Sighing, he shoved a hand into his pocket, searching for a coin. Already he knew she was stubborn and used to being independent. "My lucky Indian coin. I'll flip you for it. Heads I carry you, tails you walk."

Warily, she studied him. "A two-headed coin?"

"You really don't trust easily, do you?" He showed her both sides, then tossed the coin up in the air, slamming it down on his hand. It came up heads. "There, now put your arms around my neck."

Too tired to argue, Laura did as he asked. He carried her easily, heading toward the farthest door. She struggled against an urge to lay her head on his shoulder. He smelled of the outdoors, of woodsy aftershave, unmistakably male. He was so big, so solid, and it felt so good to be held, to feel safe. It had been so long since she'd given in to the very human need to just be held.

Following, Max protested loudly, but when Sean opened the door, he hopped on the bed immediately. Sean set Laura on her feet momentarily, pulled back the covers and eased her onto the bed. Her eyes felt so heavy she could scarcely keep them open as she felt him draw the comforter over her.

"There's a connecting door right there to the bathroom, if you need it," he explained, turning on a small night-light.

She sank into the soft warmth. "Thank you, for everything."

"Sure." He saw that she was halfway asleep already, her large blue eyes closing. The medicine along with all she'd been through was dragging her under. Gently, he brushed a strand of hair from her cheek, his touch lingering a bit longer than that of an impersonal doctor.

He watched Max snuggle up against her, keeping his golden eyes on their host. Sean moved to the door. "If the phone comes alive, is there anyone you want me to call for you?"

Her eyes opened as she mentally ran through the short list of possibilities. "No, there's no one."

Backing out of the room and leaving the door slightly

ajar, Sean felt a rush of sadness that there was no one
this lovely woman wanted to notify as to her whereabouts, no one who'd be worrying about her when she
didn't call or show up.

In the kitchen, he heated soup, set out crackers, poured
himself a glass of milk. He sat down at the counter and
ate disinterestedly, his thoughts elsewhere. Sean had a
logical mind, one that usually sorted things out in an
orderly fashion, studied the possibilities then came to an
informed conclusion. But, try as he would, he couldn't
seem to pigeonhole Laura Marshall.

She came from a wealthy family, that much he knew.
Her father had a good reputation for fair dealing, though
Sean was aware that many regarded him as cold and cal-
culating. He seemed to remember that Owen's wife had
died some time ago and, though his picture had been in
the paper in the society section escorting a variety of
well-heeled, bejeweled women, Sean didn't think Laura's
father had remarried. She said she worked for the family
real estate business decorating model homes. He couldn't
help wondering how she got along with Owen.

Sean took a bite of cracker and chewed thoughtfully.
She'd left her home in one hell of a hurry, taking along
only her purse and grumpy cat, heading for a cabin she'd
described as a safe haven. Why did she need one? She'd
obviously been up to their cabin often before, yet she
hadn't thought it might be snowing in mid-February,
hadn't dressed for the weather, hadn't even worn boots,
hadn't thrown a few clothes into a bag.

Because she was afraid of someone or something,
she'd confided, yet she didn't know who or why. How
would she react when she remembered? He finished his
light dinner, drained his milk glass and sat back. Traumatic amnesia was very real and pretty scary. What had

frightened her enough to send her scurrying to her *safe haven* with no luggage, no preparation?

Despite her accident, she appeared clear-eyed, lucid, honestly trying to remember. He could see it bothered her to not know what had motivated her rush to safety. She certainly wasn't in a dangerous line of work, nor was her father. A boyfriend stalking her, perhaps? An ex-husband or an admirer who'd become obsessive? Laura Marshall was certainly beautiful enough to inspire such behavior.

Or could she be in trouble, maybe running from the law? Stranger things had happened, yet he didn't think that was it.

For one thing, there was all that family money. Could someone be threatening her, blackmailing her or working some sort of scam? Or had he read too many mysteries lately and let his imagination go on overdrive?

Shaking his head at his flight of fancy, Sean put his dishes in the dishwasher and yawned expansively. He hadn't slept well last night, as he rarely did on these sojourns. Maybe tonight would be better. Laura's unexpected arrival had called a halt to his brooding, the first time anything had distracted him from remembering, from going over every detail of that fateful day trying to discover something he might have done differently.

He walked over to the portrait above the fireplace and stood staring at the smiling face so full of mischief. "I failed you, Danny," he whispered. "I'm so sorry."

Bending to make sure the fire was dying out, he sighed then walked over to check the phone. Still out. He paused by the room where Laura lay. Stepping in quietly, he saw that she hadn't moved. Her cheeks were a bit flushed, one hand softly curled by her face. Max's suspicious yellow eyes glowed in the semidark. Perhaps the cat sensed that he preferred dogs. Or maybe he could tell that, despite his stated desire to be left alone this week, he'd like nothing better than to change places with Max and curl up with Laura Marshall under the duvet.

Sean headed for his bedroom.

The light filtering in through the unadorned windows woke her. Blinking, Laura took a moment to orient herself, then realized it was a weak morning sun reflecting on snow that was still falling outside. Her headache was gone, and she was grateful for that. She dared to move her shoulder and felt a dull ache, but not the sharp pain of yesterday.

She turned toward the nightstand and saw that it was ten after eight on the Mickey Mouse clock. The lamp she hadn't noticed last night was a grinning Bugs Bunny chomping on a carrot, its base containing the night-light still on.

Curiosity aroused, Laura looked around and saw that she had slept in what was obviously a child's room. The yellow striped wallpaper had flocked Disney characters parading across one wall while a little red wagon sat in the far corner holding a rabbit with one ear. Surely they had to be the ones from the picture over the fireplace.

A dozen or more stuffed animals hung in a hammock stretched beneath two shelves of children's books. A blue-and-white hobbyhorse was next to the wagon, and a child's maple rocker holding a huge purple dinosaur was near the door to the bathroom. Atop the tall dresser was a huge pink piggy bank and one of those glass globes that you had to turn over and snow fell on an ice skating scene. A wooden train was next to it, the cars forming letters that spelled out *Danny*.

So the child in the picture wasn't Sean but rather a

boy named Danny whose room this obviously was. Trying to recall their earlier conversation, Laura realized that
when she'd asked Sean if he lived here alone, he had said
he actually lived in Scottsdale, that he'd built this cabin
for times he wanted to get away from the city. An evasive
reply.

Laura stretched and shoved back the covers, then sat
up. The room tilted slightly, then righted itself. Max,
who'd moved to the far side of the bed, gave her a quick
glance, then resumed his morning grooming. ''Time we
got up, lazybones,'' she told him.

It was utterly quiet, and she wondered if Sean was up.
There was a simple explanation here, she'd wager. Sean
was probably divorced and had a son named Danny who
used this room during his visits with his father. Or was
Sean still married and the boy and his mother were back
in Scottsdale?

She didn't think so. She could be wrong, of course,
Laura thought, but the masculine decor of the cabin, with
the exception of Danny's room, the lack of a woman's
touch, the absence of any pictures other than the boy's
portrait all pointed to a single man. But the most telling
thing was the way he looked at her, lingeringly, thoughtfully, heatedly. Not the way a married man in love with
his wife would look at another woman, doctor or not.

Laura ran both hands through her tangled hair. Of
course, she could be reading more into those looks than
was there. But she'd also seen his hand tremble when
he'd held out the water and pill. And again when he'd
brushed the hair from her face when he'd laid her down
on the bed. Later, dozing more than soundly asleep, she
thought she'd heard him come into the room and stand
looking down at her. She hadn't stirred, hadn't moved,

yet she'd felt his presence. He hadn't stayed long and, moments later, she'd heard the other bedroom door close.

Carefully she touched the bandage on her forehead, wondering if the concussion Sean seemed certain she had had affected her mind, as well. She wasn't one who usually read meanings into every gesture and touch. And she certainly wasn't looking for a relationship, not after the one she'd barely extricated herself from not long ago.

The short time she'd been involved with Marc Abbott should have taught her a great deal, should have soured her on quick attractions and the consequences that followed. And it had. Sean had commented that she didn't trust easily, something he'd picked up on after knowing her ever so briefly. An astute observation.

Max sauntered over and began purring, a signal that he wanted to be petted. Smiling, Laura obliged, as her thoughts floated free.

With time and distance, divorced nearly two years, Laura thought she knew exactly why she'd fallen so hard and fast for Marc. He was awfully handsome, utterly charming and knew how to make a woman feel as if she were the only one in the room. Laura had never been one to attract men like Marc.

While not exactly a wallflower, she knew from her teens on that she wasn't a raving beauty like her college roommate, Tate Monroe. Nor was she smart enough to graduate with a 4.0 like her other roommate, Molly Shipman. Ah, but she had something neither of them had had. She was rich, the only heir to her father's wealth.

Laura felt a sob build in her throat and choked it down. What a pitiful thing it was to be not the pretty one, nor the smart one, but the rich one. Her fingers drifted through Max's soft fur as she let her emotions settle. She'd long ago gotten over all that, hadn't she?

At least she'd thought she had when someone handsome and clever such as Marc Abbott had sought her out and simply refused to take no for an answer. Overwhelmed, believing herself madly in love and gloriously happy, she'd married him.

And lived to regret that foolishly hopeful indulgence.

He'd hurt her, badly. But she'd moved on, took on more work, opened her own studio, became her own person. And she'd vowed to never ever let herself be a victim again. It wasn't so bad, being alone, once you got used to it. Oh, she'd been asked out plenty, but other than business lunches and dinner meetings, she'd steered clear of letting anyone get close again. She'd never gone in for one-night stands, and everything else required a commitment she was unwilling to make.

And now she was up here, in the Gray Mountains in a snowstorm, marooned in a cabin with an attractive man who, even in her pitiful state, awakened some dormant desire inside her. But, not to worry. She'd tamp it down as she had with other occasional men who'd wandered into her life. Because she couldn't trust them, could never know if they paid attention to her for the right reasons. If it wasn't because she was gorgeous or had a personality that everyone gravitated to the moment she stepped into a room, then it was probably…because of her father's money.

Lowering her head, she nuzzled Max's fur. "No more feeling sorry for ourselves, Maxie," she whispered to the cat. "We're fine, just the two of us."

Something caught her eye at the foot of the bed, a pile of clothes. She reached for them, examining each piece. Clean sweatshirt and sweatpants, thick socks, white cotton underwear, a chenille robe and an old-fashioned floor-length flannel nightgown. Well, well. About her size, though a tad roomy. His wife's clothes? Or ex-wife's? At any rate, it was very thoughtful of him. A shower and fresh clothes would feel good.

Testing her ankle, Laura stood up. Still swollen, still painful, but bearable. She gazed out the window and saw that the snow wasn't letting up. There had to be several feet already and with the wind blowing drifts, probably higher in places. She'd never been marooned before, never spent time at a place where no one knew where she was. Saturday morning. She'd had no weekend plans, no luncheon dates or business consultations or shopping sprees with a girlfriend.

Would anyone be looking for her? Maybe, but she doubted if someone would actually worry until possibly Monday. Her father only sought her out when he had a decorating problem that needed solving or a favor he wanted from her. Everyone else would assume she'd gone away for a few days. Which, although she never did without informing someone, was a reasonable explanation.

Holding onto the bedpost, she took a step, then another then had to let go. Only three more steps to the bathroom door. Once inside, she could cling to any number of things. Her ankle felt rubbery, though Sean had said it didn't appear to be broken.

Hugging the clothes to her chest with one hand, the other outstretched to reach for the doorknob, Laura took a step, then another on her sprained ankle. That's when it went out on her and she went down with a yelp, crashing into a child's rocker. A huge purple dinosaur fell onto her, the recorded mechanism triggered by the fall.

"I love you," Barney sang. "You love me…"

Chapter Three

At the sound of the crash, Sean dropped his sketch pad and pencils onto the table and hurried to the bedroom. He found Laura on the floor struggling to free herself from Barney, who was nearly as large as she. He grabbed the stuffed dinosaur and tossed it aside, then bent to her. "Are you all right?" he asked, helping her up and hoping she hadn't reinjured her shoulder.

"I'm fine," Laura said, laughing. She teetered within his arms, her sprained ankle refusing to support her weight. "That's the first time I've been attacked by a dinosaur. A purple one, at that."

She couldn't be hurt if she's laughing, Sean realized, smiling as he steadied her. "I should have warned you. This room is booby-trapped." He noticed Max eyeing him suspiciously from the tangle of bedcovers. Sean doubted that cat would ever trust him.

"I can see that now." She looked up at him, thinking

he should smile more. It softened the hard planes of his face.

Up close against her, Sean was suddenly conscious of her tousled hair, the just-out-of-bed warmth of her, the quick awareness that leaped into her dark blue eyes as her laughter faded. She was fully clothed, as was he, yet he could feel every nerve ending go on alert with just the touch of his hand on her arm.

Laura breathed in the just-showered freshness of his hair, noticing that his broad shoulders blocked everything else from view. She watched sudden heat jump into his gray eyes and felt the reawakening of feelings she'd thought long buried. What was happening here?

Sean was the first to recover. "You're sure you're not hurt?" He forced his gaze down to her ankle, saw it was still swollen. "You shouldn't be walking on that sprain."

Laura leaned back from him, reaching a hand to brace herself on the bathroom door frame. She needed some distance, a moment to clear her head. "No harm done, really. I was just a little clumsy, that's all."

"I've got an old umbrella around here somewhere with a curved handle. It'll help you walk. I'll look for it." He had to get out of there, to move away from the womanly scent of her, the sleepy-eyed look of her. Stepping back, he bent to gather up the clothes she'd dropped, then straightened and held them out to her. "These should fit you."

"Thank you." Needing to change the subject, she gestured to include the room. "Does this room belong to the little boy in the picture above the fireplace?"

Sean's jaw clenched hard before he forced himself to relax. "It did."

Past tense. She'd better leave that alone. "And these clothes. Your wife's?"

"No!" He hadn't intended to be so sharp. "They belong to my mother. She visits sometimes and keeps a few things here." He nodded toward the bathroom. "There're plenty of clean towels. Take your time. I'll get that umbrella." Abruptly, he left the room, closing the door behind him.

So it was Danny's room and Danny's picture, Laura thought as she hobbled into the bathroom. But no wife. Or at least, no clothes of the wife's around. He'd sounded angry and bitter at the mention of her. Probably a divorce. Harsh and painful feelings often linger after a divorce. She ought to know.

Laura tested the shower, then began undressing, her mind digesting what she'd just learned.

No doubt Laura would think him quite odd when she learned that Danny was gone, yet he'd kept the boy's room at the cabin exactly the same during the four years since the child had disappeared from his life, Sean acknowledged. Of course, she didn't know the details. He supposed it wasn't quite normal behavior, whatever that was. Those first few months, he'd had trouble even coming back here. Gradually, he'd managed to visit and each year, he intended to redo the room. But when he actually stepped inside to tackle the task, he couldn't make himself pack up and put away all remnants of the laughing little boy who still owned his heart.

Sick was what Jonah told him he was, and his partner was probably right. He hadn't many quirks, but this one he'd certainly nurtured a long while. His mother had offered to do it for him, and at first, he'd agreed, only to stop her before she could begin. A shrink would have a field day with his head, Sean thought.

So be it. It was his head and his right to keep the room

any way he saw fit. Perhaps one day he'd know it was time.

He poured himself more coffee, then glanced down at the sketch he'd been working on. He'd drawn from memory Laura's face the way it had looked to him last night. Lovely. Vulnerable. Troubled. She, too, had her secrets, as did he.

It was a hell of a complicated world, Sean decided, sitting down at the maple table and picking up his pencil.

She felt better after her shower. The clothes were slightly baggy on her, but clean. She'd managed to avoid soaking the bandage on her forehead, but it needed changing. She was pleased that her face wasn't quite so pale, although she had one doozy of a shiner.

Sometime during the night, Sean had put a new toothbrush and even a hair dryer on one of the wide shelves next to the medicine chest. He said he'd built the cabin and apparently had thought of everything. She assumed there must be a second bath off his bedroom.

Laura finished blow-drying her hair just in time, for her ankle was hurting badly and standing was becoming uncomfortable. Hobbling, she made the bed as best she could, then found an old-fashioned umbrella with a thick curved handle by the door. All the amenities, she thought and left the room, leaning heavily on the makeshift cane.

He looked up when he heard her door open, but squelched the urge to rush to her side to help her over. He sensed she hated depending on him, or anyone. Besides, he wasn't certain he could handle supporting her against his body, smelling his own shampoo on her hair. But he did get up to pour her coffee and carried the cup and a tall glass of orange juice over to where she'd sat down clear across the table from him.

Was she having some difficulty handling his nearness, as well?

"The clothes okay?" She was wearing his mom's yellow sweats, their roominess emphasizing her small bone structure, making her seem more fragile.

"They're fine, thank you." She sipped the juice, her eyes downcast, feeling oddly ill at ease. It had been a very long time since she'd sat across the breakfast table from a man. Over two years, to be exact. And she and Marc had spent many of those early morning sessions quarreling before he'd leave in an angry huff.

Yes, those were the good old days. May they never return.

"Did you sleep well?" Sean asked, using his most professional doctor voice. If he could think of her as a patient, perhaps the air wouldn't be so supercharged.

"Very well, thanks." Which wasn't exactly true. She had slept soundly until the medicine wore off, somewhere in the middle of the night. Pain hadn't awakened her, her troubled thoughts had. She'd lain there trying to remember what had happened to bring her here, why she was afraid and who had made her so fearful. She'd come up empty-handed.

Laura raised her eyes to his face, caught the slight twitch of his mouth before shifting her gaze to the fogged-up window. Knowing he, too, was nervous helped her relax. "I see it's still snowing."

"Yeah. I shoveled off the porch earlier, and the steps, but they're covered up again."

Max chose that moment to saunter out of the bedroom, having completed his morning bathing ritual. He rubbed up against Laura's legs, meowing softly, wanting her attention. Smiling, she reached to pet his soft head knowing just what he wanted. "About that tuna you said you had,'' she reminded him, aware how hungry Max must be.

"Right." Sean walked to the counter and found the tuna in the cupboard, opened the can and chunked the contents into a small dish. He placed the dish on the floor by the back door, then went back for a dish of water. As he set that down, Max strolled over, but waited until Sean went back to his seat before deigning to taste his breakfast.

"Thanks," Laura said, her eyes on her cat.

Sean had been thinking about another problem involving Max. "What about a sandbox for him? Obviously, I don't have any kitty litter." And he didn't want Max to get territorial and start marking his spots.

"Hmm. Maybe you could shovel off a small section near the back door. I'll let him out and keep an eye on him. He's not one to wander."

"Fine." Sean watched her wrap both hands around the coffee mug and slowly sip. Her lips were full and looked incredibly soft. He wondered what they'd feel like, what she'd taste like and...

And he was losing his mind!

Disgusted with himself, Sean rose and went to stand looking out the window. Damn, he didn't need this right now, not this particular week. In the four years he'd been alone, he hadn't exactly lived like a monk, but he hadn't been with a lot of women, either. Mostly because at first, he hadn't wanted to, and later, he hadn't run across many who'd interested him in that way.

Besides, it wasn't fair to a woman to get involved physically when he knew he'd never again take a chance on emotional involvement. It cost too much, in pain—in loneliness, in disappointment. The fleeting pleasure simply wasn't worth it, though the lack of a love life often had him edgy. Especially when confronted with a beautiful woman in close quarters.

Laura Marshall was a mystery to him. Maybe that's why she intrigued him. Perhaps if he learned more, the fascination would disappear. In a perfect world, he would help solve her problem, the snow would stop and the roads would be cleared, which would mean they could leave and get on with their respective lives. But then again, this was hardly a perfect world.

Turning, Sean went back and sat down. "Have you remembered any more about why you left home in such a hurry?"

She shook her head, her long hair curtaining her face. "I tried, but the memory is still blocked." She narrowed her eyes, wanting badly to recall everything, for herself as well as to erase that skeptical look from his face. "I'd had a business lunch, then driven home about four. The phone was ringing as I walked in and I answered it. But I can't remember who was on the other end, or even if they were male or female. I can recall only this overwhelming need to get away. I grabbed my purse and keys, picked up Max and literally ran out the door. I don't even know if I locked up." Setting down her cup, she rubbed her temples.

"Don't try to force it. Give it time." Noticing her bandage was damp, he went to get his medical bag.

Sean removed the bandage and discarded it, then examined the cut. "It's coming along nicely." He put antibiotic ointment on a clean gauze square, then taped it in place.

"Thank you, again. It seems I'm always thanking you."

"Not necessary." He scooted his chair back, then surprised her by reaching for her sprained ankle and moving it up onto his lap. Carefully he removed the thick sock and, with practiced fingers, he felt all over, noticing her slight wince as he pressed.

He had such strong fingers, Laura thought, yet he was so very careful not to hurt her. He took his time, feeling every which way, his touch soothing yet at the same time arousing. His hands kneading her foot sent sensual waves coursing up her leg. She felt the heat rise in her face and raised a hand to her brow so he wouldn't notice.

"I think we'd better put an Ace bandage on this to give you some support."

Thankfully, he didn't seem to notice her discomfort. "Whatever you think," she said. "You're the doctor."

He gave her a pleased look. "I'm glad you finally think so." He wrapped her ankle neatly, but not too tightly, replaced her sock and released her foot. "Would you like some breakfast? There's some cereal or I could boil a couple of eggs."

"This is fine for now, but thanks." Her stomach wasn't back to normal yet. He walked to the sink to wash his hands, and she angled a couple of sketches that lay on the table around to face her. They were all of the young boy in the larger drawing. She was curious and hoped he wouldn't mind if she asked about him.

"The boy in the fireplace drawing and in these sketches, is he the Danny whose room I'm borrowing?" she asked, hoping she hadn't overstepped some unseen boundary.

Sean topped off their coffee mugs, a muscle in the side of his cheek flexing for several moments before he answered. "Yes."

"Your son?" The resemblance was too striking to be a coincidence.

He sat down heavily. "Yes." He swallowed hot coffee and didn't even feel the heat.

"I'm sorry. I didn't even ask and I should have. Your wife is..."

"Gone, and so's the boy." The screech of the captain's chair being shoved back on the wood floor startled Laura as Sean rose. In several long strides, he was across the room and pulling on his boots.

Laura reached for her umbrella cane and trailed after him. She'd learned part of it and she wanted to know the rest, but hesitated to ask more. Had they divorced and the mother had custody? Is that why he was so upset at the mere mention of Danny? "I didn't mean to upset you."

His mouth grim, Sean yanked on his sheepskin jacket, his movements jerky. "I've got to chop more wood before we run out."

"I'm sorry. I won't mention them again," she said quietly.

Sean tugged open the door and stood gazing out for several moments. "Dead. They're both dead," he said in a flat, emotionless tone. He walked out and slammed shut the door.

Laura stared after him, drenched in regret. *You couldn't let it be, could you?* she admonished herself. Feeling rotten, she hobbled back to the table.

Using more energy than necessary, Sean tossed a shovelful of snow off the porch, then bent to gather another. He couldn't chop wood until he'd cleared a path to the stacked logs at the side of the house. He didn't mind. Physical labor was what he needed just now. He needed to tire himself out so he wouldn't have the energy to think, to remember.

Crossing to the other side of the long porch, he began clearing off the newly accumulated snow. Damn stuff was still coming down, though with not quite the intensity of yesterday. Nevertheless, his experienced eye calculated that at least three feet was on the ground now and would probably reach four before the storm blew itself away. Had it been any other week, he'd have enjoyed the weather as a huge change from the endless sunshine of southern Arizona. But not now.

He was a contradiction, Sean realized. He deliberately came here to remember, yet he was getting annoyed every time Laura's innocent questions were forcing him to recall. Maybe it was because, after four long years, he still found it very hard to talk about his son, even to his own mother and Jonah. And Laura, being a stranger, knew none of the circumstances. He didn't want to go into all that, yet he wanted her to know, to explain things to her.

Odd, because he'd never before wanted to confide in an outsider. It had taken him months to tell those closest to him all the details. Perhaps he felt he might be able to talk with Laura because she, too, was troubled about something in her past. Misery loves company, or so they said.

Finished with the porch, Sean paused to catch his breath. Gazing up at the sky through the nearby evergreens, it seemed as if the cloud cover wasn't as dense today. A good sign for the snow to end soon. If only the wind would die down, he thought as he narrowed his eyes against a blast of snow-laden breeze.

His eyes were drawn to the incline leading to the gully where Laura's car had landed. He could picture all too clearly that last morning when he and Danny had dragged his new sled up to the top. He'd turned three the month before and was a regular chatterbox. Sean had zipped him into his blue snowsuit and pulled a warm knit cap onto his blond head. His mittens had been red with tiny reindeers on them.

The hill wasn't all that big, so Sean wasn't worried. At the top, he'd settled Danny on the sled, put the rope handles into his gloved hands and given a big push. The sled had zigzagged down the hill, not too fast, just enough to thrill a little boy. Danny had laughed and laughed, the sound echoing through the trees. Laughing himself, Sean had followed him down where the excited child had jumped off and into his arms.

"Do it again, Daddy," he'd begged.

And they had until both of them, tired but happy, had gone into the cabin where Kim had hot chocolate waiting. They'd all had some, even Kim's father. Danny had gone down for his nap then, almost too excited to sleep because later that day, they were going to fly to Denver where Grandpa lived for a vacation.

By nightfall, the sweet little boy with the infectious laugh was dead, gone forever.

Sean let out a shuddering sigh that sounded more like a sob. And it was his fault, all his fault. Perhaps that was why he felt the need to come up to the cabin, the last place he'd seen Danny alive and happy. It was an atonement, a penance like wearing a hair shirt, for being blind to what had been happening in his own home. Perhaps if he'd been more aware, his son would be alive today. Not that he ever felt better afterward, but then, he had no right to feel better while Danny lay dead in a snowy grave.

It would have been best if Laura Marshall had picked another week to run away. He wasn't fit company, and she had problems of her own.

Almost viciously, he grabbed the shovel and made his way around back so he could clear a path for Max.

Standing at the window, Laura watched Sean disappear around the side of the house. He'd been shoveling the porch like a man driven, then he'd stopped and stared off into the distance for the longest time, not moving, probably thinking dark thoughts.

She shouldn't have brought up his son and his wife. *Gone, both dead,* he'd said. Dear God, how awful. When had it happened? she wondered. And how had it happened? Probably not very long ago since the mere mention of them affected him so deeply. But then again, she supposed a person never quite got over something like that.

Stepping back, she wandered back to the table and looked again at the charcoal sketches he'd left there. A couple of scenes that looked as if they might have been sketched outside around the cabin in warmer weather— the stream that ran behind the Marshall property, as well, and a woodsy area where two horses grazed. The rest were all of the same little boy—on a swing hanging from a sturdy tree limb, on a sled in a snowsuit, at the same stream bending over, his hands in the clear water. There were more, head sketches, indoor scenes, one of him asleep on a striped rug on the floor in front of the fire. Sean's drawings were very good, and she wondered why he hadn't sold some of them. Perhaps they were too personal.

Thoughtfully, Laura shuffled through all of them, something bothering her. Why were there no sketches of the boy's mother?

Using her cane, she walked about the large room, thinking she'd run across one or two. Not even on the easel. Feeling as if she were invading his privacy, she hobbled down the hallway and peeked into the other bedroom, staying in the doorway. No pictures or sketches on the high six-drawer dresser or on the nightstand.

The closet door was open and, just as she'd suspected, no woman's clothes hung alongside Sean's. She'd assumed as much when he'd loaned her his mother's clothes rather than his wife's. She returned to the central room, her mind filled with questions.

Why had he removed all traces of his wife, yet kept his son's room as it probably was when the boy had been alive? Interesting. Had they been divorced before the boy and mother died? Or had he loved his wife so much he didn't want any reminders around?

Wandering over to the couch, Laura sat down, drawing her legs up in order to rest her ankle. Having finished eating, Max was already snuggled into several pillows at the far end.

No, the scenario about loving his wife so much didn't compute because he obviously loved his son and kept lots of reminders around. She wondered if his home in Scottsdale also had some of the boy's things in it, a room dedicated to Danny's memory, but all traces of the wife erased. Probably not that unusual a thing to do, but it didn't seem altogether healthy.

Stretching out, she decided that Sean's problems were his own business and she was certain he wouldn't appreciate her meddling in them. Glancing down, she saw her handbag on the floor, remembering that Sean had brought it in last night when he'd rescued Max. Maybe something inside would trigger her memory of why she'd felt compelled to leave Scottsdale in such a hurry.

Rummaging through, she found the usual things: her checkbook, her wallet, sunglasses, a small makeup case, which she really ought to make use of, a notepad with a couple of phone numbers scribbled on it. Her keys were missing, probably still in the ignition. There was a small bottle of aspirin, some tissues and two pens plus her birth control pills. Laura dry-swallowed one right away.

Still poking around, her fingers found a card, which she drew out to study. *Marc Abbott, Sales Consultant, Commercial Division, Marshall Realty.*

Staring at the card, Laura wondered how long it had been at the bottom of her purse. She felt a chill just looking at his card. She and Marc had divorced two years ago, so the card had to have been in there quite awhile. How peacock proud he'd been of his position at her father's company. Leaning her head back, she wondered all over again how on earth she'd fallen for Marc's glib charm.

Because she'd been needy. Because he'd been charming and attentive, and Laura had felt admired and desired for the first time in her life. He was a good con man, she'd give him that, and in her naiveté, she'd totally misread him. Even now, years later, she still chafed at how foolishly trusting she'd been. An easy mark for a man like Marc, a polished smoothie.

Despite the fact that she'd been graduated and out of college for two years when she met Marc, she'd been surprisingly innocent by today's standards. He'd been handsome and funny with an engaging personality that made him fun to be with. He'd joined Marshall Realty, a very ambitious young man with big plans for his future that he kept under wraps as he started moving up the company ladder.

Laura ran into him at a company meeting, only later learning that he'd maneuvered the whole thing, that Owen Marshall's only daughter and heir was very necessary to his plans. They started dating, and to say he overwhelmed her would be putting it mildly. She'd never had a serious relationship before, so quite naturally, she fell hard and fast. In short order, well aware that her father would disapprove, they eloped.

Eventually Owen came around, putting Marc in charge of commercial acquisitions, and he even began building a home for them in Paradise Valley not far from his own. Laura continued her work for the company, but her personal happiness was short-lived. It wasn't long before Marc was seldom home in their small apartment, using business as an excuse. She began to wonder if she'd married a workaholic like her father.

The first night he came home quite drunk with lipstick on his collar was a harsh awakening for Laura. When he sobered up, she confronted him. Marc explained that he'd bumped into a married friend whose wife had kissed his cheek and missed. Because she desperately wanted her marriage to work, she'd forced herself to believe him.

But there was a second incident not long after, and a third truly ugly one that occurred when Laura went out to dinner with her two college roommates on a night Marc was supposedly closing a big deal. They were scarcely seated when they spotted Marc across the room sitting close to a curvaceous redhead, holding her hand, nibbling her ear. Oblivious to those around them, they sipped champagne and smiled at each other seductively. Hurt and humiliated, Laura threw him out of their apartment that same night, tossing all his belongings onto the lawn.

Marc approached her the next day, pleading and contrite. But her father had come through for her for the first and only time in her life in a way she hadn't suspected he would. Owen informed Marc that Laura was filing for divorce and he was to clean out his desk. By the look on Marc's handsome, crestfallen face, she came to the conclusion that losing his job at Marshall Realty hurt more than losing Laura. It wasn't until the following week that she learned he'd cleaned out their two bank accounts.

By then, she was not even surprised, nor did she care overly much. It was worth it to get rid of Marc Abbott once and for all. She found it very difficult to go back to work where everyone knew of Marc's betrayal, but she disliked cowardly behavior. So, holding her head up high, she'd shown up at her office, vowing never to be taken advantage of by a man again.

Trusting blindly had cost her dearly, and not just monetarily. The residual effects were still alive within her. As soon as the divorce was final, she bought a spacious condo in Old Scottsdale and took back her maiden name, wanting no reminders of her brief marriage.

Deliberately, she tore Marc's former business card in half, then again and once more. No ashtray on the end table so she tossed the pieces into her purse and got up. A headache was beginning just above her eyes—perhaps from remembering such an unpleasant episode or maybe because she hadn't eaten since lunch yesterday.

Using the umbrella cane, she went to the kitchen and made herself a piece of toast. Nibbling on it, she looked out the window and caught a glimpse of Sean at the side of the house splitting logs. She hoped the exercise would chase away the sadness she'd seen on his face at the mention of his son. Everyone, it seemed, had problems, some worse than others.

Peeking into the refrigerator, she found an assortment of vegetables and several cuts of wrapped meat in the drawer. Sean would undoubtedly be cold when he came in and maybe hungry. Laura loved to cook, much preferred a homemade meal to eating out. Setting the makings for soup on the counter, she hobbled about the kitchen, amazed at how convenient it was with all the latest new appliances. Sean had done a remarkable job.

She found a large pot and put it on the stove, then began cleaning vegetables. So the man was a doctor with an undoubtedly busy practice, a sketch artist who probably could sell his work if he put his mind to it, and he also built this house. There seemed very little Sean Reagan couldn't do.

Impressive, talented and handsome, as well. Gazing out the window over the kitchen sink, Laura wondered what had gone wrong in his marriage, because she had a feeling something terrible had. He seemed more angry than grief-stricken. A story there somewhere, she was certain.

On the porch, his hands inside his gloves nearly numb, Sean stomped snow off his boots before going inside. The clock on the mantel told him he'd been out well over an hour. No wonder he was cold. He tugged off his gloves, hung up his coat and pulled off his boots. After slipping his feet into the moccasins he'd left by the hearth, he brushed snow out of his hair and stood warming his hands.

Pulling in a deep breath, he became aware of a delicious smell.

Glancing toward the kitchen, he saw Laura stirring a big pot on the stove. Had to be soup or stew, he decided. How long had it been since he'd had someone besides his mother cook for him? Four years now this very week.

Kim had loved to cook when they'd first gotten married. She'd collected cookbooks and experimented with herbs and spices. They didn't have much money at first, but she always managed to make something tasty. How many meals had she made that had been ruined, dried out because he'd been tied up at the hospital? She'd tried to be understanding, but he knew his hours bothered her more than a little. He'd promised her things would get better, but he knew she didn't believe him. Babies came when they were ready, not when it was convenient for the doctor.

Pretty soon, Kim stopped cooking except for Danny's meals.

Sean had modernized the kitchen in his Scottsdale home, and the one here at the cabin wasn't bad. Yet most of the time these days, he caught a meal on the run at the hospital cafeteria, seldom cooking himself. He ate out a good deal when his schedule permitted and occasionally at friends' homes. Jonah's wife, Sophie, was a great cook and was always asking him over to join them. But since Kim's death, Sean mostly turned down invitations from married couples. He felt like the fifth wheel on a wagon at those dinners.

Then there were the matchmakers, well-meaning friends who'd invite him to dinner along with a single female "to round out the table." He couldn't seem to convince them that he simply wasn't interested.

Inhaling deeply, he walked to the stove. "Sure smells good," he told Laura.

He'd seemed angry when he left and more than a little sad, but his voice sounded all right again, Laura thought with relief. "I hope you like beef-vegetable soup."

"I like most anything I don't have to cook myself." He went back to throw another log or two on the fire, stirred it up a bit, then walked to the sink to wash his hands. "You're not overdoing, are you?"

Her ankle was throbbing a bit since she'd been on it

quite awhile, and her bruised stomach ached, as did her shoulder. But she didn't want him to think she was some frail, whining woman who couldn't hold her own. He'd rescued her without knowing the first thing about her, taken her in, tended her wounds, given her a place to sleep. That counted for a lot in her book. The least she could do was cook for him even if it cost her a little pain. "I'm fine."

"Sure you are," he said, drying his hands, his eyes roaming her face and catching the small, telltale signs of fatigue. The black eye looked sore. Though she'd insisted she had, he'd wager she hadn't slept all that well, either. "Let the soup simmer. I want you to go lie down on the couch for awhile. Can't have the cook passing out on us." He smiled to take the sting from what had to sound like doctor's orders.

She went, not solely because he told her to but because she was ready to rest. He followed her over, tucked the afghan around her, then glanced down at Max. "Should I let him out?" He'd rather there were no accidents.

"I did a short time ago. He's set for awhile." She settled into the warm folds of the pillows, feeling safe. Odd how being with this relative stranger wasn't in the least alarming. Perhaps because he was a doctor. "Did you study medicine here in Arizona?" she asked, still curious about him.

He sat down near her feet, almost but not quite nudging Max aside on the long couch. "Yes, at the University of Arizona in Tucson. Interned at Phoenix General. How about you? Did you go to school locally?"

"I went to the U of A, too, mostly because I wanted to be on my own and away from Scottsdale. My mother died when I was twelve and my father was a stickler for rules, all kinds of rules. Still is. I wanted to get out from under and try my wings."

"Overly protective, is he?"

No, that wasn't what Owen Marshall was, not really. More like a control freak who wanted to run her life for her. Her only way out was to insist on going away to college, even if it was to a university just a two-hour drive from home. "My father likes having things his way," was all she'd say.

"At least you got away somewhat. My father died when I was ten and my mother couldn't bear the thought of me going away to college." He shook his head, smiling. "She was nice about it, but firm. Very firm."

She angled her head to one side, considering. "Funny, you don't strike me as a mama's boy."

"I'm not, at least not anymore. But, like you, I was the only one, and my mother's Irish. Need I say more? She can carry on with the best of them. She doesn't usually have a brogue, because she was born in Boston, but let her get upset and you'd think she'd just stepped off a boat from Dublin. She's a wonderful woman, but she can make me feel five years old with the raising of an eyebrow."

Laura smiled at that. "How nice it must be to think of a parent with such acceptance, such warmth."

Sitting back more comfortably, Sean stretched an arm across the couch back. "And you don't?"

"I cherish my mother's memory, but my father wasn't around much. From the time I was very young, all I ever heard from him was, 'Laura, you know I have to work.' His reason for not being with us was always because he had to work. My father started Marshall Realty on a shoestring, built it into what it is today, by hard work, sacrifice, dedication. He repeated that to me like a mantra regularly.''

Sean realized how lucky he'd been, for even though his father had died too young, he'd made some good investments, bought land and owned several buildings, leaving Sean and his mother well off so she didn't have to go to work after her husband's death. Ruth Reagan had seen to it that Sean had a happy childhood, had been both mother and father to him. He heard the loneliness in Laura's voice and felt bad for her.

''I don't remember us doing things together as a family, not even during holidays. While she was alive, Mom tried to get in the spirit of things, but Dad rarely showed up, except perhaps Christmas Day. When she died, he took a day off. One day. Then it was back to work.'' Her blue eyes were filled with sadness. ''I'm afraid I'm a disappointment to him because I can't buy into that philosophy. I know work is important, even necessary. But there has to be more to life than endless work.''

Sean was quiet, scarcely aware he'd picked up her feet and placed them on his lap. ''I can relate. Workaholics are a breed apart. I know because I was one.''

Was that what had wrecked his marriage? Laura thought she'd inadvertently stumbled onto the cause, but she didn't want to bring up a disturbing subject. She was enjoying their conversation too much. ''But not anymore?''

Sean shook his head. ''It takes me awhile, but I do finally learn.'' He shifted the conversation, unwilling to reveal too much. ''It must have been hard, a girl growing up without a mother.''

''It was, although after Mom died, we had a housekeeper. Greta kept the house nice and her cooking was okay, even though she didn't know much about what little girls needed. It wasn't until I moved to Tucson and met Maggie Davis that I found a substitute mother.'' Laura smiled just thinking about Maggie. "She was our housemother. My two roommates, Molly Shipman and Tate Monroe, and I moved into her home and we stayed the whole four years. Maggie treated us like her own. I hated to leave.''

"Better late than never, right?'' Absently, his fingers massaged her good foot.

"Yes, I suppose.'' His touch was so comforting, so tender. She felt a burst of longing that was as surprising as it was unnerving. She hardly knew this man, yet he aroused in her feelings she'd tried desperately to bury. She didn't want to awaken the impossible dream, to wish for a love that would last for all time. Because she knew that whole concept was flawed.

"If it's all right with you, I think I'll take a nap,'' she told him. Suddenly, she was tired, so very tired.

"Sure, you rest.'' Sean got up, carefully adjusting her legs under the afghan. He stood looking down at her a long moment, noticing that her eyes had already closed. He had an almost uncontrollable urge to reach down and stroke the silk of her cheek.

But he knew better than to start touching her. Wearily, he left her there and went in search of a book to distract his mind, knowing full well no such book existed.

Chapter Four

"This soup is wonderful, Laura," Sean told her.

She nodded her thanks. "It's a good day for soup." Taking her time, she searched her mind for a topic that wouldn't set him off again. "What's it like, delivering a baby, being the first human to see it, to touch it, knowing that you helped make the birth possible?" Laura had been wanting to ask. She'd watched those large hands of his shovel snow, chop wood and then tenderly bandage her cut. How could he be both, so physical and yet so gentle?

They were seated at the maple table, the overhead light of the kitchen on since it was already dark outside, though it was only five. Sean swallowed another spoonful of the delicious soup before answering. "This will probably sound corny, but I feel as if I'm taking part in a miracle each time." His eyes moved to her face, hoping she wouldn't think him hopelessly romantic.

She met his gaze wearing a soft smile. "Exactly as I'd imagined. I know I'd be awestruck. That tiny being, the preemies sometimes only a couple of pounds. Yet they're alive and will grow into an adult. Amazing."

Sean buttered a second piece of bread. "You sound as if you've been around birthings."

"Mostly puppies, not humans. Maggie had a female dog who was, to say the least, quite promiscuous. Lady was a mixed collie and she had two litters every year like clockwork." Laura paused, remembering. "I did assist Maggie once with the birth of a baby boy, but only on the fringes. Maggie did all the work. Among her many talents, she's a midwife."

"I've heard there are quite a few midwives around in rural areas." Sean swallowed a bite of carrot. "So you helped Maggie deliver a baby. Did the women come to her or did she go to their homes?"

Laura sat back, wiping her mouth on a napkin. "It wasn't like that. The mother was one of my roommates."

"Really?" Unusual for a young person in an urban setting to use a midwife. "Why didn't she go to the hospital? Didn't she have a doctor monitoring her pregnancy?"

"It's a long story."

He smiled at her. "It seems we have nothing but time."

"Well, you see, the three of us—Molly, Tate and I— were very close. Away from home for the first time, a little scared, a little lonely. Tate was—no, she still is— incredibly beautiful. She had so many guys ask her out that we lost track of the count. But she turned most of them down. Until this one man came along and dazzled her."

"Another college student?"

"No, he was older by eight or nine years. Anyhow, she wound up pregnant and he left town before she had a chance to tell him. Not that he'd have stuck around if he'd known, most likely. They always saw each other secretly so no one except Molly and I knew his name. Tate was determined to keep the baby, but she didn't want anyone to know about the pregnancy. So she went to classes in loose flowing clothes, but Maggie finally guessed. Bless her heart, she said she'd help Tate all she could."

Sean drained the milk from his glass and leaned back, interested in her story. "What about Tate's family? She didn't tell them, either?"

"Her mother had died and her father had worked hard to put her through college. She hated disappointing him. She knew she'd have to tell him sometime, but she kept putting it off. Then one night she went into early labor and there was no time to get to the hospital."

Even now, thinking back, Laura shivered at the memory. "I'll never forget that night. Molly and I were pretty scared, but Maggie knew exactly what to do. He was a beautiful baby. Tate named him Josh and said he was *her* son and no one else's. Afterward, Maggie took care of the baby while Tate finished school. Molly and I helped out when we could, with Josh and with her studies. She made it. She graduated with us." Laura picked up her coffee cup, then set it down. She'd had enough caffeine.

Sean pushed aside his dish, propped his elbows on the table and leaned forward. "Tate was lucky the three of you were there and that Maggie knew what to do. Contrary to what most people think, an awful lot can go wrong."

"I'm sure you're right."

"Where are Tate and her son now?"

"Good question. After Molly and I left Tucson, they stayed with Maggie for awhile. Tate went to work in a bookstore, worked her way up to manager, and they were doing okay. Until Josh's father found out about him and told Tate he wanted his son. She wasn't about to let him take Josh, so she disappeared with him."

Sean raised his brows. "Disappeared? Where to?"

"I don't know. She calls Molly and me occasionally, but she moves around a lot. See, Josh's father is a wealthy, important man now, and Tate's afraid he'll use his connections to take her son. Which is why she never tells any of us where they are. She doesn't want this guy pressuring Maggie or one of us, possibly threatening to get information."

"He'd do that?" Sean shook his head. "He sounds more like a thug than an important man."

"You're right, but to see him, you'd never know it. He's got assistants to do his dirty work. One of them called me not long ago, wanting to know where Tate was. I told him quite honestly that I didn't know, but he didn't seem to believe me."

"So, living like that, always on the run, she can't ever return home to see her family, her friends?"

"She's gone back to Tucson for short visits a time or two, once for her father's funeral, but Josh was never with her. She's got him in a safe place."

"Quite a story. Does she plan to spend her whole life running from this man? I mean, couldn't the authorities help her?"

Laura looked at him as if he were truly naive. "Did you ever try to go up against a wealthy, powerful man who has connections and is willing to do most anything to get his way? My father's a man like that and, believe me, winning against him would be next to impossible."

Sean wondered if Laura had ever gone up against her father. "Is this man married?"

"He wasn't when he and Tate were seeing each other. But he is now."

Sean shook his head. "I don't get it. Surely his wife wouldn't exactly be overjoyed with a child from a former liaison. Why is he persisting to the point of hounding Tate?"

"I understand his wife can't have children and, being a supreme egotist, he wants what he wants. I imagine he's sweet-talked his wife into accepting the situation."

"Have you met him?"

"I've never met him, but he surely sold Tate a bill of goods. For one thing, he's very handsome and probably charming. Tate's always been distrusting, certain men wanted her for her looks not herself. He must have managed to convince her otherwise. After all, we've all got a weakness or two, and he was hers. Until he showed his true colors."

Sean wondered what weakness Laura would admit to. "No accounting for taste. I suppose he made a lot of promises to her that he didn't keep, and she was young enough to believe he would."

"Absolutely. He was drawn to Tate, I'm sure, but I think she was just a fling for him while she was falling in love. After all, she was just a college girl at the time, her head full of romance. He married a woman whose family is not only rich but well connected, one that can help his career." She sighed. "Unfortunately, money and position win every time. Men have their own agendas and go after wealthy girls to help them achieve those goals. Foolishly, because she wants badly to believe in love and the fairy tale with the happy ending, a woman goes along with him, only to wake up and realize he's married her for all the wrong reasons.''

"You sound cynical."

She shrugged. "Maybe I am. Okay, not *all* men are opportunists, but many are."

He smiled to lighten his words. "You're sounding as if you're coming from personal experience on this."

"You could say that." And she'd said more than enough on the subject. Holding onto the table, she stood and began stacking the dishes.

Time to back off, Sean thought. He knew she came from wealth. Had some guy gone after her for her money, fooling her into thinking he cared about her, then walked away from her? She'd aroused his curiosity, but he could see she was closing down.

He got up, too. "No, you don't. You cooked, I clean up. House rules. Go sit down."

"Are you sure?" She felt fine, and she did want to do her share.

"Positive. Go!" He carried dishes to the kitchen counter.

She went.

It was so quiet up here, Laura thought, just as it was at their cabin. So peaceful. Summers, you could hear birds in the trees and small, furry creatures scurrying about, the occasional owl at night and the stream rushing over rocks. But in the winter, with the ground wearing a thick blanket of snow and tree limbs bending from the weight of all that white stuff, it was eerily still outside.

Standing at the bedroom window, she saw that the snowfall had been reduced to occasional flurries. As far as the eye could see, there was virginal white, a pristine covering over all. Man had yet to stomp around with footprints and shovels and snow removers to destroy the beauty. But in the morning, she was sure it would begin.

Holding onto the bedpost, Laura limped over to Danny's bookshelves, feeling out of place. Not only because she was in a child's room but, in contrast, she was wearing a floor-length flannel nightgown with long sleeves and lace at the tiny collar. The meeting of the young and the old. Sean's Irish mother must be slightly taller and quite a feminine woman.

She read some of the titles. A Dr. Seuss collection, some classic fairy tales, books about bunnies and trains. Choosing one at random, she looked inside the front cover and saw Sean's name carefully printed inside in a childish hand. The books had been his as a boy, and he'd brought them up here to read to his son. Replacing the book, Laura was impressed at the kind of father he must have been. Too many men, including her dad, didn't think being a father was as important as his chosen work.

She heard a quick knock at the door, then Sean's quiet voice. "Can I come in a minute?"

Laura glanced down at herself, covered from head to toe. She didn't suppose the absence of a robe mattered, not wearing this old-fashioned gown. "Yes, of course."

He walked in and saw she was standing by Danny's bookshelves, her slight frame backlit from the lamp on the nightstand. He was certain she wasn't aware that the thin material of his mother's gown was all but transparent from where he stood, outlining her womanly curves. Her dark hair was haloed around her oval face, falling to her slender shoulders. For a moment, Sean just stood there and stared.

"Did you want something?" Laura asked, puzzled at his unreadable expression.

He shifted his feet, breaking the spell. "I wanted to

know if you need a pain pill. After dinner, you seemed to be hurting some.''

She shook her head. ''I'd rather not, but thanks.'' She waved a hand toward the bookshelves. ''These were yours as a boy?''

He stepped closer, nodding. ''Yes.'' He touched the spine of one or two, his expression melancholy.

''I have many of the same ones. Do you still read a lot?''

''When I have time. I like mysteries, courtroom dramas. If I hadn't gone into medicine, I think I might have enjoyed the law.''

''Why did you choose medicine?'' He was standing close enough that she could make out his day's growth of beard, and she wondered if it was soft or bristly. His fair hair looked almost silky so she imagined his beard might be, too.

He was having trouble keeping his mind on their conversation. She smelled soapy clean and softly feminine, the scent playing havoc with his senses. ''My father was a doctor, a GP. We lived in the northern end of Phoenix when I was young, and it was quite undeveloped back then. Dirt roads, miles between houses. Dad used to make house calls. One of the last of a dying breed, I guess.''

''That's for sure. But you chose to specialize.''

''Yes. My aunt died in childbirth and, though I was young, it made a huge impression on me. I wanted to be a doctor so I could help women like her.''

For long moments, Sean studied her face, wanting to ask her something, yet he hesitated. He'd never asked anyone before and he felt awkward. ''You have a lovely profile. Do you think you could sit for me for awhile tomorrow? I'd love to sketch you.''

Laura was certain she looked as surprised as she felt.

No one, certainly not her father, had ever called her beautiful. "I…I'm not model material, really. I'm very average looking and…"

Sean frowned, though a smile tugged at the corners of his mouth. "Are you fishing, Laura?"

"No, of course not." She was telling the truth, as she knew it.

He believed her. "Who told you you're merely average looking?" He raised a hand and ran the backs of two fingers along one cheek. "Whoever it was, they're myopic. You have great cheekbones, flawless skin and your eyes…" He cocked his head, studying her. "They hint at something only you know. Mysterious." He wondered if he could capture that look. And her mouth…well, he wasn't going to go into that or she'd surely refuse him.

He took a step back. "So what do you say, will you pose?"

"Do you ever sell your sketches?" She wasn't sure she wanted her face hanging in some gallery. After all, she didn't for a minute believe his assessment of her assets. Hadn't her father told her repeatedly that she'd better get a good education because she wasn't all that pretty? She was the rich one, Tate the pretty one and Molly the smart one. Surely Sean could see that and was merely flattering her.

"I never have. It's just a hobby, something I enjoy doing. Are you worried I'll send your sketch off to a magazine and you'll be on the cover of thousands of issues?"

"Good Lord, no!" She hobbled over to the bed, sat down. "I just think I'd feel foolish sitting there while you studied my face."

"Look, with the snow piled up out there, it's unlikely

we'll get out of here for a couple of days yet. It'll help pass the time. If you hate posing, we'll quit. Okay?''

The man was persistent and he was her host. Even if the roads were cleared, she could hardly leave with her car jammed between two trees in a ravine and barely able to stand on her ankle. Still, she didn't owe him this, something she felt most uncomfortable about. ''I don't think so, but I *am* flattered.''

He took the rejection well, just smiled as he stepped closer and ran a hand down her hair from her crown to the very ends where his fingers lingered. Then he turned and left, leaving the door slightly ajar.

And leaving Laura staring after him, still feeling the jolt of even that light touch.

He ought to be sound asleep, Sean thought. He'd shoveled snow until he was half frozen, then chopped wood until his arms ached. He wasn't used to physically exerting himself that much in one day. He should be quite worn out. Afterward he'd had a warm, satisfying dinner, which should have made him sleepy.

Then why was it that he was still wide awake after reading for an hour and pounding the pillows for another? His discomfiture could be summed up in two words: Laura Marshall.

The week he'd planned as a quiet period of remembrance had instead turned into restless days and fidgety nights. And she'd managed to do this to him without being even slightly aware of the turmoil she'd caused within him.

While it was true that he hoped never again to commit to a serious relationship, he was a young, healthy male who got lonely at times. He hadn't sworn off women altogether, though he'd probably be better off if he could.

Yet all that had to happen was a beautiful woman literally landing in his lap during a snowstorm that maroons them together for days, and his resolve begins to slip. Badly.

It wasn't just a physical desire for Laura that was disturbing his sleep. There was something about her—a vulnerability, a sadness behind those huge blue eyes, a loneliness he sensed within her that he easily recognized since he happened to share it. She was hurting, and not just from her physical wounds. Someone or something had shaken up her world, and the awful part was she couldn't even identify it. That defenselessness appealed to a purely masculine need to protect, to hold her close and keep her safe.

How had this slender woman gotten under his skin so completely in just over twenty-four hours when many others had tried over four years and not gotten to first base?

At first, he'd been highly annoyed to have his self-imposed solitude broken by an uninvited guest. But even here, where memories flooded his mind and disturbed his emotions, Laura's very presence had distracted him, in a good way. Where before on these pilgrimages he'd walked the hills and flatlands around his cabin, weeping and moaning against the fates, since her arrival, he'd put that part of himself on the back burner. He'd spent his time wondering about her problem, trying to get her to open up so he might help her, worrying about what awaited her upon her return from whatever frightening experience she was still blocking out.

And in the process, perhaps he'd begun to heal.

She attracted him, and that was wonderful. Not that he would do anything about it, even if she'd invite him to, which seemed unlikely. But knowing that a woman was attractive to him again made him feel normal, on the road

to recovery. For most of the past four years, he'd doubted
he'd ever feel anything close to attraction again, and it
had frightened him.

His thoughts weren't sexual, not yet, at least, though
he supposed they could swing that way easily enough.
For right now, the need to protect, to safeguard her was
enough. To erase that agitated look that she'd get when
she tried to remember and replace it with the soft smile
she'd worn when she'd spoken about assisting in the birth
of her friend's baby. He wanted to lie with her, run his
fingers through that glorious cloud of hair as he'd started
to earlier tonight, to shield her while she slept and keep
watch.

Sean shook his head as if to clear it and swung his
legs over the edge of the bed, wondering if he'd truly
gone round the bend this time.

It was then that he heard a cry of alarm coming from
the direction of the next bedroom, followed by a stran-
gled sob. He was on his feet and running before he was
totally aware he'd left his room.

He found her thrashing her head on the pillow in the
narrow child's bed, her arms flailing about as if she were
fighting off someone instead of merely wrestling with the
comforter, her eyes tightly closed as she muttered and
whimpered.

"No, no, not my things," she sobbed out. "Broken,
destroyed. Oh, God, no, please." One hand flew to her
forehead as if trying to rub out a headache. "Why, why
me? Who did this?"

She'd even scared off Max, the cat cowering in the
corner, his yellow eyes open wide.

Sean approached the bed and took hold of her gently
so as not to frighten her out of the dream too quickly.
"Laura, you're having a nightmare. Wake up, come on.

You're all right.'' He slipped his arm under her, drawing her against his chest as he arranged himself on the bed, brushing her hair from her face with his free hand.

"The picture," she wept out. "Even the picture. No, no.''

Would he have to slap her awake? Sean wondered as he tried to settle her against himself. "Laura! Wake up!'' He stroked her cheek, then cupped her chin and spoke her name again, louder than before.

Her eyes fluttered open. "What? What's wrong? Why are you here?'' She struggled to sit up.

"You were having a nightmare and crying out.''

Half-leaning into him, half-seated, she pushed back her hair with both hands. "Yes, a dream. I was back in my home in Scottsdale, just before I left. Oh, God!''

Sean kept his arm around her. "Did you remember what happened?'' Whatever she was recalling seemed to be frightening her badly.

Laura drew in a shaky breath. "Yes, it was like I was reliving it.'' She shook her head, closing her eyes. "Awful.''

"Do you want to talk about it?'' He placed the two pillows against the headboard behind her.

She leaned back. Maybe if she talked to him about what she now remembered all too vividly, she could come to grips with it herself. She was tired of running from her problems, tired of trying to make sense of it alone. Sean had a no-nonsense way about him; perhaps he could view it all unemotionally and help her see.

By way of an answer, she scooted toward the wall, making room for him on the narrow bed. So wrapped up in her lingering nightmare was she that she didn't consider that he might construe her invitation as sensual, but rather as practical. He couldn't very well sit in a child's rocking chair while they talked.

Sean sat down alongside her, his back to the headboard, and stretched out his legs. He waited, letting her talk if she felt like it.

Laura gazed off in middle distance, beginning by telling him about returning from college, going to work for her father, meeting Marc Abbott and being swept off her feet by him. Her emotions swamped her as she struggled for composure.

"Thinking of him now, I can't imagine what I saw in Marc, but back then, I think I wanted someone to pay attention to me, to notice me since my father seldom did." Briefly, she met his eyes, saw he was watching her intently. "How pathetic does that sound?"

"Not pathetic. Normal. Very normal."

She recognized sympathy in his eyes and eased back from it. "Poor little rich girl, right? Don't feel sorry for me. I had more than most."

Yes, she did, he thought. Except love and joy and affection.

"I only told you that to show you why I fell so hard for Marc. He'd been a football star at ASU, the golden boy whose pro possibilities ended with a knee injury in his senior year. So he had to rely on his good looks and charm to get what he wanted, and he was clever. He figured out very quickly how to win the boss's daughter. A few dates, a little flattery and I was his. God, I hate the thought that I was so needy that I believed all he said." She wondered if she sounded as bitter as she felt.

"Are you saying he deliberately set out to romance the boss's daughter?" Con men were a dime a dozen, but Sean hadn't thought a woman as lovely as Laura would fall for one. But he was also aware that insecurities ran deep and often weren't visible to the casual observer.

"Oh, yes. Later, he told me that he'd done research on me, like for a term paper. He learned the restaurants I preferred, my favorite foods, that I enjoyed horseback riding, baseball and old movies." Marc had told her a lot of things she wished she could forget. *Did you think someone like me would actually fall for a little mouse like you? You're not even good in bed!*

The bastard, Sean couldn't help thinking, his hands fisting. Bad enough to do it, but then to brag about it to her—unforgivable.

She'd come this far, humiliated herself this much, she might as well reveal the rest, Laura decided. So she told him about her father putting Marc in charge of commercial acquisitions shortly after their wedding and then starting to build them the house of their dreams. Only her dream fell apart when she began to suspect Marc of playing around while presumably working. By the time she caught him at it, her feelings for him had all but died.

"Why didn't you do something about it the very first time, maybe even go to your father?" Sean felt that if someone did it once, they'd likely do it again.

"Because I was ashamed knowing I'd made such bad choices. Dad hadn't thought in his wildest dreams that I'd marry someone I'd known for such a short time, but I was so swayed by Marc's aggressive pursuit that I did. Oh, maybe a part of it was a sort of rebellion. Then I stayed in a miserable marriage longer than I should have because I was too humiliated to admit I'd made a terrible mistake."

"You wouldn't have been the first to jump into marriage and regret it."

"Probably not." She wondered if he, too, had regretted his marriage. The one time he'd spoken of his wife, he'd seemed more angry than sad.

Sean frowned, trying to sort out what she'd said and relate it to her nightmare. "I'm a little lost here. What's your marriage to Marc Abbott got to do with why you were so frightened that day?"

"I'm getting to that. When I reached my front door that day, it was slightly ajar. It was probably stupid of me, considering someone could have still been inside, but I pushed it open. I nearly collapsed. The place was trashed, drawers pulled out, books on the floor, lamps overturned, in every room."

"And you think Marc did the damage?"

"Who else? I lead a pretty quiet life. If I have enemies, I sure don't know who they might be. Besides, Marc had broken in once before, *after* he'd cleaned out our two bank accounts, and hauled away several valuable wedding gifts we'd received. You see, after our breakup, my father fired him and also made sure he wouldn't be hired on by any other realtors in the area. Maybe that was going too far, but that's the way Dad operates."

"I believe I agree with your father on this one. Were more things missing?"

"No, that's the surprising thing. Last time, he'd just taken everything valuable he could carry and left the rest the way it was. This time, it seemed as if he'd been searching for something, hadn't found it and had gotten so mad that he'd trashed the place in an angry fit. He…he'd even broken the ceramic frame I kept on my nightstand with my mother's picture, something Marc knows I cherish."

Always logical, Sean had a question. "Okay, so he broke in, searched everywhere, then trashed the place. Do you have any idea what he might have been looking for?''

''Not really. I don't keep money in the house. The papers from my desk were all over the floor, and I didn't look through them, but I can't imagine he'd want anything there. We've been divorced for nearly two years.''

''Well, maybe he's trying to get something on you to blackmail you.'' At her raised-brows look, he dismissed that thought. ''Just trying out theories. Do you remember calling the police or maybe your father?''

''I'd called the police after the first break-in and they'd come out and made a note of what was missing, but they told me I had no proof that it was Marc who'd done it. Still, they questioned him and, of course, he denied everything. He'd also probably hocked everything by then. He'd come to me before that and asked me for some seed money so he could set himself up in a small business, since it was my father who'd ruined him, according to Marc. I told him to use the money he'd taken out of our bank accounts, but he'd already spent that. Marc liked to live well and had gotten used to it in the year and a half we were married. He'd stormed out of there that time and told me that one day I'd be sorry.''

''I'd say that constitutes a threat.''

''My word against his, the police would say.''

''How about a restraining order?''

''Based on what, a break-in and theft I couldn't prove, a threat no one else heard? The police aren't real helpful unless you've got solid proof.''

''How about your father? He's got connections. Couldn't he get someone to point out the error of his ways to this guy?''

''I told Dad about the first break-in, and he berated me for not getting a security system installed as he'd advised me to do. I didn't call him this time. Subconsciously I think I felt that he'd be critical of me yet again for everything including having married the man in the first place.'' Laura sighed, wondering if she'd been better off not remembering that awful day. ''You have no idea how violated you feel when someone comes in and handles your things and does so much irreparable damage. The thought of having to return and face all that...'' She put a hand to her forehead, rubbing absently at a headache.

''Maybe you're not giving your father enough credit here. If he learns you could be in danger, surely he'd help.''

''Maybe, but I'm not sure I want to risk that. He's a man who prides himself on being able to handle anything that comes along, and doesn't have much respect for someone who doesn't. I'm not like that always. Someone invaded my home, destroyed my security. At the time, it seemed like the last straw. I...I ran. I guess I'm a coward.''

''I think you're being way too hard on yourself.''

''No, I'm being bluntly honest. Sometimes parents have too high expectations for their child. I never quite made mine proud of me. Grades not high enough, beauty not great enough, talent not strong enough. Married a mistake that keeps popping up and presenting more problems. Dad would *not* be understanding.''

Sean angled his body so he was facing her, then took hold of her chin so she'd turn his way and look at him. ''Laura, your parents' opinion of you, or your version of that, isn't necessarily the true one, the right one. For instance, what grade point did you have when you graduated from college?''

''A very average three point five.''

''That's a B+. Average is a C. So much for grades not

high enough. Talent? How well do you do in your business? Got a lot of clients, make a decent income?''

"I guess so. Aside from the work I do for Dad's company, I have six commercial and over a dozen individual accounts.''

"In what, six years, seven?''

"Five, actually.''

"I'd say that's doing quite well.'' He eased back from her, looking into her eyes, wondering if he could give her the confidence she needed. Wondering, too, who other than her father had persuaded her otherwise. "As for the beauty part, what would someone have to do to convince you you're right up there on any guy's top-five short list? You've got gorgeous hair, lovely skin, eyes a guy could get lost in and a terrific shape.'' Silently, she watched him out of those midnight blue eyes. "You really should believe me. In my work as a doctor, I see a lot of women, and most can't hold a candle to you. You're special, Laura. Believe it.''

She wished she could, but old habits die hard. She shifted, suddenly aware of his nearness and her own response to his close proximity. She hardly knew this man and she was sprawled on a bed with him, wearing only a thin nightgown. And he had on only a pair of skimpy gray knit shorts. Her face grew warm. "Thanks, I appreciate you trying to make me feel better. I'm sorry I woke you.'' She shivered involuntarily, remembering the powerful dream.

He caught that and guessed at its cause. Perhaps they'd talked enough for one night. "Why don't you snuggle down and get some rest? I'll stay until you fall asleep.''

She marveled at how easily he'd read her mind, that she dreaded being alone after a nightmare. Scooting down inside the covers, she let him arrange her pillows more comfortably. "Thank you," she whispered, and closed her eyes.

Sean sat gazing at her in the dim glow of the night-light. He hadn't been putting her on—she was every bit as lovely as he'd said. That fool she'd married had obviously been too self-involved to see it. And now he was hounding her, trashing her home. Maybe when they got back, he'd have a talk with Marc Abbott, Sean thought. Often as not, his size alone intimidated most people. Not that he was a threatening man, unless he had to be. Laura's father apparently wasn't in on what was going on. Someone had to help her through this.

There was that protective urge again. He hadn't felt that way in a very long time. Maybe it was a good sign.

His arm was still around Laura, though she was turned away from him. Her breathing was not yet deep and even. He decided to close his eyes for just a moment and wait her out.

Chapter Five

Her shoulder was hurting. Still half asleep, Laura shifted, trying to get comfortable. Nothing worked, so she turned over with her back to the wall and…and saw in the dim glow of the night-light that Sean was stretched out alongside her. His big frame seemed to dwarf the child's single bed. He was sound asleep precariously perched on the very edge of the bed. It was amazing he hadn't fallen off.

She remembered he'd said he'd stay until she fell asleep. Apparently, he'd succumbed, as well. Lying very still, she studied him. In repose his face lost some of its seriousness, making him look more accessible. She recalled the way he'd touched her hair last night so gently, the way he hadn't tried to persuade her to sit for him once she'd said no. She liked that about him, that he didn't push.

He frowned fleetingly, then it was gone, and Laura

wondered if he was dreaming, and if the dream was disturbing. It was difficult to even imagine losing both your wife and your child. The pain, she was certain, never really went away, yet Sean was pleasant most of the time. She'd opened up to him about her fears, about her disastrous marriage to Marc, and he'd been an attentive and sympathetic listener. If he chose to confide in her about his family, she'd certainly be there for him.

He lay on top of the comforter, wearing only gray knit shorts, his chest sprinkled with tawny hair, his legs long and muscular. He must be chilly yet he gave no indication. His hand lay inches from her own, his long fingers slightly curled. She found herself wanting to take hold of that hand, to lace her fingers with his, to feel his warmth. He seemed to personify strength and safety, something the men in her life so far had been sorely lacking. Marc had neither and her father, well, he was strong enough, but Owen was much too self-centered to believe that she'd never really felt safe with him. And she badly needed to feel safe.

The thought of having to return to her ransacked home to clean up the mess Marc had made filled her with anxiety. Why was he doing this to her? What did he want, besides money? She was sorely tempted to write him a check with the stipulation that he leave town, but she knew blackmailers never quit. How was she going to rid herself of her ex-husband?

Her gaze returned to Sean's face, his thick eyelashes resting on tanned cheeks, his full lips and a tiny dimple in one corner of his mouth that she hadn't noticed before. There was dark blond stubble on his face that didn't detract one bit from his appeal. She remembered how he'd looked when she'd told him about Marc's infidelities, his big hands curling into fists. Here was a man who'd fight for his own without hesitation, she'd wager. Why couldn't she have met him before Marc had destroyed her trust?

What had his wife been like? Laura wondered. Had they been happy together? Had this cabin been their private getaway, one he'd built for her with that beautifully designed kitchen? Probably, since there were no guest rooms. They'd likely brought their young son here, and the three of them had shut out the world and just enjoyed one another.

She drew in a breath as a swift longing for just such a union swept through her. Growing up, she hadn't wanted a marriage like her parents had, one always gone amassing a fortune while the other one sat home alone. Neither of her roommates had done well in the love department. Molly's first marriage to a man who'd dumped her because his family hadn't approved of her had caused her friend to back away from men entirely until recently when Devin Gray convinced her to take a chance on him. Tate's experience with men, though vast, was no shining example of love conquering all.

Laura sighed. Was there such a thing? Were there men in this world who'd love a woman for who she was, not what her family had? Many of her friends envied her for the silver spoon she'd been born with, but Laura thought of her family's money as more of a curse than a blessing. How could she ever again believe a man wanted her for herself alone?

Studying Sean's face, she had the feeling he might be one of those men, but she'd been wrong before. Maybe he had been before tragedy struck, but now, she had a feeling he was struggling with his own demons. As a doctor, he probably made plenty of money, but he had other problems. The last thing either of them needed at this stage of their lives was an entanglement.

But a girl could dream, Laura thought as she raised herself up on one elbow and reached with her other hand to ever so lightly brush back a lock of his sandy hair. He awoke instantly, his eyes a deep pewter in the soft light. He didn't move, but his breathing stepped up as he watched her.

Laura wasn't a risk taker, nor was she very impulsive. But there were times when everyone had to act out of character. Perhaps she could blame it on her concussion; a bonk on the head could easily change a person's personality momentarily.

Before she lost her nerve, she leaned over and touched her mouth to his.

His lips were warm, soft and unmoving. Fear of rejection emboldened her. She increased the pressure ever so slightly, then, just as she was about to pull back and apologize for reading him wrong, Sean's arms went around her at the same time he shifted their positions so she was on her back pressed into the mattress and he was leaning into her.

His mouth was moving now, kissing sweetly then more deeply. His arms crushed her to him and he drank from her like a man who'd wandered the desert a long while without water. He changed angles and sent his tongue in to explore her mouth as a small moan escaped from Laura.

She felt his need, too long denied, like her own. She felt those big hands of his kneading her back, making her feel fragile beneath his touch. It had been so long since she'd been held, been kissed like this—or had she ever? All she'd ever wanted was to be loved, to be everything to one man. She didn't kid herself that this man was offering that, but she could pretend, for just a little while.

Pretend that he needed her as much as she needed someone, to fill the long, lonely times. Pretend that he had no other agenda, that the feelings would be real and lasting. Wanting to give to him, she reached up and drew him closer as his kiss drew her in.

He'd almost forgotten how the softness of a woman, a willing woman, could make a man feel, Sean realized. He wanted to sink into Laura, to block out the world and know only her. He wanted nothing else to matter, not his sad and troubled past nor her fears or unhappy marriage. He wanted her to make him forget.

But sometimes we want too much and the gods get tired of listening. Sean eased back from her and pulled in a deep breath, letting his pounding heart settle. He leaned back even farther, confused and conflicted. "Thank you for that. It was good of you to try to make me feel better." Since he'd told her that Danny was gone, he'd noticed her eyes fill with sympathy nearly every time she looked into his.

A frown creased her brow. "Is that what you think I did?"

"What else could it be?" He sat up and swung his legs over the side of the bed, then ran a trembling hand over his face. "I shouldn't have crowded you like that on this small bed. I'll go now so you can rest."

He was leaving her like this, with his misconception firmly in place? No!

Laura grabbed his hand as he stood. "Sean! I wasn't trying to make you feel better about anything. I…I kissed you because I wanted to know what it would be like."

"Well, now you have and now you know that I'm a normal, red-blooded man who is attracted to you more than I'd planned on. But it doesn't change anything and it doesn't solve either of our problems.'' He checked the clock and saw it was just after midnight. The witching hour. How appropriate.

A bit unsteadily, he walked to the door. "Get some sleep." He left the room.

Get some sleep? Like she could just turn over and go to sleep after that.

Staring after him, Laura lay wide awake and worried. She'd kissed a number of men, and not one had ever thought she'd done it out of charity. Did Sean consider himself so pathetic as to arouse pity instead of desire in a woman? Why?

She shifted the pillows into the center of the small bed and rearranged the comforter, trying to sort things out. There was much she didn't know about her reluctant host. Somehow, these feelings of his were wrapped up in how and why his wife and son died. If only she could get him to open up.

Because that kiss had rocked her to her very soul. And although she wasn't vastly experienced, she could tell he'd been plenty moved, as well. While it was true that she didn't want another relationship just now and was still wary of trusting men, when a simple kiss blows off the top of your head, there's usually something there. Something she wasn't about to walk away from without further exploration.

His bedside clock read three in the morning and he still wasn't asleep. His bed was large, warm, comfortable—yet he lay staring at the ceiling, turning and tossing, pounding the pillows. And reliving that kiss.

He never should have responded. Sean almost laughed aloud at that crazy thought. Like he could have stopped his mind and body from responding to the giving warmth of her, the generosity, the sensuality. He'd known even as he said the words that she hadn't kissed him out of some misplaced sympathy. But as an exit line, he'd thought it worthy of a try. Of course, she'd seen through it. Who wouldn't have?

He'd had to get out of there before he let his baser instincts take over, before he'd yanked back the comforter and ripped off that flannel nightgown that seemed more tantalizing to him than some skimpy revealing scrap of material might have. Though she seemed oddly unaware of it, Laura Marshall was a lovely woman. And although he couldn't explain it, even to himself, he felt something for her that went well beyond a physical need.

Perhaps her vulnerability had seduced him. Certainly her easy acceptance of her less-than-pleasant circumstances had impressed him. The tears he'd seen in her eyes that she'd refused to shed when she'd told him about her rotten ex-husband had filled him with admiration and conflicting emotions. Fury for the man and tenderness for the woman who'd given her heart to someone who'd wanted only her money. He knew she was left doubting her own judgment now, afraid to trust.

Yet she'd kissed him.

Sean kicked off his covers, the heat of his thoughts offering more than enough warmth. Maybe he shouldn't read so much into that kiss. If he hadn't taken over, she'd probably have stopped at one small taste and explained the kiss away by saying it was a thank-you gesture.

The hell it was! There was fire in that woman, ready to boil over. He'd felt it held in check at first, then released as he'd deepened the kiss. She'd responded wholeheartedly, hungrily, passionately. And that's when he'd forced himself to pull back before he'd tossed his good sense to the winds and buried himself deep within her giving warmth.

He had too much baggage he was dragging around to be good at another relationship just now. Even if he could make himself stop these February pilgramages to the cabin each year to wallow in his pain and remember the death of his wife and child, that wouldn't mean he'd be over the grief.

And to tell the truth, Laura had a fair amount of baggage of her own. A stalking ex-husband who'd gone a bit far this last time. A control freak of a father, wealthy and powerful. Traumatic amnesia bouts that hadn't been cleared up altogether yet, for she'd not remembered everything. The next man who'd be important in her life would have to be vastly understanding and focused on making her the center of his universe, for she hadn't been paid nearly enough attention up to now.

They'd met each other at the wrong time in both their lives, he finally decided. Though they looked like two normal, successful people, they were both hurting in different ways. They needed to come to terms with that pain before entering a new phase. Maybe one day, when his problems had eased, and hers, too, they'd meet up and try again.

Meanwhile, they still had two, three, maybe even four days before they'd be rescued from their snowed-in hideaway, Sean reminded himself. It would have been far easier to get through those days if that kiss had never taken place. Now, it would sit between them like an eight-hundred-pound gorilla they'd both pretend they didn't see.

Sean flopped over onto his stomach and slammed the

pillow over his head, fervently wishing morning would hurry and arrive.

By six he was up and dressed in old jeans and his U of A sweatshirt, in the kitchen putting on coffee. It was still dark outside, of course, though the snow-covered ground lent some light. Peering out the window, he saw that several drifts were piled really high.

He turned on a couple of lamps, then laid a fire and lighted it, waiting until a good blaze was going. Nothing like a cheery fire to chase away the blues, he thought. Right!

Sean stifled a yawn and walked over to turn the furnace up a notch to help take the morning chill off the house, then sat down on the hearth to tug on his boots. He might as well get some shoveling done while the coffee perked. Just in case, he checked the phone, but it was still out. Usually, that was the last to resume normal operation.

Zipping up his jacket as he stepped onto the porch, he saw that the snow was no longer coming down, but they had plenty to deal with as it was. There had to be five-foot-high drifts in front of his garage door, and he imagined Laura's Bronco was totally covered. Grabbing the shovel he'd left alongside the door, he guessed that today the snowplows would be out clearing off the main highways. However, they wouldn't get to his side road for days. Telephone repairmen and electricians would be out en masse working to restore service. Most of the time, such delays didn't bother him up here because he was usually not in a hurry to go anywhere.

This time was different.

He wanted to get back to Scottsdale, not because of his practice, for he was certain that Jonah was handling things like the true professional he was. No, it was because of his growing attraction to Laura.

Scooping snow onto his shovel and tossing it off the porch, he bent to his mindless task, his brain busily thinking things through. Spending the next couple of days in close quarters with her now that he'd admitted to himself that he wanted her was going to play havoc with his self-control. She was not a woman easily ignored. Already he recognized her scent, a subtle cologne she must have had in that leather bag, even after she left the room. When he closed his eyes, he could picture her luxurious ebony hair, though she often pulled it into a ponytail. He preferred it loose about her shoulders like it had been last night, spread on the pillow. He'd made half a dozen sketches of her, and she hadn't posed for him even once. She was etched in his memory, and he wondered how that could be after so short a time.

Finished with the porch, he began a path around back, knowing he'd have to redo Max's potty. He ignored the occasional gust of snowy breeze, his thoughts occupying him fully. He drifted back in time, recalling how he'd met his wife one June day and hadn't asked her out till September. They'd dated occasionally, then more steadily, their romance and their love developing slowly. Basically, he was a careful man who planned out his life, then worked the plan.

But Laura Marshall had come barreling into his life and knocked the pins out from under him. Trying to think dispassionately, he knew he'd loved Kim, but he hadn't focused on her so completely the way he was with Laura. Perhaps that was because they were confined in a small space for days on end. Or perhaps it was something else again, something Sean was reluctant to put a name to.

At the pile of stacked wood, he stopped and used his shovel to brush off accumulated snow so he could later carry in more chunks of cut wood for the fireplace. Mov-

ing along, he kept clearing a path, finishing with a circular section by the back door. He propped the shovel
there and opened the back door.

That's when all the lights went out. The furnace
wheezed off, the blower shutting down with a great
whoosh. Now what? Sean wondered, closing the door
again and retracing his steps to where his generator sat
alongside a back wall. It was an eight-year-old unit, new
when he'd built the cabin. He'd checked it all out last
fall in preparation for the coming winter. What could be
wrong?

It took him less than five minutes to find out. The
generator had been running night and day for over thirty-
six hours, and it was out of gas. That wasn't the worst
of it. He'd forgotten to fill up his spare storage tank.

Annoyed with himself, Sean planted his fists on his
hips and stared up at the sky just beginning to lighten.
He'd meant to get the extra gas, but it had slipped his
mind. Of course, he hadn't thought they'd get this large
a snowstorm, but still, he should have been prepared. It
wasn't like him not to be.

Trudging around front, he saw that the two-mile stretch
to the main road was covered with a minimum of four
feet of snow in most places. Even if he managed to free
his garage door and the large apron, he doubted he'd have
the energy to shovel a two-mile path so he could go get
the gas, especially after a maximum of two hours of sleep
last night. The most he could hope for was the phone to
get back in service so he could call a private snow-
removal company, knowing they'd be really busy now,
but at least get on their list.

Sean walked around to the woodpile and gathered several pieces into his arms. At least the fireplace would
keep them warm as long as they stayed near it. Shoul-

dering in through the door, he walked over to the wood bin and dropped his load. Removing his gloves, he looked up and saw Laura wrapped in his mother's old chenille robe standing in his son's bedroom doorway.

"What happened?" Laura asked. "Something wrong with the generator?"

Sean frowned as he sat down and went to work removing his boots. "The generator's fine but it won't run without fuel and I forgot to fill the extra gas tank. I'm really angry with myself right now." He set his boots aside and took off his jacket, his movements jerky, before hanging it on the wall peg.

He was a man who blamed himself when things went wrong, large or small. She'd noticed and wondered why. "You couldn't have known there'd be a snowstorm that would last this long. I'm sure they're working on the power lines by now. It'll be back on soon."

Moving to the kitchen, he saw that her hair was wet. "Caught you in the middle of your shower, did it?"

Laura reached a hand to her hair. "Yes." There were no windows in the bathroom. "Suddenly it got really dark in there."

Sean poured himself a cup of steaming coffee. "Good thing I plugged in the pot before I went out to shovel." He sipped slowly, letting the heat warm him. Feeling grimy from his workout, he carried the cup toward his room. "I think I'll grab a quick shower before the hot water cools down altogether. Then I think it's cold cereal for breakfast."

"That's fine." She watched him walk past her, aware that his eyes didn't meet hers. The kiss they'd shared last night was on both their minds, yet neither wanted to mention it. Laura backed into her room to dry off and get dressed, wondering just how they'd avoid the subject all day.

At least he didn't have to worry about shaving since he'd brought only an electric razor, Sean thought as he left his bedroom wearing clean jeans and a tan V-necked pullover with his moccasins. He spotted Max eating tuna near the back door and was glad he'd stockpiled in several cans. What else did cats eat, anyhow? he wondered.

He found Laura seated at the table eating a banana, her coffee at her elbow. Her hair was a riot of curls, so much so he couldn't help but comment. "I had no idea you have curly hair."

She shrugged. "I usually blow-dry it straight. I'm not fond of this look, but I don't have a choice right now."

Sean topped off his coffee. "I like it."

She made a face. "You don't!"

He took the chair opposite her. "Yeah, I do. Makes you look, I don't know, younger, I think." He drank deeply, then dared to ask the question most women hated. "How old are you?"

"Twenty-nine," she answered without hesitation.

He raised both brows. "You're kidding! I would have put you at twenty-five, tops. With that hair now, maybe nineteen." He sipped, watching her finish her banana. "How old do you think I am?" Why did he care what she thought? Sean asked himself, but the question was out.

Sitting back, Laura scrunched up her face, closed one eye, considering. "Mmm, I'd guess thirty-one."

His jaw dropped. "How'd you do that?"

She grinned. "Just a wild guess." They drank companionably for a few moments, and Laura thought perhaps the kiss would stay on the back burner.

She pointed to the sketch pad that he'd left on the table. "I took the liberty of glancing through those while you showered. I hope you don't mind." And been surprised to see her face, front view and profile, looking far better than her mirror reflected. "It seems that you don't need me to pose. You've already done half a dozen sketches of me."

He dropped his eyes, a bit embarrassed. "From memory only, usually when you were out of the room. I could do a lot better if you'd pose." His hands itched to pick up his pencils right now, to get her down on paper with her hair curling wildly about her face, that lovely oval face completely free of makeup and those huge blue doe eyes. Even with technicolor strokes of black and beige and yellow beneath one eye, she looked sensational.

She looked as if she were thinking it over, then shook her head. "I think not." Wrapping her arms around herself, she shivered. "The cabin sure cooled off fast." She was wearing a thin turtleneck and sweatpants.

"Go sit by the fire," he told her, then detoured to his room and came back with a red-and-black plaid big shirt, placing it around her shoulders as she sat on the couch.

"Thanks, that's a lot better." And a lot worse, for the shirt smelled like him—the faint hint of masculine cologne and that indefinable male scent. Settling back into the pillows, she drew the ends of the rough material around her, trying not to inhale too deeply.

Sean bent to poke at the fire to get it going, then sat down beside her, though not too close.

"Thanks for shoveling Max's section. I let him out first thing. I hope you don't mind I opened another can of tuna?" Her eyes on him, she wondered how it was that his unshaven look appealed to her so much when she'd never before been attracted to that look.

"No problem. He's got to eat." As if he knew he was being discussed, Max sauntered in and glanced up at the couch. He must have decided it was too crowded because he jumped up on the hearth instead and stretched out, his yellow eyes beaming in on Sean. "I wonder why he doesn't like me."

"Don't take it personally. He doesn't like men, period. I got him when I moved back to Scottsdale after college and he was already five years old. He'd lived with a woman friend who moved to California and he'd not been around men much. He positively loathed Marc and…"

"I see Max has good taste, after all."

She decided to leave that alone, though she agreed. "…and he hides under the bed when my father comes over, which isn't often."

Sean liked the way the firelight danced over Laura's skin, turning it gold one minute, peach-colored the next. He grabbed onto the topic she'd introduced, one that would hopefully get his mind off her face and how much he'd like to draw her.

"Now that you're on your own, do you get along better with your father?" he asked. The father who'd largely ignored her most of her life, the one she was certain would still judge her harshly, from what she'd already told him.

Laura shrugged, gazing into the fire. "He seems to respect my work, though he's not big on compliments. The way I can tell is that he'd likely let me go if my work wasn't up to his standards."

"Even though you're his daughter?"

Slowly, she turned to look at him, her eyes in shadow. "If he'd gotten complaints, if his bottom line was in jeopardy, sure he would. He's not in the least sentimental.''

Sean found himself disliking Owen Marshall without ever having met him, despite the fact that he didn't consider himself quick to judge. He had every reason to believe Laura was telling the truth. ''I've often wondered why some people have children when they have absolutely no parenting skills. I've been delivering babies for seven years now and I'm to the point where very little shocks me. I had one set of parents ask me how much I thought they could get for their newborn son.''

Laura frowned, then tried to give them the benefit of the doubt. ''Perhaps they had many children already and felt they couldn't afford another mouth to feed.'' Though to sell your child—good heavens!

''No, he was their first. They were a handsome couple and figured they'd have a great-looking child. I'm afraid I was barely polite to them, but I'm sure they found some desperate infertile couple who paid quite a bit.''

''Maybe the child's better off. Think what hell on earth his life would have been with two people like that.'' The sadness of that swept over her, and she went back to studying the fire.

He'd tried to divert her and only succeeded in making her melancholy again. Then he got an idea. ''Do you like hot dogs?''

Surprised by the sudden change of subject, Laura looked up as he stood. ''I guess so, why?''

''I haven't had anything but coffee today, and all you had was a banana. What do you say we roast some hot dogs in the fire?'' Without waiting for her answer, Sean went into the kitchen where he busily assembled hot dogs and buns he'd purchased before coming to the cabin, condiments, two small bags of chips and topped off the tray with a couple of cans of cold soda pop.

"How do you cook in a fireplace?" Laura asked as he set the tray on the hearth.

"Just you watch." Back into the kitchen he went for two long wooden shish kebab sticks. "Here we go." He pushed a dog onto the end of each stick, then held them out. "Come on over. You have to cook your own."

Slipping her arms into the oversize sleeves of the plaid shirt, she walked over to sit on the opposite end of the hearth as he opened the mesh screen. She wasn't even very hungry, but he seemed as excited as a kid so she hadn't the heart to not join in.

Sean noticed she was moving more easily, her ankle less painful apparently. He handed her stick over, then stuck his into the fire. "You've got to watch closely or they'll char." He watched as she hesitantly held her stick toward the heat. "Kind of move it around so it gets cooked inside and kind of singed outside." He demonstrated, waving his stick like a baton.

Laura laughed. "I see you're an expert at this."

"First time I've done it." He was using a stabbing motion now, up and back, over and around. "Wish I'd have thought to get some marshmallows."

So he and his wife hadn't cooked hot dogs in the fireplace, hadn't had playful fireside dinners. "Have you ever stayed in the cabin during a power outage before?"

"Once." Danny had been a baby, and Sean had had reason to be grateful that Kim was nursing him, for they'd run out of most of their food before the plows cleared their small road. Kim had been furious with him, for not being prepared, for coaxing her to spend time at the cabin, blaming him for everything, even the storm.

Laura saw his lips form a thin line and realized she

shouldn't have asked. He was undoubtedly remembering that time, and the memory wasn't a happy one. Why? she wondered.

"Whoa! Your hot dog's on fire." He took the stick from her and blew out the flames. "I guess you could say this one's done." And so was his.

They busied themselves smearing ketchup and mustard on their dogs. "I sure hope the power comes back before everything in the fridge spoils," Sean commented as they returned to the couch to eat their meal.

Laura had to admit it was good, and she was hungrier than she'd thought.

"Mmm," Sean murmured. "The only time a hot dog tastes better than cooked over an open flame is at the ballpark. Did I hear you say you're a baseball fan?"

"Yes, even more since Arizona has the Diamondbacks. That Randy Johnson is some terrific pitcher." She made her way down the hot dog.

"Maybe we could go sometime, when we get back home." Where had that come from? Sean wondered, but found he rather liked the idea.

Those deep blue eyes studied him a long moment. "Maybe." The thought seemed to suggest a future together, even if it was a tentative one. Isn't that what she'd been shying away from?

Sean finished and crumpled up his chips bag before taking a long swallow of his drink. He noticed that Laura had eaten the hot dog but not even opened her chips, setting aside her plate and the unfinished can.

With a sigh, she leaned back. "That was good. Thanks."

He scooted closer, intrigued by a long curl on her shoulder. His fingers wound into the silky softness, unable to resist touching her. When she swung her gaze his way, he saw a dab of ketchup at the corner of her mouth. "Hold still," he told her, then used a fingertip to clean the spot since he'd forgotten napkins.

His hand suspended mere inches from her mouth, he saw the awareness leap into her eyes, saw them turn smoky blue and wary. He should move back or get up and walk away, Sean told himself. A moment longer he watched her while his blood pumped heavily through his veins.

Ah, to hell with it, he decided and gathered her to him, his mouth taking hers. She stiffened for the briefest of seconds, then let herself be held. She tasted of ketchup and mustard and some female essence that drew him to her. With a low sound in her throat, she returned the kiss, her arms encircling him, at last giving herself permission to enjoy.

During a long, troubling night, Sean had almost talked himself into believing his reaction to her during that first kiss had been a fluke, a once-only response brought about by years of abstinence. But no, this was no fluke, no minor happening. He held her tighter and took her under.

Floating, she was floating. Or was she flying? Laura wondered. In either case, she'd left the ground, her feelings soaring. His mouth knew just what to do to make her want more, and more yet. His hands traveled over her, bringing her skin beneath the layers of clothes alive with need. His lips seemed made for hers, coaxing then searing, his teeth nipping then kissing away the tiny love bites.

She was everything he wanted and shouldn't want, everything he needed and hadn't the right to take. The abrupt thought intruded, breaking the spell for Sean. He pulled back from her, his breath coming in huffs, his eyes burning into hers. "We can't do this. We can't."

Not again, Laura thought. Her eyes hazy with lingering passion and filled with sudden questions, she stared at him. "Why not? Is it me, Sean? Is something wrong with me?"

He moved away from her, gritting his teeth in frustration, running a shaky hand over his hair. "No, it's not you." Looking pained, he got up on legs he wasn't sure would work and walked across to stand gazing into the fire, one hand braced on the mantel. "It's not you. It's me."

Chapter Six

Sean watched the fire lick away at the logs, listened to the sizzle and pop, yet heard and saw neither. Instead, in the flames he pictured Laura's face as he knew it must look—confused, hurt, possibly angry. She had every right to all those emotions. He was sending her mixed signals: I want you; no, I don't. If their positions were reversed, he'd probably be furious.

Slowly, he turned and saw her huddled in the corner of the couch, hugging herself as if needing that small measure of comfort, her huge eyes puzzled. He hadn't the right to put her through this.

Walking back over, he searched his mind for the right words. He sat down and leaned forward, resting his elbows on his knees, his eyes on his clenched hands. "I need to explain," he began.

Relieved that finally he might open up to her, Laura turned toward him. "I'm listening."

"I know my actions aren't consistent. Things happened and I...I'm not the man I was four years ago. Back then, I still believed that life was good, that there was much to look forward to." Sean gazed up at the sketch of his son hanging above the fireplace and swallowed around a huge lump. "When Danny died, everything changed, everything fell apart for me."

She could only imagine the depth of his pain, yet her heart went out to him. He'd been grieving four years and still he hurt so badly. She wasn't quite sure what all that had to do with the kiss they'd just shared, but she'd try to be patient until he got around to that part. "Have you tried a grief counselor?" she asked, reaching to touch his arm. "I understand some of them are very good."

"They can't help me." Sean ran a hand over his face, then leaned back, his eyes haunted. "You see, it's my fault Danny died."

Surprised, Laura frowned. "How do you mean?"

He was quiet so long she wasn't sure he'd answer. Finally, he drew in a shuddering breath and began explaining. "Four years ago this weekend, the three of us— my wife, Kim, Danny and I—were here at the cabin. My partner and I were still building our practice, working long hours at the office and the hospital. Kim was getting awfully tired of being alone, so I managed to squeeze in a little time off, hoping a few days away would help our relationship, which I knew had been strained, but I didn't realize how badly. When we got here, nothing I did was right. Suddenly Kim hated the cabin, hated the isolation, the cold weather."

Laura watched him as he gazed at the fire, knowing he was picturing things as they'd been back then. She let him tell it in his own time in his own way.

"Danny and I loved it here." He wasn't aware he was

smiling at the memory. "That morning, I'd taken him out on his new sled, the one I'd bought for his birthday. He'd just turned three. We were having fun, laughing, our faces red from the cold."

He was being much more open than she'd expected, Laura thought. Maybe he needed to talk about this.

"After a while, we went inside and I put him down for a nap. Kim's father had arrived that morning. Her parents lived in Colorado where Hank Rozelli owned several ski equipment stores. He'd been flying his own twin-engine plane for twenty years or more. He'd housed it at a friend's private hangar just north of here. The plan was that I'd go back to work and the three of them would fly to Colorado for a week's vacation. The grandparents just loved to spend time with Danny. I'd promised Kim I'd try to get away and join them near the end of their trip and we'd all fly back together. She was restless, anxious to be on her way, disinterested in hearing yet another of my promises."

Sean shook his head, as if trying to deny what came next. "I didn't want them to go—I'd never been away from Danny, not even overnight—but Kim wore me down with her argument that she needed time with her parents, that she was sick of being alone in our apartment while I worked eighteen hours a day. Guilt can make you agree to lots of things, even against your best judgment."

"Had they flown in her father's plane before?" Laura asked, fairly certain she could guess by now how the accident happened.

"Kim had, but I'd always refused to let Danny go. Hank had never had an accident, she'd told me over and over. But then, it only takes one when you're flying a plane. Kim was certain they'd be fine and Hank kept asking me if I thought he'd knowingly risk the lives of his only daughter and grandson. So I gave in, drove them to the plane and saw them take off about four o'clock. I went back to the cabin and...and spent some time packing up, then drove to Scottsdale. I hurried into our apartment because Kim was to call as soon as they arrived. I waited and waited. Nothing.''

Aware the hard part was coming, Laura moved closer, her hand resting on his arm. She didn't want to interrupt though she was anxious for him to finish.

"Finally, I called Laura's mother, and the phone was answered by a neighbor. I could hear sobbing in the background. The plane had crashed just outside of Denver in a snowstorm that had come up so unexpectedly it had caught even the Weather Bureau by surprise. No survivors.''

His voice was a flat monotone, more chilling than if he'd displayed the emotion she knew he was reliving. "Oh, Sean," she whispered, her arm slipping along his shoulders.

When he looked at her, he saw that compassion had softened the blue of her eyes. "Hank had checked the weather twice. I heard him. No one could explain why they hadn't had even a hint of that impending storm. Even so, it was my fault. I never should have given in to Kim and Hank. I should have followed my first instincts and protected my son. I let him down, and he died because of my failure to speak up.''

"Sean, that's simply not so.'' Her hand moved to cover his tightly twined fingers. "You said it yourself, no one could predict that storm. How could you have known?''

His eyes had grown misty, his throat thick with unshed tears. "It's a father's job to protect his child. I didn't do my job. I gave in to Kim because we'd been arguing and

I wanted to please her, to let her spend time with her folks. I gave in to Hank, who was this big, burly guy used to having his way, because he made me feel rotten that I'd even think he wouldn't take good care of Kim and Danny. So I sent my son to his death.''

"You're wrong, Sean. Sometimes there's nothing we can do to stop a tragedy. Even if you'd have forbidden your wife to go, she might have defied you anyway.''

He ran a hand over his face, as if trying to erase the past. "Maybe if our marriage had been happier, Kim wouldn't have wanted to go. Maybe I could have stopped them somehow. But I didn't.''

She reached to stroke his cheek, turning his face toward her. "I don't think *anyone* could have stopped them, Sean. Sometimes fate takes over.''

"Maybe you're right.'' He shifted his gaze to stare into the fire. "You know, I go about my work most of the time, thinking I'm adjusted to losing Danny. But sometimes, tears ambush me. I'll see a boy of six or seven on the sidewalk playing and I think, Is that what Danny would be like now? Then the tears come and I can't stop them.''

"Then don't even try. You need to let it out.''

"Now do you see why I find it so hard to let another woman into my life? I'm not the workaholic I was back then. However, my hours are still crazy, even with a partner. Let's face it, my work will always be demanding. I'm a doctor.''

Yes, he was a doctor and a very troubled man. Laura had an uneasy feeling that he hadn't told her all of it. She chose her words carefully. "Sean, millions of doctors are married and their wives adjust to their hours. As do lawyers and executives. All sorts of jobs require long hours, especially when you're getting started. Your wife just couldn't adjust. Or wouldn't.'' She had to walk a careful line here between being too critical of the woman he'd married and yet supportive of him.

Sean went on as if she hadn't spoken. "And what if a second wife and I had children? I'd never trust her to not take him away from me at the slightest disagreement."

"Slow down here." Laura leaned back. "Somehow we've gone from a kiss to strolling down the aisle. Not every relationship leads to forever after, Sean." She shoved the sleeves of the big shirt up to her elbows, suddenly warm. "I'm not anxious to get entangled again, either. You might recall I seem to have a bit of a problem with my ex-husband even two years after our divorce. You need to relax. It was just a kiss, for heaven's sake. No big deal."

"No big deal?" He rose, drawing her up with him. His eyes burned into hers, his need to convince her warring with another kind of need he couldn't seem to tamp down. He saw confusion in her gaze and a hint of nerves. His arms encircled her as his mouth crushed hers.

She should push away, Laura thought at first contact. He was trying to make a point and she already knew the outcome. She hadn't denied wanting him, not even to herself, though they both knew it was unwise. They were both in a shaky place in their lives, unsettled, troubled. A lousy basis for a friendship, much less more.

Yet she longed for this, to be held like this, to be wanted so undeniably. No one had ever wanted her like this, as if he were fighting himself and his desire for her was winning out over his good sense. And oh, she ached for him in return, a man who was the walking wounded, one she should run away from. Yet instead, her hands on his back were urging him closer, her mouth opening to him, her heart pounding against his.

Sean was in trouble and he knew it. What had started as a demonstration of his case had suddenly accelerated into something he wasn't sure he'd ever experienced. Seemingly with a will of their own, his hands molded her soft, womanly body to his and the flames spread throughout his system. One quick kiss to show her, he'd told himself. How wrong, how naive he'd been.

But how could he have known that one small taste would only make him crave more, that one kiss with this woman would never satisfy him? The wind outside the cabin dashed a clump of snow against the nearby window, and the weak winter sun went to hide behind a gray cloud. The fire in the grate crackled and spit, but he heard only her quick intake of breath as his hand grazed the side of one breast. He shifted the angle of the kiss, breathing in deeply, his shampoo mingled with the scent of woman.

And his arms around her tightened.

Laura found she had much to give and there was so much pleasure in the giving. She let him drink from her and in turn received so much more. His hands moved into her hair, exploring, exciting, while his mouth made love to hers. It was sheer madness to want a man she'd known merely hours, not weeks or months. Yet her knees nearly buckled as she clung to him, passion clouding her mind.

He could take her now, Sean thought, just pick her up and carry her to the big bed where he'd wrestled the covers thinking of holding her like this. She might protest at first, but then she'd give in. They could strip off their clothes and slip beneath the comforter, to lie together and be able to touch to their hearts' content. But even as he felt her tremble, he knew he wouldn't, couldn't do that. Laura with the fragile beauty she couldn't seem to recognize was not someone to toy with, someone to chase away his loneliness with.

Just as he was about to ease back, Laura broke the kiss, then stepped back and bowed her head as she struggled to control her breathing. Sean swallowed hard, his hands gripping her arms in order to steady them both. He was shaken to his core and knew he was the one who had to break the uncomfortable silence. "If that wasn't a big deal," he managed in a husky voice, "then I'm not sure I'd recognize one."

Slowly, Laura raised her head, and there was the beginning of tears in her eyes. "If you don't want to get involved, why do you keep coming back for more?"

"Damned if I know." He took a step back to give himself some room and ran a shaky hand through his hair. What was there about this small, fragile woman that made him bare his soul, then kiss her until they were both trembling with need, two things he'd promised himself he wouldn't do?

He looked at her again and saw her turn, brushing aside one small tear that trailed down her cheek. He felt like six kinds of a heel. "Laura, I…I want to be perfectly honest here. As I said before, I'm attracted to you. That's obvious. I have been since that first night I carried you in here. You're the first woman since Kim died who's made me feel anything, and it's not just physical. I have feelings for you, feelings I hadn't planned on, and I admit that scares me. I want you, yet I don't want to make the same mistakes."

Laura sat down, trying to pull herself together. This thing between them was almost more unsettling than her accident. He had feelings for her, he'd said. Were they the same feelings she'd begun to have for him?

"I appreciate your honesty. And you've undoubtedly

guessed that I'm attracted to you, too. But I got involved somewhat impulsively once before and lived to regret it. You have nothing to fear from me. I'm not looking for permanence, either. And, for the record, you're the first man I've kissed, much less thought about, since Marc.''

He was feeling marginally better. ''Also for the record, I'm not after your money or your father's influence, so you can rest easy.'' He was surprised he could find a smile. ''Do you think we could go on from here and be friends?''

Laura felt as if she'd fought a battle with no winner and two losers. ''Sure. Why not?''

He held out his hand. ''Shake?''

They shook hands, and Sean's arm slipped around her, easing her into a hug. ''Thanks,'' he said into her hair, ''for understanding. I should have explained myself sooner.''

''No harm done.'' Except she felt battered, bruised.

But his eyes turned serious. ''I wouldn't want to hurt you, Laura.''

He was still filled with guilt, she decided. Or was it something else? ''What makes you think you might?''

The ringing phone prevented him from having to answer. ''It's working again,'' Sean said, rising to get it.

Her mind still on all he'd told her and that soul-jarring kiss, Laura scarcely heard his end of the conversation until he hung up and walked back. ''That was the state police checking. I told them we're fine. Looks like we'll be able to leave soon.'' Feeling oddly dismal about that, Sean reached for his phone book. ''I'm going to call about getting snow removal and towing service for your Bronco. Then you can let your father or whoever know you're all right.''

Sean noticed that she turned back to face the fire without a word, her expression suddenly sad. Was she as reluctant to end their snowbound captivity as he? What was she feeling—concern about returning to face whatever she'd been running from? Was she anxious to get back to her busy life? Or was she wondering if after they got back, they'd ever see one another again?

And the biggest question of all: why did he care?

"Hello, Molly? It's Laura." Curled up in the corner of the couch, Laura held the old-fashioned black phone in her lap, glad she'd found her friend at home.

Shifting her five-month-old son more comfortably onto her hip, Molly tucked the phone into her shoulder so she'd have one hand free to heat the baby's bottle in the microwave. "Laura! I was getting worried about you. Didn't you get the message I left a couple of days ago?"

"I haven't been home." How could she explain her hurried trip from her house and her frantic drive up north to her close friend without sounding like an idiot? Laura wondered. "I set out for our cabin in the Gray Mountains last Friday. I needed to get away for a few days, you know." That was skirting the truth without outright lying, yet Laura still felt guilty.

"Really? I heard there was a storm up that way over the weekend. I hope you missed it." Patiently, Molly unclenched her son's little fingers from where they'd locked onto her hair.

"Not exactly. I'm still up here." It was easier to let Molly assume she was at her own cabin and explain things later. "Listen, Molly, it's a long story, which I'll gladly tell you later. Right now, I need a *huge* favor."

"Name it, kid." Molly tested the milk, found it just right and went to sit down in the rocker in the living room where her daughter, eight-year-old Emily, was lying on the floor on her stomach watching television.

Laura blinked back a rush of tears, wondering why her emotions were so on the surface today. She would have bet good money that her friend's reaction would have been exactly as it was, ready to help without even knowing what was needed.

"I hate to ask, but Daddy Dearest is unavailable, as usual." Which was probably for the best, as she'd rather have Molly's help, which came without strings, than her father's, which didn't. She searched for the right words to explain her situation without alarming Molly. "The reason I left town was that when I got home last Friday around four, I found that someone had broken in and trashed my apartment."

"Marc again?" Molly asked, guessing the obvious, for she knew all about her friend's history with her ex.

"I don't know, but that's my best guess, too. I do know that I panicked and bolted. I'm not even sure I locked the door." Laura knew she sounded very out of character and hoped Molly would understand.

Molly found herself growing angry just thinking about all that Marc had done to Laura through the years. "I don't blame you for being upset. That's a shocking invasion of your privacy. I wonder, was he after something or did he just want to mess with your head?"

Laura closed her eyes for a moment, for she'd asked herself that same question. "I don't know that, either."

"In either case, it's time to report this to the police, Laura. You can't live like this, never knowing when Marc's going to show up and do damage or steal something or threaten you."

"I know and I will, but I was wondering if you could go over and see just how badly the place is wrecked. I remember seeing my mother's picture on the floor, the frame broken as if someone had deliberately stepped on it. The desk had been emptied, drawers upended, books and papers all over the floor.'' Laura's voice trembled as she pictured the scene she wished she didn't have to remember.

"Don't worry, please. Devin and I will go right over and put things to rights." Knowing that the picture of Laura's mother was the only copy she had, Molly's heart went out to her friend. All her life, Laura had been looking for love, since she never got it from her father, which was probably why she'd mistaken Marc's greedy attention for love. She deserved better than that jerk. "Do you want Devin to talk to the police about Marc?"

"I'll be leaving here soon. I think I'd better handle that myself, but thanks." Laura heard gurgles in the background and found herself smiling. "Is that my little Dev I hear? Kiss him for his godmother, will you?" After a disastrous first marriage, her former roommate finally had the family she'd been certain she never would, and Laura was so very happy for her.

"I sure will." Molly paused a moment to nuzzle her baby's cheek, but concern for her friend was uppermost on her mind. "Are you sure you're all right, Laura?"

All right? Sure, if you didn't count being stalked by an ex-husband, crashing her Bronco in the middle of a blinding snowstorm and winding up staying with a man who had just kissed her senseless a few minutes ago, messing up her mind and shattering her resolutions. "I'm fine. I'll bring you up to speed when I see you. And Molly, I can't thank you and Devin enough for doing this for me. The thought of going in there alone again…"

"Not to worry. I'll leave you a note. Be safe and call me when you get back."

"Thanks, I will." Slowly, she hung up the receiver and raised her eyes to the doorway where Sean stood watching her, his eyes shadowed. She put on a false smile and hoped he couldn't see through it. "All set. You need to use the phone, call your partner maybe?"

Sean was certain she had no idea how lost and vulnerable she looked right now. In the small cabin, he'd overheard her end of both her calls and was grateful she had a friend like Molly. Especially after the all-too-brief moment Laura had had with her father's answering machine. Apparently Owen Marshall was out of town and couldn't be reached unless there was an emergency. Great father material, that man.

He pushed away from the arch and wandered over to where she sat staring into the fire again, something she'd been doing a lot. He wanted to get that brooding look off her face, to take her mind off her problems. Bending, he reached into the drawer of the end table and drew out a box. "Do you play gin?" he asked.

Tugging herself back from her troubled thoughts, Laura looked at him, puzzled. "What?"

"Gin rummy. Do you play?"

"I haven't in years, probably not since college." She watched him remove the pack of cards from the box.

"That long, eh?" He wiggled his eyebrows up and down twice, affecting a sinister grin. "Step into my parlor, said the spider to the fly."

She had to smile as she followed him to the table. "So you think you're going to trounce me, is that it?"

Sean lighted the chunky vanilla candle in its brass holder. Though it was still daylight, the cloud cover didn't allow the sun to peek through. He shuffled the cards, showing off. "The thought had occurred to me." He fanned out the deck, then whipped the cards back into a neat stack. "What shall we play for? Go easy on your-self, but make it interesting."

Watching his strong physician's hands deal the cards, she considered possibilities. "Toothpicks? Match-sticks?"

"Puh-leeze. How about strip gin? Lose a game, take off an article of clothing." Again, he wiggled his eye-brows menacingly as he saw her cheeks flush and her mouth drop open. He laughed out loud. "You should see your face! Just kidding. Okay, overall champ gets to lie on the couch while the loser makes dinner. How about that?"

He'd had her going for a minute there. "How hard can making dinner be with no electricity? Make a sand-wich?"

"Let's not forget the four food groups. We'll need carrot sticks and celery, maybe chips and an apple. And a glass of milk." He picked up his cards and held them close to his chest, peeking at one at a time.

"I think I can handle that," Laura said, checking her cards. "However, I might not have to. Did I tell you I paid my way through college on a gin rummy scholar-ship?" Her lips twitched.

He laughed again. "Sure you did. Okay, I dealt, you draw first."

Laura was so intrigued with the way his face, serious most of the time, looked when he laughed that it took her several seconds to pick a card. Now if only she could keep her mind on the game instead of reliving that stun-ning kiss...

"Wait a minute!" Laura was indignant. "That's not fair, going down first thing without even giving me a chance to draw one card."

"Sure, it's fair. You go down when you think you can beat your opponent." He leaned forward, egging her on. "Come on, let's see what you're holding."

They'd been playing at least two hours, and Laura had yet to win a hand. With a feigned aggrieved sigh, she threw down her cards. "All right, I give up. You win."

"Aha! And how many points do you lose on this hand, Ms. Card Shark Extraordinaire?"

"Fifty-five, but you cheat!"

"Do not." Smiling smugly, Sean shuffled the cards. "Are you ready to say uncle or do you want to go on?"

"Uncle, uncle." Laura shifted in her chair and raised both arms in a stretch to relieve her cramped shoulder muscles. Her recently dislocated shoulder felt fairly normal finally, and the swelling in her ankle had all but disappeared. Her middle was still discolored from the bruising, though her stomach was no longer sore. She felt fine again except for this restlessness.

Rising, Laura stuffed her hands in the pockets of the oversize shirt she wore and wandered over to stare out the window.

Sean set aside the cards and gave in to a big yawn. He hadn't been sleeping well, and the reason for that was standing across the room from him. Still, he followed her over. "Are you all right?"

Without turning, she answered him with a question of her own. "Is that the doctor asking or the man?"

"Both."

"I see. Well, Doctor, I think I have cabin fever."

"A malady that can be cured in several ways. You could pose for me, which would occupy several hours. Or we could go out and build a snowman."

Smiling at that, Laura turned, then stopped when she realized he was much closer than she'd thought. Her smile slipped as she looked into warm gray eyes studying her closely. This had to stop.

Sidestepping him, she walked away. "I don't feel like posing or playing in the snow." She strolled toward his overflowing bookcase. "Maybe a little reading..."

Wondering why he didn't just leave her to her own devices and spend some time with his sketchbook, Sean found himself following her yet again. "Lots to choose from. What do you like to read?"

She scanned titles, noticing books on gardening, on illustrating, some science fiction and loads of mysteries. He'd mentioned he liked to read just about everything. "Quite an eclectic collection."

Sean shrugged. "You never know when an author will grab you and draw you into his story." He removed a paperback that looked well read. "Take this one, for instance. Patricia Cornwell writes about a fictitious medical examiner who runs into all manner of cases. Her autopsies get a little gruesome, but they have the ring of truth because the author actually worked in a pathology lab."

"Yes, I've read her. She's very good." Still looking, she pulled out a book by Anne Morrow Lindbergh. "Here's one I wouldn't have guessed you'd read—a book of poetry."

He replaced his book and leaned against the wall, crossing his arms over his chest. "I bought and read that shortly after Danny died. The Lindberghs also lost a son, and I hoped she might give me some insight into accepting my son's death."

"Did she?"

"Mmm, I'm not sure. Everyone handles death differently, I've come to realize. But her writing is very moving."

There was a lot of depth to this man, Laura was beginning to realize. She'd wager that most if not all of the men she'd known would steer clear of poetry.

Just then, the furnace gave a mighty wheeze and rumble, and two lamps alongside the couch went on.

"The power, finally," Sean commented.

"I suppose this means you'll want me to cook an elaborate dinner since the stove will be working," she teased.

"You got it." He walked over to the small radio on the kitchen counter and turned it on. Searching through the static, he found a station featuring a rousing country and western tune. "Sounds like line dancing," he said, returning to her. "Do you know how?"

"I don't think so."

"Come on. I'll show you."

"Aren't you supposed to have several people for a line dance?"

"We'll improvise. Just follow my lead." He took one of her hands and guided her arm across his shoulders, then took hold of her the same way. The area in front of the bookcases near the door leading to the garage had plank flooring and was good-size. Sean maneuvered her there, moving in time to the music, demonstrating the steps, getting her into the swing of things.

He was smiling at her, as excited as a little boy, Laura thought as they made their way around the floor, first to the left, then shuffle and switch to the right, continually moving forward, then backward. She couldn't help but smile back at his enthusiasm. Maybe she was good for him, keeping his mind off his sadness, as he was for her, making her forget her troubles. Laughing as they picked up the tempo, moving faster and faster. Somehow, she managed to keep up without straining her ankle.

Long minutes later, the musical number ended as Sean hugged her close, both of them laughing.

''Well, that certainly put a little sparkle in our day, didn't it?'' she asked, feeling upbeat.

But Sean was drawing her against his body as the next song began, a slow-dancing fifties number. Without skipping a beat, he had her swaying with him to the old ballad.

''You-oo-oo, thrill me, honest you do…''

Laura's heart beat faster during this slow song than it had during the hectic line dance. It had nothing to do with the music and everything to do with the man whose hand at her back pressed her closer as she felt his breath warm her cheek. This felt like a mistake. It felt like madness to deliberately put herself into his arms. Yet it felt so good.

Her hand was damp in his, Sean realized, and wondered if it was from the heat of the fire, the fast polka or being molded to him. A saxophone moaned in the background, the sound filled with longing. He guided her away from the fire, into the shadows. His stomach muscles tightened as he draped both her arms over his shoulders and shifted her even nearer. Swaying with her, he wondered why he was putting himself through this exquisite torture when he was the one who'd put the brakes on during their last encounter.

Because he couldn't seem to help himself, he realized.

Laura could feel his heartbeat even through the thickness of the heavy shirt she wore, as erratic as her own, thudding against her breast. Unable to stop herself, she touched the hair curling at the nape of his neck, running her fingers through the softness.

What on earth was she doing?

Since her divorce, she'd avoided situations like this. It was so easy in and around Scottsdale, going to functions with a select few men she'd deemed tame and solid. A business dinner, a concert, a play—then a quick hug or perhaps a peck on the cheek at her door before she dashed safely inside. No hurt feelings, no soaring emotions, no racing hearts to contend with.

Only there was nothing tame or safe about her feelings for the man who held her now, the man who in two and a half days had her emotions churning and her blood heating. The simple truth was, she had feelings for Sean Reagan. Complicated, warm and tender feelings, and she wasn't the least bit happy about any of it.

Especially since she had an uneasy feeling he was holding back, not telling her something. Yet he caused ripples of sensations inside her that were as surprising as they were unwelcome. She'd deliberately turned from her sexual responses since her marriage to Marc had floundered, burying them. Or thought she had. Trapped here alone in a cabin with an attractive man was no time for them to emerge, operable and screaming for attention. Even as she wondered how she'd come so far so fast, Laura rested her head just under his chin, as if it belonged there.

He hadn't imagined it, Sean told himself. She smelled like wildflowers, soft and fragrant in his arms, unbelievably responsive. She probably wasn't what he needed, but she was what he wanted. And despite declarations to the contrary, he couldn't seem to stop wanting, to discipline himself not to touch her, he who was so disciplined in every aspect of his life save this one.

At first, he'd thought her to be a little like Kim, but he'd soon realized there was a major difference. Kim had kept herself distant from the beginning. Even during lovemaking, she'd always been in control of herself, single-minded, centered. Laura could be distracted with a touch, a look, a laugh. He pictured her in his four-poster bed in his home in Scottsdale, wild and abandoned, carried away with passion as he was certain she could be. And his imagination was making him hard and hurting.

But there was more. She touched him deep inside where there were empty places, so many empty places. He didn't know her, yet he knew her all too well.

Laura felt the change in him, the tightness of his body and the heat of his flesh under his cotton sweater. She leaned back and stared into eyes hot and hungry. The song ended on a high note as she took a step backward, brushing her hair back from her flushed face.

She cleared her throat, sure her voice would be husky, and gave him the first excuse that popped into her mind. "Listen, I think I'll lie down a while. My ankle is hurting again." To give value to the lie, she limped toward the couch.

Sean didn't move, just stood where he was, watching her. Even if he hadn't been a doctor, he would have noticed that she hadn't favored her sprained ankle all day. He knew why she was withdrawing from him, and thought it was probably for the best.

Feeling guilty being untruthful, she glanced over her shoulder. "I hope you don't mind."

"No, I don't mind." She needed to be alone, and so did he.

"Okay, then." She hobbled off, closing the bedroom door behind her.

Sean thrust unsteady hands through his hair and strolled over to gaze out the window. The snowplow should be here soon, if not today, then surely early tomorrow. Then the service station would send its tow truck. He didn't envy those men the job of hauling out her big Bronco, stuck between two trees and covered with snow.

He rolled his shoulders, trying to ease some of the tension that had his muscles coiled like finely wound springs. He had no one to blame but himself for his present condition.

Cursing himself for a damn fool, he sat down on the hearth to pull on his boots. An hour or two of shoveling snow might help.

Then again, he wasn't certain there was a cure for what ailed him this time.

Chapter Seven

The sound of a motor straining and metal scraping woke Laura. Coming awake slowly, she figured it had to be the snowplow. The Mickey Mouse clock told her it was a few minutes past seven. A heavy and very warm cat was snuggled up against her back as she lay on her side. Shifting Max over, she yawned then stretched. Lying in a cocoon of comfort, she wasn't sure she wanted to crawl out. Or did she just not want to face the day?

It was Monday, she realized, and tried to remember if she had any pressing appointments for today. She'd have to call the real estate office and talk with Marcy, the secretary, then call her own office and check in with Tina, her secretary and gal Friday. She wondered just when her father would be back in town since his vague message had said very little. She wondered if he'd think to call her. Not likely, unless he needed her for something. The model homes for Marshall Realty's new subdivision in the east valley wouldn't be ready for her decorating services for at least another week. Probably nothing else on her calendar she couldn't postpone.

In either case, she had no choice but to remain until her Bronco was towed to a station. If Sean wasn't planning to go back just yet, she'd have to rent a car.

Sean. Unbidden, the memory of their dance and that kiss crept back into her mind, as it had been doing most of a restless night. She'd left him standing in the middle of the room and gone in to lie down, though she'd known sleep wouldn't be possible. She'd lain on the bed, her mind jumping from one impossible thought to another, until she'd heard Sean rattling around in the kitchen. Remembering that she'd lost the gin rummy bet and was supposed to make dinner, she'd gone out then, wearing a breezy smile, determined she wouldn't let him see just how deeply he was getting to her.

They'd eaten a bowl of reheated soup, and she'd fixed Sean a sandwich, though she hadn't wanted one. She'd made a pot of tea and managed to sit across from him sipping from her cup and making small talk. Just when she'd been congratulating herself on what a fine actress she was, he'd touched her arm as she cleared the table, startling her so that she'd dropped a dish. It had shattered into a million pieces.

Apologizing profusely, she'd bent to clean up, explaining that she wasn't usually clumsy. Silently, Sean had swept up the mess, then framed her face with his large, gentle hands, his silver gray eyes meeting hers. "It's all right," he'd whispered. "Everything's all right."

Only it wasn't, and they both knew it. She'd spent the rest of the evening curled into the far corner of the couch trying to read a mystery even as the words blurred on the page. Sean stayed in the kitchen at the table, sketching she knew not what. By the time the mantel clock chimed nine, she'd been more than ready to escape to her room.

There was no denying a powerful sensual pull here, one she'd never experienced before. If things were different, if Marc wasn't making her life a living hell and if Sean wasn't haunted by guilt and feelings of distrust, she might eagerly pursue a relationship with him. Because how often did a woman find a man who could make her heart beat faster with just a look, whose mere touch could send her flying? Definitely something a sane woman wouldn't walk away from.

But then, hadn't Marc been charming and attentive and intriguing when they'd first met? And how long after the wedding did she begin noticing changes in him, a month, two? Of course, Sean was no more interested in another marriage than she was, for his own reasons. If she were a different sort of woman, she could enjoy him for the physical pleasure she was certain he could bring to her, then go on with her life.

But let's face facts, Laura told herself. Her greatest fear was that she'd fall hopelessly in love with him, and he'd break her heart. How many times can a heart be broken before it shrivels up and dies? How many encounters with handsome and charming men was it going to take before she learned her lesson? For two years now, living on her own, supporting herself with work that she loved, she'd told herself repeatedly that she didn't need a man in her life to feel complete.

Wasn't it time she believed that simple truth?

Bored with her tossing about, Max moved to the foot of the bed and curled into a ball, not yet ready to start his day.

Laura's feet touched the floor, and a shiver raced up

her spine. Hurriedly, she made her way to the bathroom.
Perhaps a long, hot shower would clear her head.

Sean stood at the front window, one hand in the pocket
of his jeans, the other curled around a mug of hot coffee,
watching the heavy truck use its blower attachment to
clear snow from the hill leading to the area where Laura's
Bronco was stuck. He'd gone out as soon as he'd heard
the plow and offered the driver a fee if he'd clear a path
to the stricken vehicle and another bonus if he could man-
age to blow it free of snow. He wasn't sure just how
close the truck could get due to the many trees, but the
driver had been more than willing to try when he'd seen
the money in Sean's hand.

He'd talked with Phil Dawson at the service station, a
man he'd gone fishing with on several occasions. Phil
had said he had no doubt he could get the Bronco out,
but his tow truck wasn't equipped to clear snow. Now he
was waiting for a call from Sean to let him know the
Bronco was ready. Even so, the way it was wedged in
there, Sean was certain it would take awhile to haul it
up.

The way the big four-wheel-drive had hit its front end,
then spun about from the looks of it, he couldn't even
estimate what the damage might be. Hopefully Phil could
repair it, but much would depend on Laura's insurance
company, whether or not they thought the repair bill was
worth it. However, not yet a year old, the Bronco hopefully could be fixed up like new.

He drained his mug and wondered what next. What
would Laura do about her ransacked home when she returned? It didn't seem likely that Owen Marshall would
be of much help; in fact, she seemed as though she might

not even tell him what happened since he was so hyper-critical.

Sean's thoughts shifted to Marc Abbott, Laura's ex-husband. What was he after that he felt was in her condo? They'd been divorced two years. Or did he invade her privacy just to harass her? He'd read about stalkers who get fixated on someone; they basically have their own twisted reasons for pursuing that person. Maybe he could do a little checking, find out just what this guy was up to.

But wait a minute. Hadn't he told himself he wanted no involvement? If he started checking into Marc's life on Laura's behalf, that was unquestionably involvement. Perhaps he should just forget it, forget her. Yet even as the thought formed, Sean was sure it was already too late. Laura Marshall was not that easily forgotten.

He walked back to the counter and poured himself more coffee just as her bedroom door opened. But only Max emerged, sauntering out, haughty as ever. The big cat strolled past Sean without so much as a glance, went straight to his dish and stood looking down into its empty depth. Slowly he turned, gazing at Sean over his shoulder, his yellow eyes asking where his breakfast was just as surely as if he'd spoken aloud.

"What she sees in you, chum, is beyond me," Sean muttered as he opened the cupboard. Good thing they'd be leaving soon. Only one can of tuna left after today's. He picked up Max's bowl, washed it out and spooned in the tuna, then gave him fresh water. Stepping back, he met the cat's golden gaze.

"Well, go ahead and eat. Isn't that what you wanted?" Unaccountably annoyed, Sean turned away just as Laura came out.

She was wearing the outfit she'd arrived in, a blue

sweater over snug designer slacks, her hair once more blown dry and straightened, falling softly to her shoulders, framing a face that had been carefully made up. Her black eye, however, was still visible. After seeing her in his mother's loose-fitting sweats for several days, her face freshly washed, her hair in wild curls, it was quite a shock. This was Laura Marshall, designer for Marshall Realty, not simply Laura, a waiflike little thing who'd stumbled into his home needing his help. The change was remarkable, causing a muscle in his jaw to tighten, leaving him speechless.

"Good morning," Laura said, wondering what was causing his almost unfriendly expression. "Is Max giving you a hard time?"

Sean forced himself to relax, even to find a smile. "Nah, he's just being his ornery self. He's sure a one-woman cat."

Pouring her coffee, Laura had to agree. "He's so protective you'd think he'd been a watchdog in another life. I have a cleaning woman who comes in once a week. I have to lock Max in his cat carrier for the morning when she's there. He's actually leaped at her, hissing away." She sipped her coffee and saw the tension lines on his face ease.

"So it's not just men he doesn't like, eh?"

"No, he's cranky with most everyone except me."

Up close alongside her, his eyes roamed her lovely face. He'd found her attractive and appealing in her natural state, but like this, she was downright beautiful. And she seemed totally unaware of her beauty, a fact that puzzled Sean. "Max has excellent taste in women," he said, his voice low and intimate.

Laura's eyes settled on his, trying to read his thoughts while her heart rate moved into double time. Once they were out of this small cabin and back in the real world, would she still react this way to him? she wondered. "Thank you."

"Would you like some breakfast, now that the stove's working again?" Yesterday, all she'd had was one hot dog for lunch and a small bowl of soup for dinner. No wonder she was so slender if this was the way she ate all the time.

"Thanks, but I'm really not hungry." She took another sip. "Your coffee's great. Not every man can make..."

The pounding on the door stopped her in mid-sentence. Setting down his mug, Sean walked over and invited the driver of the snowplow to come in.

Pulling off his heavy gloves, the tall man stepped inside and removed his knit cap. "I cleared a path to the Bronco wide enough for the service truck to get in there. And I blew the snow away from the vehicle, all except for some crusted on the windows. Windshield's broken, and I didn't want to make it worse."

Sean reached in his pocket and handed the man several folded bills. "I sure appreciate you helping out. Hope I didn't put you behind schedule."

"Nah. I'm going to be clearing roads till quitting time." He shoved the money into his pocket. "Thanks again, Doc." He left, closing the door behind him.

"I'm going to call Phil at the service station and tell him he can come anytime now," Sean told her, walking to the phone.

"You paid that man to clear the snow from my Bronco. I want to know how much so I can repay you. And for the food I've eaten and..."

Frowning, Sean dialed the phone. "Forget it." Phil answered on the second ring and they spoke briefly before he hung up. "He'll be here within the hour with a

couple of his men to help him haul the Bronco up. After
that's done, I guess we can pack up and go back home.''

Laura sat down at the kitchen table. ''Sean, I always
pay my own way. Please tell me how much or I'll just
have to guess and write you a check.''

''Tell you what,'' he said, walking over. ''I'll flip you
for it.'' He dug his lucky coin from his pocket and held
it up.

''No. I want to pay you.'' The last thing she needed
was to be beholden to a man, any man.

''Okay, how about we Indian wrestle for it.'' Sitting
down, he propped his elbow on the table, his hand open
and waiting. ''Come on.''

''Hardly.'' She shook her head. ''I'm serious and
you're clowning around.''

Sean stood his ground. ''What'll it be, wrestle or coin
toss?''

Resigned, she sighed. ''Coin toss. I call tails.''

Up went the coin and landed with a smack on his hand.
It was heads. He grinned.

''Let me see that coin,'' she demanded.

Looking innocent and injured that she'd think he'd
cheat, he handed her the coin, then watched her examine
it thoroughly.

''I still think you cheat,'' she said, handing the coin
back to him.

''I'm wounded. That coin was given to me by my
grandfather. It always comes through for me.''

''Uh-huh.'' Laura watched him over the rim of her
cup, but her eyes were smiling.

Sean noticed Max standing at the back door, so he
went over and let him out, then came back and sat down.
''Do you think your friend Molly will have your condo

back in shape by the time we get there late this afternoon?''

"Yes. I can always count on Molly. And her husband, Devin, is wonderful, too.''

"It seems that the second time around was the charm for her.''

Laura nodded. "They're lucky to have found one another.'' She drank more coffee, wishing the serviceman would hurry. Now that they'd come this far, she was anxious to get going. Yet a part of her was also fearful. "I'll have to have the locks changed. Again.'' She was scarcely aware she'd spoken out loud.

Sean leaned forward. "Laura, would you like me to have a chat with your ex-husband? Maybe I can get something out of him as to why he can't seem to leave you alone.''

Laura blinked rapidly against a rush of tears. Kindness always did that to her, turned on the waterworks. "I thank you for your offer, but I can't have you getting mixed up in my problems. You've been wonderful, taking me in like this, fixing my shoulder, my ankle. I don't know how to repay you. I wish you'd let me do something.''

A weekend in my four-poster bed would be a start, Sean thought, then turned aside, hoping his face didn't reveal how he felt. What in hell was wrong with him?

"I told you, I don't need you to do anything," he managed. "You've already thanked me." He got up and placed his mug in the sink, then walked over to pick up his jacket. "I'm going out to wait for Phil." Hurriedly, he stepped outside.

Laura watched him leave, wondering what she'd said or done to cause these up-and-down emotions in him.

* * *

Phil Dawson was six feet of solid muscle sporting a head of brown curly hair, windburned cheeks and a ready smile. "Man, that baby was really wedged in there," he commented, knocking snow off his heavy boots. Standing on the cabin's porch with Sean and Laura, he tried to keep his eyes on his friend, but they kept drifting to the woman huddled in what looked to be an expensive leather jacket. He hadn't seen a woman here with Sean since his wife died, and this one was a knockout. "You were lucky to get out of there with only minor bruises," he told her.

Wearing Sean's mother's boots, Laura had climbed the short hill and gazed down at her Bronco's resting spot before Phil's men had pulled it up. She'd been shocked at its precarious position, especially the tree limb jutting into the windshield. "I sure was," she told Phil. "And lucky that Sean was here and heard the crash."

"Yeah, Sean's a good old boy." Phil gave his friend's shoulder a playful punch. "You going back now?"

"Yes," Sean answered. "I'm going to drive Laura home."

"Please call me when you've assessed the damage," Laura said, handing him her card. "You should be able to reach me at one of those numbers, or just leave a message and I'll get back to you."

"Sure thing, but I might not be able to get to it for several days. I've got several stuck cars to haul out from other accidents and four already in the shop." Phil pocketed the card as he turned to walk down the steps. "When you coming back up this way, Sean?"

"Not for awhile. I think I'll wait for the spring thaw."

Phil's laugh was hearty. "Good idea. Let me know and we'll get some fishing in."

"Will do." Sean watched the big man make his way

back to his truck where his two helpers waited. The Bronco rested on a flatbed attached to the truck.

"That front end looks pretty bad. I wonder if he can even repair it." Laura had her doubts.

"Phil's a pro. If anyone can do it, he can." Hand at her back, he guided her back inside the warmth of the cabin. "Are you all set? Want something to eat before we go?"

Nerves had her stomach jittery. "No, thanks. I'm ready when you are." She had nothing to pack, only to grab her purse and pick up Max.

"I'll just be a minute." He disappeared into the bedroom.

Laura wandered the big room, gazing at Danny's picture for long minutes. This cabin had been like a haven for her when she'd needed it most. Three days spent where no one knew where she was, no one could stalk her or make her feel threatened. She found she was loath to leave, although she knew she must.

She picked up the phone to call Marcy at Marshall Realty and learned that her father was due back sometime today. Also, Robb & Stucky, a furniture store she used for some specialized pieces for the upscale models, had called to say her order was in for the Beaumont house. Ray Beaumont was a friend of Owen's, which was why her father had volunteered Laura's services to him in redecorating a mansion-style home he'd recently purchased on Camelback Mountain. Ray was loud, demanding, lecherous and highly annoying. Laura hated working with him, wouldn't have given him the time of day if her father hadn't insisted. Now she told Marcy she'd call the store tomorrow from the office.

Phoning her own office, she explained to Tina that she'd be in tomorrow and to reschedule her one appoint-

ment at a tile dealership. That done, Laura wandered over
to the kitchen table where a stack of Sean's sketches
caught her eye. There had to be a dozen, all of her—
head drawings, profiles, full body wearing sweats that fit
far better than his mother's had. He'd added his artistic
imagination and had her looking far more beautiful than
she was.

Or did he really see her like this?

No, she warned herself. Don't go getting a swelled
head over a few pencil sketches. An artist's vision was
different than reality. Her looks were okay, but certainly
not exceptional. She studied one head shot that caught
her looking quite melancholy with huge, sad eyes. None
depicted her smiling, which was odd since she thought
of herself as fairly upbeat. A camera never lies, it was
said, but does a sketch artist sometimes inject his own
feelings onto the subject?

She heard footsteps and turned to see Sean carrying a
leather suitcase. As she walked over to where Max lay
on the hearth, Sean packed his sketches, pens, pencils
and erasers into a large, flat case, then zipped it all
around.

"That's it, then. Phil's mother has a key, and she'll
stop by to clean up and take home any food that would
spoil before I return." His eyes were drawn to Danny's
portrait where they lingered for a long minute. Then he
shook off the mood and shrugged into his jacket. "Let's
go this way," he said, leading her to the connecting door
of the garage.

Reluctantly, Laura gathered her cat into her arms and
followed him.

In under an hour, the weather had changed drastically
and for the better. The sun was shining brightly on High-

way 17 as they headed south, the temperature moving up every mile, it seemed. The scenery was beautiful if somewhat boring, endless acres of undeveloped land where mesquite grew wild and saguaro cacti, some that had been standing for over a century, guarded the uneven terrain. The road wound and twisted, the occasional horse ranch visible off in the distance, the red rock mesas adding color to the bleak desert drive.

Sean scarcely noticed, his thoughts turned inward. Maybe he should sell the cabin, filled as it was with memories good and bad that shadowed his visits. He could build another one in a different location where every rock and hill didn't remind him of the brief time he'd spent with Danny. If he sold the place, he could end these yearly treks to wallow in self-pity. Besides, though his mother visited occasionally and seemed to enjoy a change of pace, no one else ever stayed there except him.

Until Laura.

Inevitably his thoughts drifted to the slender woman in the bucket seat alongside him, large sunglasses hiding her expression. She'd been silent since they left, lost in her own thoughts, as he was. Did she dread returning to the home she'd fled in such anguish? Was she worried about another encounter with Marc Abbott? Was she concerned about her father's reaction to all this?

Would she quickly put out of her mind the three days they'd spent together, the long talks, the sharing of some difficult memories, the soul-shattering kisses? They lived less than ten miles apart, worked at locations even closer to one another. Scottsdale was basically a small town. Would they run into each other? Did she want to see him after today?

What about his feelings? Sean asked himself. He tried to think things through logically. If they became friends, dated occasionally, dinner and a show, as he'd suggested, would that work? Confined in that small cabin for over seventy-two hours, they'd shared more than many couples who date for six months. Would that bond remain? Or would they be awkward with one another in different surroundings?

Maybe he should stop overanalyzing and take things as they came, Sean decided.

The cat prowled the back seat, grumpy as usual. "I think Max will be glad to get back on familiar turf," he commented.

Laura glanced back and gave her cat an affectionate smile. "Yes, I think you're right." But as each mile brought her closer, she felt more and more apprehensive about entering her home.

"You're sure Molly cleaned up your place by now?"

"Yes. Molly's the kind of friend who never lets you down." As best she could recall, it would have only involved straightening up tossed books, papers, et cetera. She didn't remember anything actually broken except her mother's picture.

They crossed over from Phoenix into Scottsdale, and Sean saw a temperature reading on a billboard. "It's sixty-eight degrees and climbing. I guess I can turn the heat off." He reached to do just that, but saw her hands were tightly clenched in her lap, her gaze directed out the side window. "Laura, are you all right?"

She didn't turn to look at him. "A little nervous, that's all."

"I plan to go in with you and check out the place and I know a locksmith I can get to come over quickly." Instead of touching the temperature control, his hand covered her two, reassuring her.

Laura swallowed hard, moved by his kindness. He

didn't miss much. "Thanks. I'd appreciate that. As I said, I think the door was ajar when I got home. I don't know if he jimmied the lock or if somehow he's got a key, but it wasn't actually broken."

"It's not that hard to get hold of some small tools that will allow you to bypass a lock, if you know the right people."

She turned to look at him. "Really? Somehow I can't picture Marc rubbing shoulders with the criminal element."

Sean swung onto Scottsdale Road. "He wouldn't have to. There're all kinds of places you can get things like that, spy shops, the Internet shopping channels, even garage sales."

"You're kidding. Why do we bother to lock our doors, I wonder, if it's that easy for anyone to get in?"

"Good question. I saw this special on television awhile back. They were interviewing a B and E man who'd been in prison for several years for dozens of robberies. He said that the house hadn't been built that he couldn't break into if he set his mind to it, even with newer sophisticated security systems."

"Comforting thought."

"What you need is a dog, a big dog. The average guy looking for a random house won't bother trying a home with a dog that'll bark and wake the owners or cause neighbors to hear, or even go on the attack once he gets inside."

"I'm not sure Max would like that." She glanced back and saw the cat lying on the back seat, his eyes on hers registering annoyance.

"Maybe not, but it's worth thinking about." He crossed Camelback Road heading into Old Scottsdale. "Where do we go from here?"

"It's about two miles down yet, then to the right."
Laura watched the familiar neighborhood fly by, trying
to calm the butterflies in her stomach. "You know, invasion of privacy, of having someone enter into your private living space uninvited and paw through your things,
is one of the worst things that can happen to a person.
You feel violated and vulnerable from then on."

"Do you own the condo? Maybe you should consider
moving. I know a good Realtor…"

"Cute. I just hate to move. I've got the place fixed up
just the way I want it. Besides, I dislike being chased
from my own house. And what if he followed me to the
next place? You said these guys can break in anywhere
they want. I can't keep moving every few months."

"You could move back in with your father. He must
have one hell of a security system."

Laura's jaw clenched for a moment, then she forced
herself to relax. "That's not an option." She pointed just
ahead. "Turn right at the next intersection."

"Then I guess you know the only solution is to confront your ex-husband and find out what's motivating
him. Is he searching for something you have and he can't
find? Or is it simply harassment, in which case you could
get a restraining order. It might not stop him, but you'd
have some leverage with the police if he tried it again."

Laura brushed back her hair with both hands, a nervous
gesture. "Why won't he simply leave me alone? I've
thought and thought and I can't imagine what I'd have
that Marc wants."

"Have you asked him outright?"

"No."

"My offer still stands. I'll go with you if you want."

Her eyes roamed his large, strong frame, noting his big
hands, his broad shoulders. Never mind that those hands

belonged to a doctor, a man of healing, and they could be wonderfully gentle. And no matter that those muscular arms around her had made her feel safe, and much more. Marc, who was barely five-ten though he worked out at the gym, would be intimidated by Sean. "I might have to take you up on that." She turned to peer out the windshield. "It's there on the left in the cul-de-sac, the one with the green shutters."

Parking in her drive, Sean went up the front walk with her, carrying a protesting Max as she unlocked the door.

"See, it wasn't broken. He must have those tools you mentioned because he's never had a key to this place."

Cautiously, she walked in, noting that Sean was close behind.

The large living room had everything restored to the way it had been before Friday, the bookcases once more filled, her desk put to rights. Strolling through the arch into the dining room and on to the kitchen, she saw nothing amiss.

"Molly and Devin did a terrific job, thank heaven." Laura took off her jacket.

Sean set the squirming cat down and looked around. He might have guessed she'd choose peaceful pastels— pale green, peach and ivory. There were plants, lots of plants, plus pillows everywhere, large and small. The place seemed well suited to her.

Laura noticed her mother's picture in a brand-new mosaic frame on the dining-room table and silently thanked her friend's thoughtfulness. Next to it was a note with her name on it. She picked up the folded paper and recognized Molly's neat handwriting. "It's from Molly asking me to call when I get home."

"Well, looks like everything's in order, unless you'd

like me to check out your second floor." Sean glanced up the staircase.

"I'm sure it's fine. Thanks for coming in with me. You must think I'm truly a scaredy-cat."

"No, I think some caution in this situation is definitely in order." Drawn to her desk, he saw the message light on her answering machine blinking. "You want to play this before I go, in case Marc left you a message?"

Laura punched the Play button. The first message was from Molly, who'd called on Friday morning, before the invasion, asking when they could have lunch. The second was dated Friday just before noon, a gruff man's voice.

"Laura, it's Rafe Collins. I've left you several messages and you haven't called back. I told you I need to talk with you. This can't wait. I'm running out of patience. Call me now."

Frowning, Sean looked at her. "Who's that?"

"This thug I told you about who works for the man who fathered my friend Tate's son. I talked with him a couple of weeks ago and told him I have no idea where Tate is, and that's the truth. He keeps hounding me, wants to meet with me in person. I refuse to do that so I just ignore his calls."

Sean looked thoughtful. "Do you think he could be behind this break-in?"

Laura shook her head. "He's a roughneck, more of a bodyguard than an associate. But I can't imagine he'd break in. I have absolutely nothing they would want. Besides, his boss is a big shot. If word ever got out that he was harassing a woman, the scandal would harm him. No, it's not Rafe. He's just a bully who thinks I'll fall in line when his boss crooks his little finger."

She punched the play button again and the machine registered eight hang-ups, all Saturday and Sunday.

"That's odd. Oh, well, I guess they'll call back if they really want to talk."

Sean placed both hands on her upper arms. "You're a tough cookie, aren't you?"

"Not really." She could feel the warmth of his touch through her sweater, could feel her heart step up its beat. Funny how she was all right until he touched her, then the confusion began all over again.

"Are you going to be all right?"

"Absolutely. Listen, I can't thank you enough for all you've done for me. I still wish you'd let me pay you...."

Her words stopped as his mouth settled on hers. Her thoughts stopped, too, as he gathered her into his arms, easing her closer, closer. His tongue danced into her mouth and she forgot her own name.

She tasted like the first sweet spoonful of thick new honey in the spring and smelled like a field of summer wildflowers. Back at the cabin, he'd asked if they could be friends, meaning a relationship free of entanglements, for he couldn't abide the thought of her completely gone from his life. After all, they were two adults, both having been married, not young kids wrestling with their first attraction. He had lots of women friends, wives of his buddies, patients. He should be able to handle one more.

But Laura wasn't like any of those women he knew. She tasted sweeter, smelled fresher, kissed better than anyone he'd met so far. She made him forget all his lofty resolutions that sounded so good in the planning stages. She made him yearn, had him dreaming, shook him to his very core.

What in hell was he going to do about Laura?

Moments ago, Laura had wished he'd hurry and leave so she could relax, could start getting over this very con-

fusing weekend by putting it in perspective. Now she
clung to him, she who detested clinging women. She
kissed him back wholeheartedly, as if it were the last time
she'd know the wonder of his mouth on hers. Because it
might be.

So she'd drink from him while she could, let her fingers wander through his thick hair, let him press her willing body close to his. Because this felt very much like
goodbye.

Chilled by that thought and hoping desperately to hang
on to a semblance of her pride, Laura eased away from
him, then stepped back. She pressed a trembling hand to
her stomach to quell the nerves that danced there before
finally looking up. "What was that for?"

Sean couldn't quite carry off a nonchalant shrug. "I
wanted you to stop talking about paybacks." He turned
toward the door, needing some time and space, but he
couldn't leave her like that. "Laura, if you need anything,
anything at all, just call me. Will you?"

She nodded, not knowing what to say.

He glanced at his watch, saw it was only three. "Make
arrangements to get your locks changed as soon as I
leave, promise?"

Again that silent nod.

"Get dead bolts this time." At the door, he again
paused. "I'll call you."

Finally she found her voice, for she didn't want him
to feel responsible for her. She'd been running her own
life for some time now. "It's not necessary, really. I'm
fine."

Sean battled twin emotions of wanting to stay and
needing to go, of desiring her and yet fearing involvement. A hell of a dilemma. Maybe the best thing he could
do would be to let her be.

''Take care,'' he said, then was gone.

Slowly Laura walked over and locked the door, then turned to lean against it, closing her eyes. She hadn't cried in a long time, had steeled herself not to. Which was why she was faintly surprised that her cheeks were damp.

And the funny part was she wasn't even sure why she was crying.

Chapter Eight

Laura pulled her rented white Taurus into her designated parking space alongside her father's building in downtown Scottsdale. The car seemed small after her SUV, but its trunk was good-size and held all the samples she'd removed from the Bronco's back seat. Fortunately, nothing had been ruined by the snow.

The Marshall Building, only two years old, loomed in front of her, two stories high, housing a commercial division, a new homes development as well as the used housing department. Marshall Realty had its own title insurance company, affiliation with a mortgage company and even a moving van business. All offices were glass-enclosed, facing a huge atrium with southwest vegetation including a tall palm tree that swept up to the second story. The entryway flooring was Italian tile but each office had plush carpeting, conservative piped-in music and soft lighting. The total effect was of comfort, wealth and serenity, designed to put clients at ease and primed to buy.

Laura had designed the interior, choosing every stick of furniture, the colors, the paintings, sculpture pieces, plants, the lighting, even the music. She'd won two prestigious awards for creating an ambience that had upscale clients feeling right at home. The awards ceremony had taken place at the Arizona Biltmore and had been attended by hordes of the movers and shakers in the Scottsdale-Phoenix area. Owen Marshall had been out of town and unable to be present.

Stepping out, she noticed her father's black Lincoln in its usual place and braced herself for an inquisition. Then again, she hadn't left a message on his answering machine, so perhaps he didn't know or care that she'd been gone.

No such luck, she realized as she entered through the double glass doors and saw Owen leaving her office across the atrium from his own. Naturally, he spotted her and waited, a scowl on his face.

Maybe she could placate him with a show of friendliness. "Good morning, Dad," she said, a smile in place. "You're looking well." But then, when wasn't he? With his naturally slim build, his golfer's tan, his thick dark hair with becoming white sideburns and his custom-tailored clothes, he was the epitome of a successful businessman.

Without preamble, Owen said what was on his mind. "I just got off the phone with Ray Beaumont and he's *not* happy. He's giving a dinner party on the weekend and he wants to know where the furniture you promised him is."

No greeting, Laura thought, no acknowledgment that she was his daughter, much less his employee. She might have been a delivery clerk for all he cared. Why was she surprised? Laura asked herself. It had ever been thus.

She shifted her briefcase to her other hand. "I'm taking care of that this morning. Robb and Stucky called, and his pieces are in. And, for your information, I didn't promise Mr. Beaumont a particular delivery date because every item is custom made and the store refused to commit."

Owen had an answer for that. "Next time, get the store to commit. Go to the top, if you must. Or tell me and I'll talk to them. Ray's not only a good client but a friend. I don't like my friends being upset."

But you don't mind upsetting your daughter. Laura forced herself to stay calm, hoping he couldn't read her expression. She hated starting off the day with a confrontation. But often as not, her father gave her no choice. "If you don't like the way I'm handling the Beaumont account, by all means, take it over." She held steady, her gaze challenging.

Owen's eyes narrowed, trying to assess her uncharacteristic remark. "What's gotten into you? Decorating is your department. Take care of it. First priority." Turning, still without a personal word, his long-legged strides carried him into his office, the glass door silently closing behind him.

First priority, Owen's favorite phrase. He'd said it to her a million times, meaning whatever he wanted done had to have first priority.

Laura let out a tense sigh, wishing he'd taken the bait and taken over his screwball friend. This would be the last job she'd do for Ray Beaumont, and if her father wanted to replace her as Marshall Realty's interior designer, so be it. Maybe it was time for the inevitable split. She had no doubt she could concentrate on her own business and do even better if she weren't constantly being dragged off to do her father's bidding. Working with that overbearing, pompous jerk Beaumont simply wasn't worth it.

Trying to put both men out of her mind, she entered her office and smiled at Marcy seated at the semicircular secretary's desk. "Good morning. How are you today?" Laura liked Marcy, a sweet-faced woman in her mid-forties who was efficiency personified, and who often shared her aggravation with her father.

"Fine, thanks. You're looking especially lovely today." Peering over her half-glasses, Marcy checked out her boss's cream-colored silk blouse and matching trousers. "You must have a luncheon date."

Walking on into her private office with Marcy trailing behind, she nodded. "You guessed it." An easy guess since Marcy was used to seeing her in casual clothes, jeans and shirts mostly, because she spent a good deal of time in storerooms and tile yards and lamp warehouses.

Laura placed her briefcase on her desk and set down her shoulder bag. "All right, other than our dear Mr. Beaumont, do we have any other problems pending?" Picking up a small stack of mail, she absently sorted through it.

"Just a couple. The development out Pinnacle Peak Road has had its opening date moved up a month, so they'll need models furnished earlier." She placed that file on Laura's desk. "And Tina called from your other office. Eleanor Hemmings wants an appointment."

Laura raised a quizzical brow. "*The* Eleanor Hemmings?" The heiress to a cosmetic fortune her late husband had left her, Mrs. Hemmings had recently moved into the valley and into a twenty-two-room mansion.

Marcy's smile was wide. "The one and only."

"I wonder how she heard of me."

"You won't believe it. She met your father at a charity fund-raiser and he gave her your card. She told me so herself."

"Interesting." Laura sat down in her leather swivel chair, her mind racing. Was Mrs. Hemmings after her father and trying to ingratiate herself by using his daughter to decorate her home? Or had Owen, who'd been known to pass out business cards at a funeral, been pushy? It would be fascinating to find out, since Owen rarely recommended her services outside his own circle.

"I can see the wheels turning," Marcy went on. "There was a picture of Owen and Eleanor in Sunday's society section, probably taken at the same fund-raiser. Then Monday she calls you. Methinks the lady's after him."

"Good luck to her. Many have tried and all have failed. Dad likes his freedom too well." And it was difficult finding a woman he could totally control. "When did Mrs. Hemmings's husband die?"

"Two months ago. She's not wasting time, eh?"

"That's how some women get to be millionaires," Laura stated, removing her oversize sunglasses. "Marry 'em, then bury 'em."

It was Marcy's turn to raise a brow. "You're a little cynical today." She leaned across the desk to take a closer look at Laura. "Is that a cut on your forehead? And, good heavens, a black eye?"

Laura's hand raised to her face self-consciously. She'd applied a concealer to cover both the healing cut and the skin beneath her eye. It had fooled her father, but not Marcy. "I had a little accident with the Bronco. It's in the shop, which is why I have a rental car."

A worried frown creased Marcy's pleasant face. "I

wondered when you called yesterday from up north if you were all right. You sounded sort of…distracted.''

Yesterday. Up in the cabin, with Sean, still marooned. She'd spent a restless night with thoughts of him intruding on her dreams and into her waking hours. Yes, he'd been a big distraction. "I was lucky. The accident happened on the property of a doctor. He patched me up.''

"I see. Well, I'm glad you weren't seriously hurt.'' Marcy set several pink message slips on the desk. "These are just notes on a couple of calls, nothing important.'' She started to leave, then turned back, her expression speculative. "This luncheon date you have, could it be with the doctor who patched you up?''

Marcy had been with Marshall Realty since Laura was a little girl, which made her an interested friend as well as a trusted employee, one who could ask a personal question now and then. And she often tried fixing Laura up with a ''nice young man'' since her divorce from Marc, a man Marcy had not approved of.

"No, Dolly Levi,'' Laura answered, addressing Marcy by the matchmaking title character in *Hello, Dolly.* "I'm meeting Molly at one at the Quilted Bear.''

"Oh, darn. I suppose he was old and gray with a paunch and a fat little wife, eh?''

"Not quite. Are you going to let me make these calls before Dad marches in here and fires me?''

Marcy didn't look a bit contrite. "You should be so lucky.'' But she did leave the office, closing Laura's door.

Laura read through the messages and scribbled a few notes on her calendar regarding future appointments, then called the furniture store and set up a delivery date for Beaumont's pieces. Next, she called Ray Beaumont to tell him. He approved the time and date, but insisted she be there when the furniture was delivered so she could make sure everything was as ordered. Also he wanted to talk to her about redecorating his bedroom.

Terrific, Laura thought, hanging up. Just what she needed, strolling around the lecherous old goat's bedroom while he talked to her in double entendres, reeking of expensive cologne and finding reasons to *accidentally* brush against her. Maybe after she checked the delivery, she could find a graceful way to refuse any more work just now, explaining that her schedule was too full.

Only Ray would pick up the phone the minute she left and call Owen. Was she ready to leave Marshall Realty over one disgusting client? Perhaps she could make her father see just how obnoxious his friend was?

Right. The day pigs fly.

As she opened the file on Marshall's newest development, the phone rang. Her thoughts on the Pinnacle Peak homes, she answered somewhat distractedly. But as soon as she heard the deep, masculine voice, she closed the file and leaned back in her chair. "Hello, Sean," she said, her heart stumbling.

"Hello, yourself. I called your other office, but your secretary said you'd be at Marshall Realty this morning. I just wanted to know how you were doing."

Laura stared out the window at Camelback Mountain in the distance, but she saw instead a tall man with broad shoulders and thick, sandy hair, his gray eyes smiling, then darkening with passion, his beautiful mouth damp from her kisses.

She cleared her throat. "I'm fine, thanks. Are you calling from the hospital?" She'd heard a voice paging in the background.

"Yes. I just finished a delivery with another in labor. Jonah delivered six while I was gone, almost one a day.

Must be the full of the moon. I've got office hours later, but I thought I'd call first. I'll bet you had a good night's sleep in your own place after that narrow single bed.''

Bed. Did he have to bring up beds? Involuntarily she thought of him lying alongside her in that small child's bed, and the first kiss they'd shared. Her hand tightened on the receiver. "Slept like a top," she lied. In reality, she hadn't slept well since meeting Sean Reagan.

"No more hang-ups?" He told himself he'd called just to make sure she was all right and for no other reason. But, hearing her soft voice, picturing her as he'd last seen her with her mouth slightly swollen from his kiss, he had to force himself to stay focused on their conversation.

"No, thankfully. Probably someone had a wrong number." She wanted to believe that.

"And you haven't heard from Marc?" What was he doing, getting involved when he'd vowed he wouldn't?

"No. I did get the locks changed, late last night. Dead bolts. The place is like a fortress now."

"Good." Stretching his legs out and propping his feet on the coffee table in the doctor's lounge, Sean stifled a yawn. He'd been at the hospital since five after about four hours sleep. This had to stop. "But you still need a dog."

"I have a cat, remember?"

"How is good old Max?"

Laura smiled. "He misses you."

Sean laughed out loud. "Yeah, I'll bet." He heard another page, and this time it was for him. "I've got to run. Take care of yourself, Laura."

"You, too. And thanks for calling." Slowly, she hung up, struggling with conflicting emotions. One part of her wanted to be back up at the cabin, in Sean's arms, with no obstacles between them. Another part, the sensible one, wanted to forget all about this past weekend, to make the intelligent choice to stay free of entanglements.

He hadn't said he'd call again, Laura realized. Probably for the best. He'd called just now to be polite, that's all. Like a doctor checking on a patient. One of them, at least, was being rational.

Laura picked up the file, determined to get to work and get her mind off Sean Reagan.

Dr. Jonah Evans crossed his legs as he leaned back in the chair facing Sean's desk, a thoughtful expression on his round face. He was as dark as Sean was fair, as chubby as Sean was lean and as outgoing as Sean was reserved. Jonah was also a big baseball fan.

They were in Sean's office having just finished discussing a couple of patients before afternoon appointments began. Sean sat at his desk toying with his pen while Jonah pounded a baseball into his old catcher's mitt. "Are you going to tell me what happened this past week, or am I going to have to guess?"

Sean eyed his closest friend and partner. "Look, you know I'm usually moody after I come back from one of these February sojourns. Then there was that storm to make matters worse, and I'd forgotten to buy gas so the generator went out on me. Not fun."

"Uh-huh. No, not the weather. It's something else. You're not moody, you're revved up. You've had three deliveries already and it's not quite one, up half the night, yet you're raring to go, filled with energy. What did you do, find the magic elixir of life up there, old pal?"

If anyone on earth knew Sean, it was Jonah. They'd met in the third grade and been friends ever since. He'd been with Sean when his father had died; they'd gone through college and med school together, been best men at each other's weddings. Jonah had tried to hold Sean together after the plane crash, and Sean had been there for Jonah when his wife, Sophie, had had three miscarriages in three years. Finally, Sophie had managed to carry a baby to term, and Sean had delivered baby Chrissie two years ago and was her godfather.

Jonah knew that Sean usually came back from the cabin filled with remorse, sullen and sad for weeks. The February chill, Jonah called it. But not this time.

Sean had been joking with the nurses at the hospital, brought flowers to their receptionist and had had the patients giggling this morning. Highly unusual.

"Come on, tell Uncle Jonah. What's up?"

Sean never could fool Jonah. Or his mother, who'd already given him the third degree on the phone. Maybe he should just get this over with. And maybe Jonah, who always seemed to see things so clearly while Sean saw things murky and confused, would lend some insight. "All right. I met someone."

Jonah sat up straighter. "Well, hot damn. I've been waiting to hear you say that for four years. Who is she? How'd you meet? What's she like?"

"Hold on." Sean tossed down his pen, wondering how much or how little he wanted to reveal. "She had an accident near the cabin on Friday night. Luckily, I heard the crash and took her in. Dislocated shoulder, mild concussion, sprained ankle. Nothing too severe. The snow kept coming down and we were marooned."

Jonah was grinning. "Sounds like a romance novel, pal. Go on."

Sean shrugged. "Nothing much more to tell." At least nothing he would tell. "Yesterday, Phil pulled her Bronco out and I drove her home. End of story."

"Oh, no, you don't. Between Friday night and Monday

morning, something happened or you wouldn't be so different. Might I remind you that in four years you've never mentioned a woman. So, what's so special about this one?"

Sean tried for nonchalance. "She's nice. Great looking. Divorced with an ex-husband who's been stalking her. A control freak of a father. Carrying a fair amount of baggage, but then, who isn't these days?"

"What's her name?"

"Laura Marshall. Her father's Owen Marshall of Marshall Realty. She's an interior designer."

Jonah whistled long and low. "Big bucks there. I hear Owen's shrewd but mean as hell."

"I've heard that, too. They don't get along. Her mother's dead. She lives with a grumpy old cat."

Jonah watched his friend's face closely, reading his expression as well as listening to what he wasn't saying. The man was definitely interested. "When are you going to see her again?"

Sean swiveled sideways to stare out the window. "I don't know. I want to, but…well, you know."

Jonah knew all too well. "You're thinking she'll turn out like Kim." Jonah stood, gazing down at his friend. "Sean, isn't it time you stopped running? We've talked about this before. Life without someone special is too damn empty. You, of all people, should know that. Now, suddenly, along comes someone you maybe could care for. Don't blow it, pal. Despite the risk of being hurt, it's worth checking out. We all know there're no guarantees, but you could hit gold."

Sean looked up, knowing that his friend was right. Yet he couldn't help hesitating. "It's easy for you to say. You lucked out the first time at bat." Jonah and Sophie had been married eight years and were as much in love if not more than in the beginning.

"You're right. Okay, so you struck out first time. But you're up to bat again. Quit worrying about all her old baggage and yours, too. If it's right, you can work out all that stuff. No one walks into the game with a clean slate. Bases are loaded, buddy. Grab that bat and slam it out of the park." Having said all he had to say, Jonah walked to the door, opened it. "But first, bring her around so I can check her out." With a grin, he left the office.

Sean sat there, pondering his friend's advice, wondering if he dare take a chance. His hand went to the phone, picked up the receiver. But he'd already called her this morning. Maybe...

A knock at his door was followed by his nurse sticking her head in. "Dr. Reagan, I've put your first patient in Room Two."

"I'll be right there," he told her, replacing the receiver and rising. Perhaps tomorrow.

"Honestly, Laura, we were glad to do it." Molly took another bite of her crab salad. "That SOB sure made a mess of the downstairs. Even pawed through your bedroom. Devin took Polaroids of each room in case you want to show the police."

Laura opened a package of crackers. "I've got no proof it was Marc." She took a cautious taste of her clam chowder and found it delicious.

"Who else would it be? Have you had any run-ins with anyone else?"

"Yes, my father. He's forcing me to decorate Ray Beaumont's new place." Laura shuddered. "The man's got these little piggy eyes and fat fingers. Yuk!"

Molly laughed. "Like that guy who kept hanging around in freshman year wanting to date Tate, remember?"

"Do I ever. And Maggie caught him on a ladder peeking into our upstairs bath. I never thought that pudgy guy could run that fast as when she chased him with a broom." They both laughed over one of their shared memories. "Speaking of Tate, have you heard from her lately?"

Molly considered a roll, then decided she might as well and reached for one. "Not in weeks. I got a call from that creepy Rafe Collins last week looking for her. He got downright nasty and demanding. That guy never gives up."

"No kidding. He's called me several times and I've told him repeatedly I don't know where Tate is living. Now, he wants to meet with me in person."

Molly frowned. "You're not considering it, I hope."

"Certainly not. Mostly I let the answering machine take my calls, then I simply don't call him back. There again, we can't go to the police because we promised Tate we wouldn't reveal Josh's father, and Rafe works for him."

"Yes, I know. Devin thinks we still should call them. What if something's happened to Tate and that weasel knows all about it?"

"I told Sean no one would believe me because Rafe's boss is this big shot and...what?" Molly was looking at her quizzically. "What'd I say?"

"Sean? Who's Sean?"

Damn her slip of the tongue! Laura thought. But maybe it was for the best. She could use a friendly ear. "A man I met over the weekend." She might have guessed old eagle ears would catch her.

"Is that right?" Signaling the waiter for coffee, Molly sat back. "All right, let's hear all about this Sean."

So, between spoonfuls of cooling chowder, Laura told her friend about her frightening experience Friday night that she at first remembered only snatches of and which later had been labeled traumatic amnesia. And about driving in the snowstorm, the accident, waking up on Sean's couch, his attending to her injuries, the power failure, his wife and son dying in a plane crash, all of it.

Well, almost all of it.

Watching closely, Molly knew just when Laura began hedging in her storytelling, when her eyes wouldn't meet hers and she became fascinated with her napkin, hemming and hawing around, her words hesitant. "I see. So would it be fair to say you're attracted to this handsome and charming doctor?"

"Mmm, I suppose. But it has nowhere to go, Molly. He's still tied up in knots over his son's death, blaming himself for not stopping him from going. He visits that cabin on the anniversary of their death every year as sort of a pilgrimage, and just thinks about them and mourns."

"That's not healthy, not for four years." Molly dribbled cream into her coffee. "But he wasn't grim the whole time you were together, was he?"

"No, not at all. We played cards and cooked hot dogs in the fireplace and...and danced. He's so gentle, Molly, and very talented. He sketches and you should see his work." Unaware her eyes were shining, Laura set down her spoon.

"You should see yourself, my friend," Molly said quietly. "You've fallen in love with him, haven't you?"

"No! I...well, maybe a little. But I shouldn't. It's just that he makes me feel so much. Molly, you can't imagine how I feel when he...when he..."

"Uh-oh. Have you gone and done the big deed?" This was definitely not like Laura.

Laura frowned. "What?" Suddenly, she understood. "Oh. No, no, of course not. We were only together three days."

Long enough, Molly thought, remembering her own overwhelming feelings when she'd met Devin Gray. "Like the love songs say, sometimes it only takes a moment...."

"Well, this was only a kiss or two. All right, several. The man sure knows how to kiss." She leaned forward, whispering. "Molly, he makes me feel beautiful. Is that crazy?"

"Of course not. You are beautiful."

Laura shook her head. "Not really. Not like Tate or..."

"For heaven's sake, none of us can compare to Tate. But we're not exactly chopped liver." She looked into her friend's confused eyes. "If he makes you feel beautiful, Laura, I'd say he's a keeper."

"Is that how it was with you and Devin?"

"Exactly how it was. Still is. Even when I was big as a house carrying the baby."

A baby. She'd wanted children with Marc, at first, but he'd nixed the idea immediately. Now, she was glad they hadn't had any. But how would Sean feel about having a child after having lost a son?

Oh, Lord, she was getting way ahead of herself here. "Well, it's nice to dream," she told Molly, "but chances are, I'll never hear from him again. He was just being polite and kind. After all, he's a doctor. It's part of their nature." She picked up her coffee cup and sipped.

"What's his name again?" Molly asked.

"Sean Reagan. He's an obstetrician."

Molly nodded. "I know the name. He volunteers a day every two weeks at a clinic near where I used to live before Devin and I married. He donates his time to un- insured women and indigents."

Laura smiled. "Yes, I can imagine him doing that. He's very kind."

Sitting back, Molly studied her friend. Laura had al- ways lacked confidence, had never realized how lovely she was. Her father had drummed it into her that she wasn't pretty enough, smart enough, probably so she'd be on guard against someone turning her head with com- pliments and marrying her for her money. And it had happened anyhow.

With all her heart, Molly hoped that Dr. Sean Reagan was different. It was about time Laura had a break.

Bagels and Such was a popular deli near Sean's office, one he often stopped in to buy a quick corned beef on rye for lunch, which was what he did on Friday just be- fore afternoon appointments. He waited through a fairly long line at the meat counter, casually looking over the goods displayed, inhaling the appetizing smells. Hand in his pants pocket, he rattled his change impatiently, not wanting to be late getting back.

To pass the time, he glanced back toward the small dining area where four booths and two tables were squeezed into a space for half that many, with waiters lugging heavy trays through crowded aisles. Not a seat to be had and people waiting there, too. Not a problem for him since he planned to get take-out and eat at his desk while looking over a few charts.

He was about to turn back when he spotted someone he realized looked familiar. The woman with the wild cloud of black hair was seated in the furthest booth wearing a red sweater and plaid slacks. Sean craned his neck trying to make sure, then he heard her laugh. Laura Marshall.

Sean felt his heart do a quick somersault. He deliberately hadn't called her since their brief conversation Monday, hoping out of sight would mean out of mind. Despite Jonah's encouragement, he wasn't sure he should pursue this attraction. So he'd kept busy with work, and an evening of tennis with a friend plus a day at the ballpark plus his usual Wednesday night dinner at his mother's.

It hadn't worked. He'd still thought of her long after he turned off the lights at night and first thing each morning. Concern for a patient, he told himself, one under a great deal of stress. He wondered if her ex had bothered her again and if her father had given her a hard time about the break-in. Most of all, he wondered if she ever thought about him.

He studied the booth surreptitiously, like a cop who had two suspects under surveillance. Laura's companion, whose back was to the door, looked to be tall man with black hair just touching the collar of a tan jacket. Whatever he was saying must be hilarious, for Laura laughed again.

She hadn't laughed that much in the three days she'd been in his cabin. Who was this comedian she was lunching with, anyhow? Surely not her ex-husband. Too young to be her father; besides, from what he'd heard of their relationship, Laura wouldn't be having a fun lunch with Owen Marshall.

Sean stepped up in the line automatically, his eyes never leaving the back booth. He'd checked and knew her office was close by, so it wasn't odd that she'd be having lunch here, or even that they'd run into one another. Scottsdale was basically a small town.

However, what might be considered odd was that she was having this cozy luncheon with another man after kissing him like there was no tomorrow just four days ago. Sean didn't exactly consider himself an expert on women, but he knew damn well there was no way she'd faked any of those kisses. Then who was this guy who, even now, was reaching over and taking her hand?

Frowning, Sean continued watching as the man tugged Laura's hand to his lips and kissed her fingers. How chivalrous. How corny. Was this the sort of behavior that made her eyes light up? If so, he didn't think he could carry it off in a million years. He simply wasn't the Cary Grant type.

"Hey, bud, what'll you have?" the man with the ponytail behind the counter repeated, raising his voice in Sean's direction.

Stepping up, Sean placed his order, then turned back in time to see Laura and her hand-kissing companion rise and make their way through the tables toward the door. They'd have to pass him in order to get out. He tried to keep his expression unreadable as he watched, catching the moment when she spotted him.

"Sean. How are you?" Surprised to see him, Laura smiled.

"Fine, and you?" he answered, but his eyes drifted to the tall Oriental man who'd moved close up behind her in the crowded aisle.

"Good." Laura angled her body, drawing the man in. "This is Bobby Chan. I'm designing the interior of his third restaurant opening in Fountain Hills in two weeks. Bobby, meet Dr. Sean Reagan."

"Good to meet you," Bobby said, reaching to shake

Sean's hand despite being jostled by another couple leaving the deli.

"Same here." A business luncheon, he supposed she'd call it. Sean had attended quite a few, with his accountant, his lawyer. Never, ever had he kissed their fingers. "I've seen your original restaurant at Fashion Square."

"That's the one my dad opened twenty years ago. He likes traditional Chinese decor, but wait'll you see what Laura's done with my new place. It's as beautiful as she is. Stop in some time. I'll show you around." His left hand was on Laura's shoulder, ready to guide her out the door.

Which was why Sean noticed that Bobby was wearing a wedding ring. He decided to get nosy. "Your family work with you?" he asked.

"Just my wife. We don't have any children yet."

"Sean's an obstetrician," Laura told Bobby. "When the time's right…"

"Yeah, I'll keep you in mind, Doc." Bobby smiled, revealing very white teeth.

Sean had always hated to be called Doc, but everyone did it. He could afford to be expansive now that he knew Bobby was safely married. "You do that." He turned to Laura. "Do you have plans for tomorrow night?" he asked before she could slip away.

"Uh, no, not really." Taken aback, she seemed hesitant.

"Good. I'll call you." Sean heard the counterman trying to get his attention. He smiled at Chan. "Good meeting you."

"You, too." Bobby ushered Laura out through the crowd.

Sean paid for his lunch, then made his way toward the door. But he was delayed by a patient carrying a cuddly baby that Sean had delivered six months ago. By the time he admired the baby and mother, he stepped out into the parking lot just in time to see a sleek Jaguar with Laura in the passenger seat pull out into traffic. He stood watching the car glide down Scottsdale Road for a minute, then hurried to his own car.

He wasn't jealous, he told himself as he climbed behind the wheel. That wasn't why he'd asked her out. The fact that he'd seen her with another guy, looking happy and even laughing, had nothing to do with his sudden desire to take her out. After all, he'd been thinking about her daily, wondering how she was. This would be his chance to find out.

Sean left the lot and hung a quick right, wondering just when it was that he'd begun lying to himself.

Chapter Nine

Laura felt whipped. Pulling into her garage late Saturday afternoon, she decided she was more mentally than physically exhausted. She'd spent a most uncomfortable two hours at Ray Beaumont's home, supervising the arrival of each piece of furniture from Robb and Stucky. The upscale store was known for its attention to detail since they mostly dealt with moneyed clientele. She'd had no reason to believe there'd be any problems with the four chairs, the couch and love seat, the three tables. And there hadn't been.

The problem had been Ray himself.

He'd boorishly berated the deliverymen without cause, inspected every inch of each piece as if a hanging thread might be reason for rejection and screamed at one of them for tracking a piece of dirt onto his marble foyer. Through it all, Laura had bitten her tongue until it nearly bled, all the while mentally writing scenarios on just what she'd like to tell Ray he could do with his house, the furniture in it and his friendship with her father.

But, as usual, she'd swallowed the harsh comments, disgusted with herself for doing so. Was she, at nearly thirty, still afraid of her father's reaction if she told one of his friends off, even though he deserved it? Was she too professional to consider showing her true feelings, knowing that Ray would waste no time in spreading the word that Laura Marshall was rude and improper, shifting the onus on her despite his ill-bred behavior? Or was she simply maturing and learning to accept that when one dealt with the public, one had to put up with all kinds of people?

Entering her house, she thought there was probably a little truth to all of those things. She'd been ready to grin and bear it until the incident. That put another whole slant on things.

Tossing her purse and keys on a chair, Laura double-locked her door. Max sauntered out of the coat closet where he liked to nap, yawned expansively and went to her for his usual head scratchings.

"Old man, you sleep twenty-two out of twenty-four," she told him gently. "If I could do that just once, maybe I could handle things better." Straightening, she went to the kitchen for a cool drink.

Perhaps if she told her father what Ray had done, he'd finally see his friend for the pig he was. Then again, Owen might not even believe her. No one ever knew which way he'd go.

Laura squeezed lemon into her tall iced tea, then took a long swallow. She hadn't overreacted, which was probably what Dad would say. After the furniture was finally all in place and approved, as Laura was about to take her leave, Ray absolutely insisted she accompany him to his bedroom ''just to make a few suggestions,'' even though she'd adamantly informed him she couldn't handle any more work right now.

She'd taken out her yellow pad and pen, but she hadn't gotten far in her note taking because Ray had made a pass at her. Not an accidental touch, but a full-blown pass, grabbing her, pulling her into his arms, trying to kiss her. Fortunately, even though she'd been thrown off balance, Laura was in great shape from running several mornings a week and an occasional workout at a gym where she had a membership. Unfortunately for him, Ray was fifty pounds overweight and thought exercise was a four-letter word.

She'd broken his hold on her in mere seconds, then shoved him a good one, causing him to fall on his well-padded rump on his thick wool carpeting. Furious, she'd warned him to never, ever call her again before she'd hurriedly left his hilltop mansion. In her kitchen now, she shivered, remembering his sweaty smell, his seeking hands, his hot breath.

How had such an obnoxious man ever become a friend of her father's? Of course, it was good business for Owen to label everyone he sold a home to a friend. But there had to be limits. Maybe the best way to handle this was for her to tell Owen before Ray put his own spin on things. The best defense was a good offense, or so they said.

Laura strolled over to her desk phone and saw the message light blinking. Her first thought was that Sean had said he'd call yesterday when she'd met up with him at the deli, so she hit the Play button. Her look of anticipation soon became a smile as she listened to Sean's voice ask her out to dinner tonight. He wanted her to leave a message for him at the hospital since he was there monitoring a woman through a difficult labor.

She listened to the message twice, knowing that if she accepted this invitation, she was also inviting him back into her life, not as someone he'd rescued from a disaster, but as someone he wanted to get to know better. Did she want that, too? Laura asked herself.

She dialed the number, but though they paged him, she was told he was already in the delivery room. She left a message saying she'd be happy to have dinner with him and asking him to call as to the time and place. Hanging up, Laura stared at the phone, hoping she'd done the right thing.

The truth was, she did want to be with him. He'd acted a bit peculiarly at the deli, not terribly friendly toward Bobby Chan, and she'd been wondering why. Perhaps he'd had a patient on his mind. She paused, trying to plan what she'd wear, thinking he'd probably take her to a fairly casual eatery since nearly every dining establishment in Scottsdale was informal.

Just as she was reaching for the phone to call her father and get the Ray Beaumont discussion over with, it rang. Smiling, sure it was Sean getting back to her rather quickly, she answered with a warm hello.

"About time you got home," a gruff voice said. "Where have you been? I've been trying to reach you for over a week now."

She recognized the caller immediately and wished she hadn't picked up. "What do you want, Rafe?"

"You know damn well. Tell me where Tate is. I'm running out of patience. My boss is getting annoyed, and he's not a good man to mess with. And neither am I."

Laura felt a shiver of apprehension race up her spine. "I've told you repeatedly that I don't know where Tate is. I haven't spoken with her in weeks. I'm sick of you bothering me. Stop calling here."

"I will once you give me Tate's address. Or phone number. We know she's in touch with you and Molly regularly. Unless you want me to go over to Maggie Davis's and see if I can persuade her…"

Heat rose in Laura's face as she struggled with a spurt of anger mingled with fear, yet she kept her voice controlled. It wouldn't do to let this bully realize she was afraid of him. "Are you threatening me? You'd better not go near Maggie, Rafe Collins, because if you do, I'll go to the police. Tell that to your boss." She hung up the phone with a slam that she hoped jarred his eardrums.

The nerve of that two-bit hood masquerading as an aide to a wealthy and important man, one whose hands were no cleaner than the thugs he hired. But what could she do? If she went to the police, they'd undoubtedly want to know every detail, and that would be betraying Tate's trust. She simply had to locate her friend.

Sitting down at her desk, Laura flipped through her address book and found Tate's page. There were at least five numbers for her listed there, then crossed out. Nevertheless, she'd try them all. She picked up the phone.

Ten minutes later, frustrated even more, Laura hung up. Either the numbers had been disconnected or Tate was no longer staying there. She'd even checked the bookstore where Tate had worked more recently, but the person who answered didn't know a Tate Monroe and the manager wasn't in on Saturday. At least that might be a possibility for Monday.

Maybe she should call Maggie in Tucson since she usually knew of Tate's whereabouts. But, glancing at her watch, Laura realized she didn't have much time to get ready for her dinner date, and she knew Maggie would keep her on the line a good half hour. And she had yet to call her father.

All right, she'd call Maggie tomorrow. Slowly, she dialed her father's number at home, but got the answering machine and left no message. Then she tried his office, knowing someone was always in at the realty. Owen wasn't in there, either, but they knew exactly where he was. He'd been called away from a meeting because a friend needed to talk with him.

Heart in her throat, Laura asked the friend's name. The real estate agent told her it was Ray Beaumont. Sagging in her chair, Laura thanked him and hung up.

Too late. Lord only knew what Ray was telling Owen right this minute. Taking a deep breath, she straightened her spine. No matter. She knew she was in the right no matter what Ray told her father. If Owen chose to condemn her for her actions, she'd quit working for Marshall Realty. She no longer needed that job anyway. Let him replace her. There were some things she simply wouldn't put up with from anyone, and Ray had crossed the line.

Rising, determined to put the matter out of her mind for now, since nothing could be done at the moment, Laura climbed the stairs, deciding that soaking in a long, hot bath would soothe her nerves and get her mentally relaxed for a lovely evening.

Jerome's was a popular eatery in Old Scottsdale featuring aged beer, fresh fish and a jazz combo that was mellow and unobtrusive. Sean slipped the young parking attendant five dollars to make sure his Mercedes would be close to the building in case he needed to get out quickly for a delivery.

"I've got someone in labor and I'm on call," he told Laura as he guided her through the beveled glass door.

"It's her first, though, so chances are she won't go for a couple more hours. Hope you don't mind."

Laura walked into the dim room with its long oak bar, enjoying the feel of his hand at her back. "No, of course not."

They strolled the length of the bar toward the maître d's station at the arched entrance to the restaurant proper. Halfway there, Sean heard his name called.

"Sean, hi," said a silky-smooth feminine voice.

Stopping, he noticed the blonde seated on a stool sipping a margarita from a large frosted glass. "Lisa, hello."

"Haven't seen you around much," Lisa said in her throaty voice, her eyes drifting to Laura, sliding down the length of her and back up.

"Yeah, well, I've been busy." Sean caught the maître d's eye. "Looks like our table's ready. Nice seeing you, Lisa." He saw the disappointment on her face as he gently urged Laura along to where the smiling maître d' greeted him, then led them to a table for two in a secluded corner. "Thank you, Karl," Sean said.

"My pleasure." With a flourish, Karl handed them menus and a wine list.

"Would you like a glass of wine?" Sean asked Laura.

"No, thank you."

"None for me, either, Karl. I'm on call." He handed back the wine list. "Thank you."

Laura opened the large menu, still amused at the fairly obvious woman at the bar who'd looked so crestfallen.

Sean leaned forward, setting aside the menu for now. "So, you and Bobby Chan are just…business associates?" he asked pointedly.

"Yes, of course." Laura glanced toward the archway leading to the bar. "And Lisa, she's an old friend?"

"More of an acquaintance, I'd say."

"Mmm." A smile tugged at her lips. "She seems nice, if you can get past the tattoos and the wart on her chin."

"Tattoos? Wart?" Sean shot a quick look toward the bar, then heard her chuckle. "Oh, so that's how it's going to be. Well, I could see at the deli why you'd want to have lunch with Bobby." He reached for her hand, raised it to his lips and began kissing her fingers, one by one. "Yummy."

They both laughed, breaking the ice.

"Bobby's very courtly with every woman he knows," Laura explained, "despite being madly in love with his wife. It's the way he was raised."

"I noticed. As for Lisa, she's kind of a sad case. She's my partner's patient, but I've seen her on rotation. We've never dated. As a matter of fact, I think she's married."

"A wedding ring doesn't seem to stop some people from flirting, or more."

Sean knew she was thinking of her unfaithful husband and wished he'd kept quiet about Lisa.

Laura took another look at the menu. "So what's good? I've never been here."

"Almost everything." He told her about some of the choices. A mustached waiter appeared and took their orders. "Have you gotten any more hang-ups?" Sean asked, admiring how she looked in a simple white linen dress and jacket with a wide leather belt emphasizing her small waist. She'd put her hair up in some sort of a French twist when he'd have preferred it softly touching her shoulders. He wanted to take back the hand she'd rescued from his finger kissing and hold it in his, but he thought better of such an outward show of affection.

"No hang-ups, but I did talk with this big bully who's a bodyguard or whatever to Tate's son's father. He just can't seem to get it through his thick head that I don't know where to reach Tate. I thought I'd warn her, so I called every number I have, but I couldn't reach her." Concern darkened her blue eyes. "I hope she's all right."

Their food arrived, and Laura picked up her fork. The salmon was wonderful, she discovered, but she wasn't very hungry. The late lunch, she guessed, or perhaps she was just nervous. She tried her best, but her heart wasn't in it.

Sean loved lamb shanks, and these were particularly good. But a couple of bites and he didn't want any more. Glancing at Laura's plate, he saw she was having the same problem. He looked up and saw her watching him. "Not hungry?"

"I guess not. I'm sorry." Their first real date, and she had no appetite for the expensive dinner he bought her.

"Don't be. I'm not, either." Sean tossed down his napkin and signaled the waiter. "Let's get out of here."

Outside, he helped Laura with her jacket, then took her hand. "How about a walk?" They were very near the Fifth Avenue Shops, over three hundred stores featuring everything from silver turquoise jewelry to Indian artifacts to southwestern boutiques and eateries of all sorts.

"That sounds good." She felt him take her hand in his large, warm one and started strolling down the avenue alongside him. He was so tall, so solid, a man who made a woman feel protected. After her break-in and the upsetting phone call from Rafe Collins, Laura needed to feel protected.

Halfway down the second block, Sean tucked her arm through his and drew her close to his side, still clinging to her hand. Going on nine in the evening, the crowds had thinned to only the occasional couple ambling by. Slowly they continued their walk, gazing into store win-

dows, commenting on the leather goods, the fringed out-
fits, a fragrant cigar shop and finally pausing in front of
a place that sold only Christmas items.

"Oh, look at that lovely angel on top of that tree,"
Laura pointed out. "She looks so fragile."

Gazing down at her, Sean thought she resembled a
fragile angel, one who'd landed in his life and turned it
upside down. "I'm afraid I've forgotten how to date,"
he confessed. "It's been too many years."

"For me, too." Her eyes on an animated Santa in the
window in a rocking chair alongside Mrs. Claus offering
him a plate of cookies, Laura sighed. "I was never very
good at dating even in my teens. Thinking back, I think
my father ruined dating for me."

"You mean no man could measure up to him?" Which
wasn't the way he'd thought she felt about Owen Marshall.

"No, not that. It's just that he'd drummed it into my
head since I first noticed boys that all of them would be
after his money and that I had to be ever vigilant. Try
relaxing on a date with that thought in your head."

Sean guided her over to a long bench alongside a
wooden Indian who held a container of cigars. They sat
down and still he held onto her hand. "My problem was
I was always falling asleep on dates. I carried a double
load in college, wanting to get through quickly. Once
you're in med school, all you do is study. Then there's
interning and residency where you can't remember the
last time you slept. Not conducive to fun dating."

She turned to him, a smile on her lips. "Are we a
couple of misfits?"

"I hope not. I tell you what, let's forget we're on a
date. Let's pretend we're just a couple of friends out for

an evening. Takes the pressure off.'' He smiled down at her, squeezing her hand.

''Works for me.'' Leaning back, she forced herself to relax as she gazed across the street. ''Oh, look over there.''

He saw the ice cream parlor with soda fountain tables and chairs arranged in front under a striped awning. Despite a chill to the air, people were lining up for cones and cups. He tugged her to her feet. ''Come on, let's get some.''

Crossing the street with him, Laura frowned. ''It's a little decadent, having dessert when we didn't finish our dinners.''

''I won't tell if you won't.'' Inside, he studied the long list of flavors. ''I want chocolate praline almond with sprinkles. How about you?''

''That's pretty wild. I think I'll try bubble gum. I haven't tasted that since grade school.''

In moments, they were back to strolling the avenue, licking huge waffle cones and laughing like teenagers. It was more like when they'd been in the cabin, Sean thought. The awkwardness was gone, thank goodness.

Later, on her porch, Sean unlocked her door and handed Laura back her keys. Inside, as she reached for the light switch, he closed his hand over hers. Turning her into his arms, he looked down into eyes dark blue and aware. He studied her a long moment, looking for some sign. Finally, her lips parted and he heard a sigh as soft as the night breeze.

He lowered his head and…and his beeper went off.

Sean touched his forehead to hers. ''Rotten timing,'' he whispered, then flipped on the light and checked the number. ''It's the hospital.''

"The phone's on my desk." Laura wasn't sure if she was disappointed at the interruption or relieved. This ambivalence—did she want him? was she afraid to want him?—was driving her crazy.

Sean hung up the phone. "I've got to go. She's ready to deliver." He took hold of her hands, trying to read her expression. "Such is the life of a doctor." He was probing, wanting to know if Laura, like Kim, would resent his hours, the times he'd be called away, the evenings unavoidably interrupted.

"But you're doing something so important, bringing a new life into the world. That's fantastic."

He couldn't help wondering if she was saying what she thought he wanted to hear, then felt guilty for not trusting her sincerity. "Nerves aside, I had a good time tonight."

"I did, too."

"I want to see you again."

She studied his eyes, trying to see deep inside him, aware he was fighting his growing feelings. As she was. "Are you sure?"

"Yes," he answered without hesitation. He didn't want to leave. With a reluctant sigh, he kissed her lightly, a mere brushing of lips. He knew if he went back for more, the woman in labor would have to deliver her own baby. "How do you feel about Wednesday?"

"Wednesday? What's happening Wednesday?"

"My mother's making Irish stew. Would you go with me?"

Oh, Lord. Dinner at Mother's and she'd known him less than two weeks. But she could think of no reason to turn him down. And it might be interesting meeting his mother. "I'd love to."

"Good. I'll call you." He kissed her forehead, then hurried off.

Deeper and deeper, more and more involved. Watching the taillights of his Mercedes disappear down the road, Laura wished she knew if she was doing the right thing.

On Monday in her own office, Laura called the bookstore where Tate had worked, but the manager couldn't give her any information about Tate Monroe. Or wouldn't. He seemed awkward and reticent. Perhaps Tate had instructed him to speak to no one about her whereabouts. Considering her circumstances, that was understandable.

Next, she called her old college housemother, Maggie Davis. "You sound good. Are you feeling all right?" she asked the older woman after a few words of greeting. She pictured Maggie with her sweet face, her white hair and intelligent blue eyes, and smiled.

"I'm fine, honey. Just fine. Molly told me about your accident. Are you all healed by now?"

"Yes. The injuries were minor."

"Lucky for you that doctor fellow found you. He's nice, is he?"

Molly and her chatty ways, Laura thought. "Yes, he's very nice. Listen, Maggie, the reason I'm calling is I wonder if you know how I could reach Tate."

"Oh, no, honey, I don't. I'm not sure where she's living right now. I haven't seen her or Josh in weeks." Maggie's voice brightened. "But one day, she'll pop in here just like she's never been away. That's Tate."

"Mmm. Has anyone else, besides Molly, been asking you where she is?" She had to know if Rafe Collins had contacted Maggie.

"Not recently. Awhile back, this man called and was

kind of insistent, even downright nasty on the phone. He demanded I tell him where Tate was. But, since I honestly didn't know, I told him that. At first, he didn't believe me, then he hung up and I haven't heard from him since. I can't recall his name.''

"Was it Rafe Collins?"

"That sounds right. Who is he, Laura?"

"Someone who works for Josh's father. Not a nice man. If he calls or shows up, don't give him the time of day. And if you see Tate, tell her I'd like her to call me, okay?"

"Sure, honey. When do you think you might be coming down this way? I miss seeing you girls."

Laura smiled. To Maggie, all three of them would always be her girls. "I'm not sure, but I'll call you when I get some free time. You take care, Maggie."

"You, too, honey."

Laura hung up, her mind for a moment back in Tucson. Little had she known that those years would turn out to be the best she'd had up to then. A kinder, simpler time. She wished she could recapture that feeling, but it was a foolish thought.

Digging in her purse, she found the card from the mechanic up north, Phil Dawson. She hadn't heard from him about her Bronco and was getting concerned. She dialed the number, and after four rings, Phil finally answered. He listened while she explained who she was.

"Oh, sure, I remember now." Phil sneezed twice, then cleared his throat. "It's still real cold and we got lots of snow. Listen, I'm way behind here. One of my best mechanics had to take a leave of absence on account of there was a death in his family in northern California. That storm brought in a lot of vehicles and there's only two of us working. I apologize for the delay. I plan to get to the Bronco in a couple of days. Hope that's all right.''

It would have to be. ''Okay, Phil. I'll wait to hear from you.'' As she hung up, she acknowledged her secretary, Tina, who'd knocked, then walked in.

At twenty-five, Tina had a degree in accounting and was taking night courses in interior design. As a secretary-assistant, she was a whiz and not easily intimidated. But she was looking uncomfortable now.

''What's up?'' Laura asked.

''I've come in to warn you. Mr. Marshall called from his car phone wanting to know if you were in. He said to keep you here because he's on his way and wants to talk with you. He didn't sound happy.''

Laura sighed. ''When does he ever sound happy?'' She'd often wondered why her father, who was very rich, still attractive, healthy and with a thriving business he loved, more often than not wore a scowl and bulldozed his way through life, hurting and harming those in his way, not even keeping track of the body count. Would he be different if her mother had lived? Laura asked herself. Probably not, since she'd been a mild-mannered woman, one Laura had never seen stand up to Owen.

Tina smiled her agreement. ''Just wanted you to know so you'd brace yourself.''

''Thanks, Tina. I think I know what this is about.'' The Ray Beaumont debacle.

Laura watched Tina close the door behind her, wishing she could shut her father out just that easily. Her first instinct was to take off before he got here, mainly because she hated scenes and this was bound to be one. But ever since the shocking invasion of her home had sent her into a traumatic reaction, she'd decided that running away wasn't the answer. If she wanted to be comfortable within herself, she needed to face her problems head-on.

In ten minutes, like a raging storm cloud, Owen entered the offices of Laura Marshall Interior Design Studio, walked past Tina and charged into Laura's private office without knocking. "I understand you've alienated one of my best clients by refusing to work for him anymore," he said without preamble.

Laura closed the book of drapery swatches she'd been searching through and sat back. "Hello, Dad," she said, as calmly as possible.

Owen's black London Fog raincoat was damp from morning showers but his dark hair was perfectly combed as he stood staring at his daughter, his manner demanding. "Well, why did you do it? I trusted you to take particularly good care of Ray since this is the third home he's purchased through us, with more to come, I'm sure. Why did you refuse him with that weak-sister excuse that you're too heavily booked?"

"Because he made a pass at me." Laura toyed with a pencil as she watched his face, first the surprise, then disbelief. Obviously, Ray's version of the incident differed greatly from hers.

"That can't be," Owen said, backing down just a little.

"Oh, but it is. He insisted I check out his bedroom and make a few suggestions as to redecorating. But when we got there, he grabbed me, tried to force himself on me."

Struggling with which version to believe, Owen frowned. "What did you do?"

"Shoved him hard, saw him fall onto his keister, told him to never call me again and then walked out. I imagine he told you quite a different story." She still wasn't convinced he believed her.

"Yes." Owen sat down in the chair facing Laura's desk. "He said you outright refused to work with him, that you obviously didn't like him, and after he's been so nice to you. He wants his whole house redone, and he's bidding on another for his daughter."

"Who's no doubt about my age. I refused to work with him even before he grabbed me. He's obnoxious, to me and the delivery men and anyone else we do business with. He's a big boor who thinks his money gives him the right to do exactly as he pleases. Well, not with me."

"All right, so he's a little rough around the edges. He made his money in construction and never had your advantages. I'll get him to apologize and…"

"No! I won't do it." She was calm, in control, but adamant, her eyes on his. Inside, she was trembling, but she wasn't about to back down. Not on this.

"Laura, he's an old friend. He lost his head, is all. It won't happen again."

"You're right, because I never want to see him again." She could tell by the tightening of his lips that Owen didn't like to take no for an answer.

"I've given you a lot of breaks, Laura. Most designers take years to make a name for themselves. If it weren't for me, you wouldn't have this studio."

"I'm aware of all that, but thank you for the reminder. I've also earned my way." She hadn't realized she'd snapped the pencil in half until she heard the crack. She leaned forward, needing him to see. "Dad, I'm good at what I do. If you want me out of Marshall Realty, I'll survive. But I won't put up with that kind of treatment from anyone." She drew in a quick breath. "And while we're on the subject, it would be nice if you took my side once in a while."

Owen seemed puzzled, for he'd never thought of his

daughter as headstrong. "I took your side with that no-account ex-husband of yours, didn't I?" He didn't wait for her response. "It seems that doctor you've been seeing has had some influence on you already."

She should have known he'd have heard. Owen Marshall knew just about everyone in Scottsdale. Someone had to have seen her and Sean together and told him. "He has nothing to do with this."

"Doesn't he?" He stood up, gazing down at his daughter with intense eyes. "I had him investigated, you know. He makes pretty good money, but not enough to take an early retirement like he could if you married him."

Laura had thought she was beyond shock over what her father was capable of. Apparently not. "You had him investigated? I can't believe you!"

"Of course I did. I lived to regret that I didn't have Marc investigated. You're the only heir to a fortune. You have to know that that kind of money can make a man start planning a walk down the aisle really fast. Am I right? Is he rushing you like Marc did? You were young then, but honestly, Laura. When will you learn?"

Stunned, she sat silently studying him. Why was she even mildly surprised? All her life, she'd heard the same words sung to a different tune from him. "You're right, Dad. I seem to be a slow learner."

Owen didn't notice how flat and lifeless her voice had become. "Damn right, I'm right. Listen, honey, you know I only want what's best for you."

There it was, his reason for everything he did for her. And to her.

"All right, tell you what," Owen said, prepared to be magnanimous. "We'll forget all this and concentrate on business. You sleep on it and you'll realize Ray's not so bad. I'll talk to him. He'll be okay, I promise.'' He checked his watch. "Got to run. Catch you later.'' Coattails flying, he left.

Laura sat for a long while, going over their conversation, trying to figure out where she'd missed the boat in convincing her father that he was wrong and she was right this time. She couldn't seem to come up with an answer.

Moving slowly, she pushed the intercom and asked Tina to come in and bring her pad. When she was seated, Laura dictated a letter of resignation to her father, withdrawing as interior designer for Marshall Realty effective immediately.

Chapter Ten

"Sean couldn't have been more than four," Ruth Reagan said as she cut generous pieces of blueberry pie, "when he spotted this stray kitten up in our lemon tree. The poor little thing was meowing his head off. He'd gotten up there but he was afraid to come down. So naturally, Sean climbed up." Smiling at her own story, she passed a dessert plate to Laura.

"But the kitten didn't know what was happening so he moved farther out on the limb. Not one to give up, Sean followed after him, coaxing him to trust his rescuer. On the ground looking up, I told Sean to come down and I'd get a ladder. But he kept on going, creeping closer until the kitten had nowhere to go. Sean grabbed him and held on, even though the frightened little animal was scratching him all over."

The hero of his mother's story accepted the piece of pie she handed him and glanced at Laura, who was listening raptly. He'd heard this tale often enough to be able to recite it in his sleep and had known when he'd invited Laura to dinner at Ruth's home that she'd get around to telling it. He saw Laura's lips twitch and decided she at least wasn't bored.

She'd seemed a little nervous on the way over, though why he couldn't have guessed. He'd explained that his mother was ultra-casual, so Laura had worn designer jeans and a simple white top with a navy sweater draped about her shoulders, her hair caught at her nape with a gold clip. She looked about seventeen.

Ruth, on the other hand, was just Ruth. Nothing much ruffled her nor surprised her. He hadn't brought a woman to her home since Kim had died, yet when he'd mentioned the possibility, she'd agreed without asking too many questions, then cooked her marvelous lamb stew. Laura had eaten every scrap on her plate, pleasing Ruth no end. The nice part was that with his mother, no matter who he'd invited to her table through the years, there was never an awkwardness. She managed to put everyone at ease quickly, which Sean always thought was a special gift she had.

He brought his attention back to the story she was telling.

"I tried to guide Sean down verbally, but he was scooting backward and trying to hang on to a fighting kitten. It was too much for him and they both fell." Ruth paused, using the knife in her hand for emphasis. "But do you know what he did? On the way down, he angled his body so that he'd take the brunt of the fall and the kitten wouldn't be hurt. And he was only four, mind you."

Laura turned to Sean, her eyes warm. "Lucky for me this rescuing habit is still a part of him."

Ruth caught the look and wondered, not for the first time this evening, just what all had happened up in that cabin. "It most certainly is. His first words on the ground were asking about that silly cat, who by then had run off. Sean had a broken arm from the fall, and scratches all over his arms and chest, but he didn't seem to mind as long as the kitten was okay." Smiling proudly, she set aside the pie plate and sat down with her own piece. "I think I knew right then that he'd follow in his father's footsteps and become a doctor."

A shade embarrassed, Sean's eyes were on his plate. "All right, Mom, I think we've had enough Sean-as-a-child stories for one evening." He sent Laura an apologetic look. "Obviously, my mother's my biggest fan."

"I can see why." She swung her gaze to the tall woman with short, salt-and-pepper hair and her son's kind gray eyes. "I have a cat who's getting old now and somewhat grumpy. He didn't take to Sean very well, but then, he doesn't like anyone much."

"I'm surprised because most animals love Sean."

"Animals and children," Sean answered, scooping up another bite. "Mom, this pie is wonderful."

"Yes, it certainly is," Laura agreed. "Mine somehow is always too runny."

"You have to cook half your blueberries with cornstarch and sugar until they thicken, then add the rest of the blueberries right into your baked shell before topping it with the cooked portion. Works every time."

"Really? I'll have to try that."

"Do you like to cook?" Ruth was aware she was asking one of those probing mother questions, but she couldn't resist the opening she'd been given.

She had to admit to a curiosity about the first woman her son had brought about since before his marriage. The looks that passed between them, the way Sean's eyes stayed on Laura's face even when she'd turned aside, the purposeful brushing of hands that reestablished contact with one another—all these added up to the first real interest Sean had shown in anyone in ages. Ruth knew what he'd gone through the past four years, how badly he'd been hurt, how he'd grieved for Danny. She'd despaired that Sean might never be able to accept his son's death and go on with his life. This bright young woman at least seemed to bring a smile to his face.

"Yes," Laura answered Ruth's question. "I only wish I had more time to cook. I get busy and eat too many meals on the run. One of these days, I'll *make* the time."

"Laura works two jobs, Mom," Sean explained. "She has her own design studio and also decorates model homes for her father's real estate company."

Not anymore, Laura thought, but she hadn't told Sean she'd terminated her work for her father.

"Small wonder you don't have time to cook." Ruth's gaze traveled about her dining room and through the archway into her living room, wondering how her simple home looked to the eyes of a decorator. "I guess this place would never appear in *House Beautiful,* but it suits me."

When they'd arrived, Laura had stopped to admire the piano in the living room where at least a dozen framed photos showed off Ruth's family. There were several of Sean, of course, and Danny. Also a tall man with thinning, sandy hair who had to be Sean's father. And above the fireplace hung another colored sketch of Danny in a small rocking chair wearing pajamas and a mischievous grin.

But not a single snapshot or drawing of Kim.

"Your home is lovely, Mrs. Reagan," Laura told her

honestly. "The colors you've chosen are soft and restful, your furniture is cozy and comfortable. It's a place that invites a visitor to sit back and stay awhile. Not too many people can carry that off."

Sean looked at Laura and decided she meant the compliment. "I grew up here," he told here, "and you're right. My friends used to tell me they loved coming here." He swung his eyes to his mother. "All because of Mom."

"The chocolate-chip cookies I usually had on hand helped," Ruth said with a laugh. "Laura, you must decorate some fabulous places."

"Yes, I do, but the warmth that you have here, it's difficult to duplicate unless the people themselves reflect that in their lives. I grew up in a great big house, three stories, seven bedrooms, a walk-in refrigerator. My father had it professionally redecorated after my mother died when I was ten. It had all the warmth of the public library." Her smile was a little crooked. "I go along with Sean. You've made this house into a home."

Ruth heard the longing in the younger woman's voice, and her heart melted. She reached across and put her hand on Laura's. "Thank you, my dear. I have a feeling that your present home is a wonderful place to be, as well." She looked at her son. "Is that right, Sean?"

She was cagey, he thought, slipping that seemingly innocuous question in so slyly. He grinned at her so she'd know he was on to her. "From what I've seen of it, Laura's home is as lovely as she is." He checked his watch, saw that it was nearly ten. They'd whiled away three hours and the time had just flown by. "Speaking of Laura's home, I'd better get her back there. I have early morning rounds." Pushing back his chair, he rose. "I hope you don't mind," he said to Laura.

"Of course not. But let's take a few minutes and help your mother with the dishes." She'd noticed on her tour of the kitchen that Ruth didn't have a dishwasher.

"Nonsense. I'm just so glad you both could come."

"You're sure?" Laura asked as Ruth, who was almost as tall as her son, saw them to the door.

"Absolutely." Impulsively, Ruth hugged the slender young woman. "I hope to see you again soon."

Sean spoke up. "You will, Mom." He leaned down to kiss her cheek. "Thanks, as always, for a wonderful dinner." He winked at her. "You done good."

"You're very fortunate to have a mother like Ruth," Laura told him on the way home. "I envy your childhood."

Sean turned onto Scottsdale Road and headed south. "She is terrific, isn't she? My dad was a great guy, too. They had the kind of marriage I always wanted to have." And thought he had there for a while. Only Kim wasn't the person he'd thought she was.

Leaning back in the soft leather seat, Laura was pensive. "I wonder why so many of us can't get it right these days. Molly and Devin seem to be one of the rare exceptions, and even that was the second time around."

"I read somewhere that most people take more time to pick out a car than to choose a mate. Wasn't true with me. I knew Kim for two years before we got married."

"It was with me. I married Marc after knowing him about two months. Not long enough, by far."

Sean turned onto her street and left the noise of a busy street behind. "If you ask me, it's a crapshoot. Some get lucky, some don't. Some get burned and are hesitant to try again. Look at your father. He never married again."

Laura didn't particularly want to look too closely at

her father's record with women, so she gave him an ambiguous answer. "My father dates some, usually attractive and intelligent women. Personally I think they figure out rather quickly that to be with him is to let him dominate, so they back away. If they're smart."

Sean swung into her driveway and cut the powerful Mercedes engine before turning to her. It was unseasonably warm for February, shirtsleeve weather in Arizona, a lovely starlit night. He was in no hurry to say goodnight. "You and he not getting along?"

"You could say that. I sent him a letter of resignation on Monday." She knew Owen had received it by now, but she hadn't heard from him.

"Something happen or just on general principle?" He felt comfortable enough with her to ask.

"I should have quit a long time ago. We see things so differently. But this last incident over the weekend where one of his friends made a very aggressive pass at me in his home while I was ostensibly there to advise him on redecorating was the last straw. Dad thought I should overlook the big oaf's pawing hands. I thought otherwise."

Sean decided he liked Owen Marshall less each time they discussed him. "He dismissed the pass as just another good old boy's prank? It seems that the friendship ties in certain groups of men are next to impossible to break. They excuse all sorts of behavior. And misbehavior. He stuck up for the guy, right?"

"Yes, he did." Laura's sigh was ragged. "I should also tell you that he's had you investigated. You might as well know all the sordid details. I never mentioned your name, but he heard through his own special grapevine that I was seeing you, I guess." She turned to him, searching his face in the spotty moonlight. "This is your cue to run away from me as fast as you can. I couldn't fault you if you did."

"Your father had me investigated?" Sean laughed out loud, surprising Laura. "Did I pass muster?"

She saw no resentment or anger in his eyes. "You're taking this awfully well. Here I want to apologize for my father's crude behavior and you find it funny."

Sean sobered, taking her hand. "I find it funny because I'm not afraid of Owen Marshall. He can check all he wants. There's nothing in my background that he can use against me or he'd have found it by now and done just that. But I'm curious. Does he check out every man you date?"

"I don't know. This is the first one he's told me about. It's probably because I married Marc so quickly—did I tell you we eloped?—before Dad thought I was serious about him. I know he regrets not having had him investigated."

"Would you have believed the report if he had?"

"Probably not. I don't believe in these character searches. Marc would have come out squeaky clean because he'd never been in trouble. He wasn't exactly a con man, not then. He turned into one when he decided to marry me in order to get ahead financially."

Sean looked down at their intertwined hands. "So then, if that theory's right, and I came out squeaky clean, does that mean your father warned you that I could still be after your money?"

"This is a silly discussion, and I'm sorry I mentioned it."

"Humor me. What did he say?"

Honesty in a relationship. It's what everyone *said* they wanted, but did they really? She was about to find out. "He said that you had a good income with lots of potential but you couldn't retire just yet on that, not like you could if you married me.''

Sean let that sink in, knowing she'd hated to tell him. Then he touched her chin and turned her head so she'd look at him. He saw her eyes were bright with unshed tears and he wondered how many other men Owen Marshall had frightened off.

''First, let me say that I don't give a damn about your money or his money, as I've said before. I make enough. Secondly, I didn't become a doctor so I could stash away piles of money as quickly as possible, then retire.'' He saw that she wanted to interrupt him, but he held up a hand to stop her. ''Let me finish. I don't know where you and I are going with this so-called relationship, Laura. I know I love being with you. I find you funny and kind and very attractive. I've also told you from the beginning that I'm not real good at being married. But, however far we go, we won't split up over money. It's the least important thing between us. Do you believe me?''

''Yes, and I couldn't have said it better myself. Thank you for understanding.'' Her emotions precariously close to the surface, Laura struggled to retain control.

''I'm sorry your father hurt you. I'm sorry that bastard Marc hurt you. I hate the thought of *anyone* hurting you. Even me.'' Her eyes were huge and seemed to be asking a question. ''What? What is it you want?''

''I just want you to hold me, hold me really tight.''

Awkwardly with the console between them, Sean eased her closer and put his arms around her. She wasn't crying, not visibly, but he thought she might be on the inside. He kissed her hair and sat holding her for a long while, neither of them saying a word.

Finally, Laura moved back, her eyes downcast. "I'd ask you in, but you said you have early rounds."

Sean had come to a decision, one he'd been thinking about for weeks. It was time to stop fooling himself. He wanted her, and waiting wasn't going to change that. "Tomorrow's my day off. I can make rounds any hour. Ask me in."

She knew what he meant by that, that asking him in was tantamount to asking him to make love with her. Though she was edgy with nerves, she knew that's what she wanted, too. "Would you like to come in, Sean?"

"Only if you want me to."

She studied his shadowed eyes and saw what she wanted to there. "I do."

Inside, he again stopped her from turning on the light as he drew her into his arms and kissed her. The kiss started off soft and tender, but escalated when her hands settled on his shoulders, her fingers clenching in the cotton of his shirt as she gave herself over to the kiss. Sean's whole body tightened and his blood began to race.

Laura knew she was quickly losing control as his mouth took over hers, drawing from her. She also knew she wanted to lose control, to experience the mindless loving she was sure this man could bring to her. In the car, Sean had said he didn't know where their relationship was headed. Neither did she. But she didn't want to live with regrets, to realize she could have known the pleasure of making love with him and had backed away out of some unnamed fear.

Yet when he urged her toward the stairs leading up, something stopped her, and she eased back. Trying to catch her breath, she sought the right words as he shifted to nibble her ear. "Sean, do you remember back in the cabin when you said something about our relationship being based on friendship? Well, I've never kissed a friend quite like that. Maybe we should slow down here, friend.''

Sean pulled in a deep breath. "I said that?"

"Yes, and I agreed. Because friendships last much longer than most love affairs."

"You've had a lot of love affairs, then?"

"No, but I'm sure that…"

"What I'm sure of is that I've never in my life wanted a woman more than I want you this very second."

Laura's heart was pounding so hard she was certain he could hear it. He was looking at her with those hungry eyes, waiting for her response. She knew he wouldn't push, that it was up to her. She watched him wet his lips with his tongue and almost moaned aloud.

"What is it you want, Laura?" he asked, his voice low and seductive.

"Please, no guessing games. I don't want to play games."

"This is no game." His arms pulled her fractionally closer where he could feel her breasts through her thin cotton shirt press against his chest, the nipples hardening. His body reacted predictably, and still she watched him silently with those huge blue eyes.

He wanted her, but unless she wanted him just as much, it was no good. He needed to hear it from her. He knew that right now Laura was sensually awakened and filled with needs too long denied. As he was. But she had to answer him. "Tell me what you want."

She read the demand for truth in his eyes. No more running, or denying. "You," she whispered. "I want you."

If she'd given him any other answer, he'd have found the strength to leave. But she wanted him, and that was all he needed to know. He lowered his head and touched his lips to hers.

She'd expected stunning passion and hot kisses, but instead, his mouth merely brushed back and forth over hers, sliding and caressing, stopping to kiss the corners, then returning to capture the fullness of her lips. He drew her bottom lip into his mouth with his teeth, nipping here and there, then kissing the corners. Swaying with him, Laura let him take over completely.

His hands on her back pressed her closer and closer yet, unhurried yet stimulating the skin beneath her thin shirt. Everywhere his strong fingers touched, he lit a fire. And still his lips merely played with hers. Losing patience, she slipped her tongue into his mouth and finally felt the response she'd been craving.

Sean pulled in a sharp breath followed by a deep moan as he met her thrusts with bold strokes of his own. His hands at her back drifted lower, pressing her soft, giving warmth into his hard, aching need. Finally, he could take no more of this standing up and raised his head.

"Is there a bed in this house?" he asked, his voice hoarse.

Under the circumstances, Laura didn't think she could laugh, but she smiled at the silly question as she led him up the stairs and to her room. She noticed Max lying on her bed, but not for long as Sean walked over, picked him up and put him firmly out in the hall, closing the door. Moonlight sprinkled in through the curtained window, and they needed no more light. She stood alongside her big bed and he came to her, his eyes devouring her.

Sean saw a slight tremble take her and slowed down, kissing her gently, lengthily. But when his fingers started to fumble with the buttons of her shirt, her hands stopped him.

She blinked twice, her eyes luminous in the pale light. "I...I'm a little nervous here. All right, I'm a *lot* nervous. When a woman finds out that her husband married her for all the wrong reasons, that he didn't want her but just her father's money, it tends to mess up her self-esteem. Forgive me, but now, when a man says he wants me, I find it hard to believe. I want to, but..."

"I know exactly how you feel." Sean took a step back, giving her her space. "It happened to me, too, Laura. Kim left me for another man." He sat down on the bed, looking suddenly weary.

"Another man? But I thought you told me she left to spend time with her parents?"

"That's what she'd told me. But after I saw them off on the plane, I went back to the cabin to pack my things. I found a note on our bed next to my open suitcase where Kim was sure I'd see it. It was short and to the point. She was tired of the long hours I worked and the dedication to medicine that she felt was stronger than my feelings for her. She didn't think I'd ever change. She'd met this other man, one who made her feel special. She was leaving me, taking Danny, saying he'd be better off without me, too. She'd already seen a lawyer and planned to stay with her parents until the divorce was final." He let out a ragged sigh. "Finally I knew why she'd insisted on going and why her father had bullied me into letting them go."

There it was, the something she'd felt all along that he'd left out when he'd told her about the plane crash. What a cruel coward his wife had been, Laura thought as she sat down beside him. "Then if anyone's to blame for them being on that plane, it was her, not you. She had an agenda, Sean, a plan she'd obviously worked out with this other man. She'd apparently convinced her father to help her.''

''I can't believe she thought I'd let her have Danny just like that. I'd have fought her in every court in the country.''

''She probably figured you would, which was why she wanted to move to the protection of her parents' home. After the accident, did her mother and you talk about this?''

''Briefly, at the funeral. I didn't mention the note, but Anne was very bitter. She'd lost everyone dear to her and she blamed me for neglecting Kim, for making her daughter so unhappy that she'd planned to leave me. She said Kim had called begging her father to come get her and Danny, that she had to get away from me.''

''That was her grief talking. Did you talk later, when she'd had time to adjust?''

''She refused my calls and sent my letters back unopened. She slammed the door on me, so I finally stopped trying.''

''It's difficult to blame someone who's died, especially if that someone is your daughter, so naturally, she blamed the only survivor. Besides, who knows what Kim might have told her.'' Her heart went out to him, having to deal not only with his wife's death, but her betrayal. Now she knew why there were no pictures of Kim at the cabin or at his mother's home. ''Ruth knows, I suppose.''

''Yes.'' He ran a hand through his hair, wondering if telling her had been the right thing to do. ''I didn't go into all this at the cabin because, frankly, it's very hard to talk about. Only my mother and my partner know all the facts. Like you, I've had trouble trusting the opposite sex after Kim's betrayal. And I guess my ego's bruised.''

His confession had moved Laura. She wanted him no

less, but her desire was tinged with a need to comfort. She reached to stroke his face. "Look at us, two survivors, Sean. We're determined not to let anyone hurt us deeply again." She paused, noticing that his eyes had lost that haunted look. "But we're still friends. Good friends, I hope."

"Yes, we are." He raised a hand to cup her face. "Let's pretend we're two people each without a messy past who happen to like each other a lot and want each other even more. Let's take things nice and slow. We have all the time in the world. And if you want to stop at any point, we will. Okay?"

After searching his face for a long minute, Laura nodded, surprised again at how easily he seemed to understand and relate to her fears. He was right, she did like him a great deal and she wanted him so very much. How could she want something so badly, yet fear it at the same time?

Sean had promised her slow, and slow was what he gave her. Pressing her down onto her big bed, he lay down beside her, then began kissing her. Slow, lazy kisses on her eyes, her cheeks, her ears, her silken throat. His patient ministrations soon had her eyes closing and her body shifting restlessly. He returned to kiss her beautiful mouth, swallowing the soft sounds she made.

But he had to soothe her mind, as well. "Do you remember I told you how long I've wanted you?" he asked, his voice husky.

She did, of course, but she wanted to hear it again. "Mmm, tell me." Was this really happening to her? Laura asked herself. Was she really going to set aside all her fears, all the negative thoughts piled up in her mind, planted there by her ex-husband and her dominating father?

"Since I carried you from your Bronco and lay you on my couch. You weren't even awake, yet I saw how lovely you were and suddenly I was reacting." With one hand, he opened the clip at her neck and released her thick hair. "I couldn't take my eyes off all this gorgeous hair." He trailed his fingers through the heavy waves. "I wanted to bend down and kiss you right then and there."

A slight frown creased her forehead. "But I'm not…"

A finger placed on her lips stopped the rest of her words, for Sean knew exactly what she was going to say. "Don't. Don't tell me again that you're not beautiful. You can't see yourself as I do, as other men do. Don't compare yourself to Tate or anyone else. You're you and that alone makes you beautiful." Leaning down to her, he stared into her eyes, willing her to believe him.

"I want to be beautiful, for you."

He just smiled at that, then bent to nuzzle her neck, breathing in the captivating scent of her skin. He felt her shiver as his tongue slipped into her ear, her hands moving up to grip his shoulders. He took his time, slowly getting her to relax, learning her body through her clothes with his seeking hands. Attuned to her, he knew just when she began losing her awareness of the outside world and joining him in one of their own making.

"Close your eyes, Laura. Forget everything and everyone. Just let yourself feel." His lips still roaming her face, he watched her eyelids shutter closed.

He wanted to shatter her control, to see her with her hair wild and loose, those big eyes dazed with passion. He wanted to inhale her feminine scent, to taste the satin of her skin when she was burning for him. The way he burned for her.

Laura felt as if she were tossing about on a restless sea. For so long, she'd been afraid to let herself feel deeply, knowing the loss was sure to come and with it, the pain. She'd denied herself this magical loving, as if by denying the need, it would disappear. Only it hadn't. Sean was awakening her senses, making her feel glorious. His unhurried attention to every part of her, the almost reverent way he kissed her, had her actually *feeling* beautiful, a major accomplishment.

Sean settled his mouth on hers, keeping her busy concentrating on the kiss while he slipped off her shirt, then went to work on her jeans. As she shifted to accommodate him, her eyes met his and he saw the hazy beginning of passion. He rose to remove his own clothes and saw she was watching him with avid interest. When the last piece of clothing fell to the floor, her arms reached out for him.

"You make me forget everything but you and this room we're in," she whispered into his ear as he returned to her. "How do you do that?"

"Maybe you need to forget for awhile. Maybe I do, too."

Her eyes burned into his. "Make me forget, Sean." She touched her lips to his and felt her pulse begin to pound in parts of her that had been lying dormant for many months. His mouth was hard against hers, almost bruising, and exactly what she needed right now.

The vulnerability, the hesitancy that she'd shown earlier, was suddenly gone. And gone was Sean's patience. Excitement thudded through him as her dark, rich taste exploded on his tongue. He felt her tremble, felt her body arch toward him and felt a wildness he had only imagined before take over. Yet he gentled his touch long enough to remove her bra and toss it aside. Then he dipped his head and kissed her breasts, the swollen peaks welcoming him. A soft moan escaped from Laura, and the sound urged him on.

His hands traveled down her rib cage before removing the last satin barrier as she shifted to allow him access. He took his mouth on a journey of her slender frame as her trembling hands settled in his hair, flexing with each new discovery. He rubbed his face against her and felt her startled response.

Then he was everywhere seemingly at once, his hands and mouth, his teeth and tongue, touching her, kissing her, driving her. Trying to keep up, Laura found her body could no longer be still. Unable to believe she could ever be this helpless, Laura felt herself buffeted by quivering waves of longing. Wanting him to be as powerless as she, her hands caressed his broad chest, her fingers tangling in the soft, tawny hair. Then her fingers moved lower and closed over him.

Sean sucked air in as a sharp gasp came from between his parted lips. He felt her hesitancy return as she caressed him somewhat awkwardly, though her touch still had the power to jolt him. His desire for her had built slowly over the two weeks he'd known her, like sand in an hourglass patiently drifting downward. Now it was raging, streaking like the winds across a turbulent sea. His fingers moved into the hot center of her while he watched her face, first the shock, then the sensual delight.

He sent her climbing slowly, her body reaching out to him. At the first startling peak, her eyes flew open in shocked pleasure. A rosy blush stole over her features and then, before she could catch her breath, he sent her soaring again.

Suddenly he was inside her as Laura's hands tightened at his back, her whole being alive and in tune with this one man who was making her feel as she'd never felt before. Making love had never been this intense, this potent, this beautiful. It felt like a breathless race, like a storm out of control, building, building. It felt like joy, like freedom.

It felt like love.

He moved with her, leading the way, guiding her home. For the first time in her life, Laura didn't feel so alone. When she was sure it was impossible to fly higher, he showed her more.

Laura took her time drifting back to the real world. Her system was slow on recovery, but perhaps it was also because she was reluctant to return. She'd known she'd find physical release when she and Sean made love, but she hadn't expected to be catapulted into a beautiful sea of sensation. No woman alive could turn away from such an experience untouched, Laura decided. Her eyes closed, she clung to the glow of the aftershocks, unwilling to lose the feeling.

Sean wasn't sure he could move, though he was very sure he didn't want to. Of course, he knew he must. "I'm crushing you," he said quietly, and made as if to roll over.

"No, no, you're not." Her hands at his back urged him to remain. Just a little longer before the bubble would burst. Had her memory dimmed or had this really been so out of the realm of her previous experience? And how was Sean feeling? Did he want to just get away from her, to hurry home, now that it was over?

He lifted his head and watched her eyes open slowly, the haze finally clearing and reflecting a wariness that surprised him. Smiling down into those gorgeous blue eyes, he kissed her gently. "I could stay here all night just like this, but I'm too heavy for you." With that, he rolled onto his side, taking her with him, settling her against his still damp body. "There, isn't that better?"

All of Laura's insecurities returned in a rush. "I thought you were anxious to leave," she blurted out.

Frowning, he angled his head so he could look at her. "Why would I want to leave? Do I strike you as a one-night stand kind of guy?"

He didn't, but she was so afraid to believe that he wanted more than what they'd just had. "Not really. But you have to get up early and…"

"My day off, remember?" However, something else occurred to him. "Unless you want me to leave."

Never. She never wanted him to leave. The word *love* that had floated into her consciousness awhile ago came back to taunt her. No, she mustn't introduce that four-letter word into their tenuous relationship. She needed to be casual, cool, nonthreatening to his freedom, or he really would go running out the door.

Laura gazed into his gray eyes and smiled. "I don't want you to leave."

"Good. That makes two of us." He held her close, adjusting her one leg over his, twining them together intimately. "I had a feeling making love with you would be like that."

"Like what?"

"Like a volcano erupting, like a free-falling dive from a plane, like the great experience it should be, but isn't always."

His words sobered her even more. "I know what you mean. I probably shouldn't tell you, but it's never been like that for me, not until tonight. You're really very… skilled."

Sean chuckled. "It's not skill, Laura. It's having the right partner." He could say that now, though during his years with Kim, he'd wondered why she'd never seemed too enthusiastic about going to bed with him, had never initiated their lovemaking, not even once. He'd dreamed of the kind of response he'd gotten from Laura, but refrained from telling her. A man had to keep a few secrets.

She thought over what he'd said as she lay in his arms, both of them quiet. So quiet it was unnerving. In keeping with her resolution to keep things light lest he discover how she truly felt, she rose on one elbow. "I don't suppose you'll believe this after that great dinner, but I'm hungry."

He laughed. "I was just thinking the same thing."

"I make a mean cheese omelette," she suggested.

"You're on." He watched her scoot out of bed and hastily gather up her clothes before she dashed into the adjoining bathroom. Funny thing about women; you could make love with them for hours, kiss every inch of them, but afterward, they needed to shield their nakedness from a man's eyes.

Amused, Sean reached for his jeans and pulled them on, then wandered over to look out the window at a half-moon hanging in an inky sky. If he were in the market for a permanent woman in his life, Laura would be his choice, he thought. She was so responsive, so loving. And a genuinely good person.

Bracing one hand on the window frame, he asked himself what he was afraid of, then. Of having history repeat itself. Of coming home one day and finding a note that she'd found someone else. Of being hurt so badly that this time he might never get over it.

Better to let things be as they were. He loved being with Laura and he certainly loved being in bed with her. He'd take things one day at a time. If you planned too much, things had a way of falling apart.

A movement outside caught his attention. A long black sedan was parked directly across from Laura's house, its motor running. Someone was inside and had opened the door briefly, then shut it quickly. He moved the curtains aside to look more closely. The windows were tinted so he couldn't tell if it was a man or woman behind the wheel, or if the person was alone.

A quick check of his watch told him it was past midnight. Who'd be out there at this hour, just sitting and perhaps watching? As he continued to stare out, the car eased away from the curb and drove off. Odd, Sean thought.

Wearing a thick terry-cloth robe that all but swallowed her slender frame, Laura came out of the bathroom and glanced over at him, her look a bit shy. With the lights on, her natural reserve returned. And there Sean stood wearing only his jeans, his chest bare, his hair mussed from her hands, looking sexy as hell.

"Ready for that omelette?" she asked.

"You bet." Throwing an arm casually over her shoulders, he walked downstairs with her. As they passed her desk, Sean noticed that her message light was blinking and told her so.

"I guess when we came in I wasn't thinking about phone messages," she said with a smile in her voice. She walked over and hit the Play button. The first message was from Marc.

"Laura, I've got to meet with you. I need a favor, and don't tell me you can't help me. Your father's seen to it that no one will hire me in this godforsaken town. You owe me. Call me no matter how late you get in."

Laura sighed. "Not again. I think I know what he wants."

"Money, undoubtedly. But if he's the one who broke

in here, would he be bold enough to call and ask to meet with you?''

"I don't know. Marc's hard to figure." She hit the button to hear the second message.

"Hey, Ms. Marshall, it's Phil at the service station up north. I finally got a good look at your Bronco and the news isn't good. Repairing the front end's going to cost a bundle, but that's not all. Someone put a hole in the brake line, fairly small, like with an ice pick. It's nothing that happened with the accident. This was done deliberately, as I see it. After the brake fluid slowly leaked out, you had no brakes, which is why you had the accident. I need you to call and tell me what you want me to do. Maybe you should consider calling the cops because someone out there's got it in for you. I left the same message at Sean's house, just so he knows, too. Hope you don't mind. Call me, and watch your back."

The blood had drained from Laura's face as she turned to look at Sean, her eyes wide and frightened. "Oh, my God," she whispered. "Someone tried to kill me."

Chapter Eleven

Sean went to the foot of the stairs and listened. Yes, Laura was still in the shower. He walked over to her answering machine and pushed the play button, wanting to hear again the message they'd listened to earlier. Marc's agitated voice sounded like a man at the end of his rope.

"Laura, are you there? Dammit, pick up the phone! I have to see you *today*. Look, I know the last time we were together wasn't exactly pleasant, and I'm sorry, really. All I need is five thousand and I'll leave town. You'll never hear from me again, I swear. I…I owe some guys this money and they're not nice people. Five thousand is pocket change to you. Bring it over to this place where I've been staying, One Hundred Tenth Street, Villa Rosa Apartments, number fourteen. I'm telling you for the last time, if I don't get this money, I won't be responsible for what I do. Today, before noon. Call first, okay?''

His mouth a thin line, Sean stared out the window. Last night, he'd spent the better part of an hour talking with Laura after they'd listened to Phil's message. It had been too late to call him, of course, so he'd held her close through a restless night. Neither had slept much. First thing this morning, she'd insisted on calling the mechanic and hearing all the details. And it boiled down to the same conclusion. Someone had sabotaged Laura's Bronco.

Despite his attempt to reassure her that they'd get to the bottom of this, Laura had withdrawn inside herself. White-faced, she'd put on the coffee after speaking with Phil, and he'd gone up to take a shower. He'd tried to coax her to share the shower in a feeble attempt to get her mind off the person stalking her, but she'd opted to wait until he was finished. He'd walked back down just as the phone was ringing with the call from Marc Abbott.

Sean hadn't thought Laura's face could get any paler, but it did as she listened to her ex-husband's threatening words. Then, as if it was all too much to take in at once, she'd hurried upstairs to shower.

Had Marc been in that black car outside last night, the one he hadn't mentioned to Laura? There were only two people Laura felt might be responsible for disabling her Bronco, Marc or Rafe Collins. Sean hadn't met either one, but his money was on the ex-husband. Whoever Rafe was working for, this wealthy and important man who'd fathered Tate Monroe's son, probably wouldn't get whatever it was they were looking for in her apartment by killing Laura. But if Sean's theory was right, Marc might get a bundle of money if Laura died.

Returning to the kitchen, Sean saw Max standing by

his empty food dish, looking annoyed, as usual. He opened a couple of cupboards and found a can of cat food. But even when he put the food down in front of Max, the cat just stared at him, probably still upset that he'd had to spend the night away from Laura's bed. "Too bad, fella," he muttered.

Sean heard the shower shut off upstairs. He poured himself a second cup of coffee, recalling their conversation last night. In searching his mind for a motive for Marc to ransack Laura's place, he'd asked Laura if possibly the answer was insurance.

Laura had told him she'd taken out a policy on herself and Marc when they'd married, each for half a million dollars. However, after the divorce, she'd canceled both. But did Marc know she'd canceled? Laura didn't think so.

Maybe he'd come searching for the policy on her, Sean had suggested, thinking it was in force and he was the beneficiary. When he hadn't found it, he'd become frustrated and trashed the place. Laura had admitted that Sean's theory was plausible. She'd even mentioned the possibility of arranging to meet with Marc, in a public place, and explain about the insurance policies. But she hadn't come to a final decision.

However, Sean had arrived at one. He listened again to Marc's last message, making a note of his address. He didn't want Laura upset any further, not after the frightening call from Phil. His schedule on his day off was loose. He'd make hospital rounds and afterward he'd be free. Then he'd pay a little visit to Marc Abbott and see if he could persuade him that backing off from Laura would be in his best interest.

Hearing her come down the stairs, Sean put on a smile. She was heart-stoppingly lovely, he thought, wearing a beige silk blouse over brown linen slacks and carrying a striped jacket. Her hair was straightened, falling softly to her shoulders. If it weren't for the shadows under her eyes and the haunted look, no one would guess she was a wreck inside.

"Want some more coffee?" he asked, moving to her and taking her hands in his, finding her fingers chilly.

"I don't think so. I'm jumpy enough as it is." Laura walked to the dining room table and picked up her shoulder bag, searching inside for her sunglasses. She slipped them on, then glanced into the kitchen and saw Max finishing his breakfast. "Thanks for feeding Max." She brushed a fall of hair off her face. "I forgot all about my poor cat."

He moved to her. "Your poor cat is just fine. Wouldn't hurt him to miss a meal, either. It's you I'm worried about. Where are you headed?"

"To my office." The only office she had now that she'd quit Marshall Realty. And still no word from her father. "I have an appointment with Mrs. Hemmings at ten. Of course, if she's more interested in Dad than in hiring me, she may have canceled after talking with him."

Sean tried to see her eyes through the shades. "Are you all right?"

Laura tried to keep it light. "Except for feuding with my father yet again, having my new Bronco out of commission till heaven knows when and some madman who's trying to kill me, I'm just fine." The words tumbled out, ending with a catch in her throat.

Since hearing Phil's message last night, Laura's mind kept inventing scenarios, all of them disturbing. Had Marc truly gone off the deep end? Midway through their marriage, she'd come to the conclusion that he didn't love her, but could he kill her for money? Or was Rafe Collins behind all this breaking and entering as well as disabling her vehicle? What would killing her accomplish, or had he been trying to scare her into cooperating? Yet how could she cooperate when she honestly didn't know Tate's whereabouts? Not that she would reveal them if she did.

Had she royally ticked off one of her clients, a service provider, a wholesaler? The only name that came to mind was Ray Beaumont, and he hadn't had a reason to retaliate until *after* her home invasion. So where was the connection? Who was doing this to her and why?

Her hands trembling, she dug out her keys from her purse, thinking how happy she'd been when she'd come home last night, how thrilled she'd been to share her bed with Sean. And how quickly this nightmare had overshadowed that fleeting pleasure.

Despite her hidden eyes, Sean could read her emotions clearly on her expressive face. Perhaps he should revise his plans. "Look," he said, taking hold of her hand again, "why don't we play hooky today? You can reschedule your appointment and I can get Jonah to make rounds for me. We can do something together, something that'll take your mind off all this." When, he wondered, had comforting and distracting Laura taken precedence over most everything else? Sean asked himself.

She found a small smile. "It's sweet of you to offer, but I'd be really rotten company." She drew in a deep breath, checked her watch and saw that it was nearly nine. "I'd better get going. Maybe we can talk later today."

They most assuredly would talk later today, after he had that chat with Marc Abbott. "All right," he told her as they walked to the door. "Do you have a cell phone?"

"No. I've always had a car phone so I didn't think I needed a cell. But now with this rental car..."

"Take a few minutes today and get one, will you, please? For my peace of mind." He took her into his arms, and she stiffened, then finally relaxed. "I care about you, Laura," he said, knowing it was true, knowing she needed to hear it.

Laura felt her eyes fill and fervently wished things were different. He was only saying that now because she was obviously afraid and vulnerable. How much better it would have been if he'd told her last night as they'd made love. She'd had a good cry in the shower, then told herself she wouldn't cry again, not over the mess her life was or the fact that she'd fallen in love with a man who wanted only an intimate friendship.

Blinking behind her glasses, she stepped back. "I know you do, and I care about you, too. I'm sorry that last night didn't turn out quite like we'd hoped."

"Parts of it were wonderful, and there'll be other evenings." He kissed her lightly and took a card from his shirt pocket, handing it to her. "These are all my numbers—my home, the office, my pager and the cell phone. Even the hospital. You can always reach me at one of them. Call me later, will you?"

She nodded as they stepped outside. It was a beautiful, sunny day, quite warm for nearly March. Locking the door, she took a deep breath. She'd get through this day, somehow.

Sean climbed into his Mercedes parked in the drive, then turned back to her as she hit the remote to open the garage. "Tell me, what kind of car does your ex-husband drive?"

Frowning at the question, Laura paused. "A black Honda, the last time I saw him. Why?"

He shrugged, feigning nonchalance. "No reason. Just curious. Talk with you later. Be careful." He backed out and was gone in moments.

Laura stood looking after his car, wondering why Sean would care about Marc's car.

It was nearly noon when Sean turned into the circular drive of Villa Rosa Apartments on 110th Street. Hospital rounds had taken him longer than he'd planned, and he hoped Marc would be at home. He drove slowly, checking the numbers, and found number fourteen around back facing a stucco fence, a large waste disposal bin and beyond that, an alley. Stray papers and a plastic cup blew across the parking lot in a soft breeze. He spotted a black Honda in the parking spot designated for number fourteen. He pulled into an unmarked space nearby and checked out the Honda up close. No, this car wasn't the black automobile with the tinted windows that he'd seen from Laura's window last night.

Looking around, Sean thought that the whole complex could use a coat or two of paint and some general repairs. The gate to the alley was hanging on one hinge, and most of the scraggly shrubs had withered from neglect. The sound of a rock band drifted through an open window from a tinny radio, mingling with a child's cry that went on and on. Walking toward Marc's apartment, Sean decided that this was quite a comedown for a man who'd lived the high life while married to a wealthy woman. It was enough to make someone consider blackmail. Or worse.

Apparently the units weren't air-conditioned, for Marc's window was open. The smell of fried onions wafted through the screen from what was undoubtedly his kitchen. Sean knocked on the door.

Almost immediately, the door was jerked open and a man about five nine or ten stood there, a frown on his unfriendly but handsome face. Barefoot and unshaven, wearing jeans and a black T-shirt, Marc Abbott with his blond hair and blue eyes looked like a thirty-five-year-old all-American boy who'd let himself go to pot.

Scratching the beginning of a paunch, his eyes narrowed as he looked Sean up and down. "What do you want?"

"I think we should talk—about Laura Marshall." Sean saw interest light up his eyes.

"Did she send you to see me?"

"Something like that. Can I come in or do you want to discuss this out here?" Sean watched him measure the four- or five-inch difference in their height, his broad shoulders, his dress shirt and slacks since he'd just come from the hospital. Though he was wary, Marc's curiosity won out over his reluctance.

"Yeah, come on in." Marc walked over to the small kitchen and turned off the stove where he'd apparently been making his lunch. The air was warm and thick with the smell of grease.

Sean closed the door and looked around. The cheap furniture obviously came with the place, used by a hundred others down on their luck, he imagined. He turned back to Marc, who was studying him.

"Don't mind this place. It's temporary. I'm working on a couple of deals." Marc ran a hand over his bristly chin. "So, are you Laura's messenger boy? You got something for me?" His voice was pathetically hopeful.

"Matter of fact, I do." Sean squared his shoulders. "A message. Don't ever call Laura again or you'll answer to me. She owes you nothing and if you bother her again, she's going to the police to press charges for harassment.

She's got all your taped messages saved. Threatening people is illegal, did you know that?''

Marc wasn't quick enough to hide the disappointment, the flicker of fear. ''Oh, yeah?'' His voice hardened, his face flushed with anger. ''What you just said, that's a threat, too.''

''Yes, but I'm not stupid enough to make it on tape. The best thing you can do is get out of town and forget all about Laura.'' He moved two steps closer, knowing his size was intimidating. ''Do you understand?''

''Who the hell are you to tell me what to do?'' But he shuffled backward a couple of steps, his hands just a shade shaky.

Sean noticed an open bottle of cheap whiskey on the counter. ''I guess you could say I'm an interested party looking out for Laura. Where she goes, I go. And if I spot you anywhere near her, your face or your car, I'll be back. Do you get the picture?''

A sly look came over Marc's face, turning handsome into ugly. ''I get it, all right. Whoever you are, you're my replacement. You're moving in, getting lined up to marry her and all that lovely money.'' His sneer was contemptuous. ''Ha! The laugh's on you, buddy. Papa Marshall isn't about to roll over and die and give you two all that cash. And he definitely calls all the shots.''

Let him think what he would, Sean decided. ''Just butt out and don't worry about us. If you ever break into her home again or go near her car, I'll…''

''Whoa, there, bucko! What are you talking about? I never broke into her place. I don't know what kind of garbage she's been telling you. Right after she threw me out, I went back and used my key to pick up a few things, like wedding gifts I figured she could live without and I could hock since her old man fixed it so I can't get a job anywhere in this stinking town. As for her car, I've never touched it. Why would I? You can't sell a car without the registration.'' Marc pulled the bottle closer and poured himself a generous shot. "I don't know where you get your information, but you're off base.''

Sean kept his face expressionless, thinking over what the man said. Either he was damn good or he was telling the truth. ·

Marc tossed back the liquor, grimaced, then swiped at his mouth with the back of his hand. "All I did was ask her—no, beg her—to loan me a couple thousand. I...I got involved with some guys who have a short fuse, and I owe them some money. If I don't pay, it could get ugly. And she can afford it. Just five grand and I'm gone. For good.''

Sean wasn't sure he believed all of it. Marc Abbott had the look of a con man who'd gotten by on his looks and quick wit all his life. "You never broke into her home, looking for something, maybe, like an insurance policy?''

"Hell, no. I called the insurance company. She canceled that policy the day we split. She's no dummy, you know. Nothing left I could hock, so what would I be looking for?''

Sean was beginning to believe him. "If I find you're lying...''

"I'm not, I swear.'' His eyes became shrewd. "What's it to you, anyhow?''

"Like I said, I'm a close friend of Laura's.''

"Uh-huh.'' Marc's gaze took in Sean's expensive clothes, his watch, even his haircut. "Well, close friend, maybe *you* could come up with the five grand. I swear I'll take off for good. You won't have to track me down again.''

Sean actually considered paying him off, if only he wasn't certain that a guy like Marc would never truly disappear. He'd be back trying to bleed them for more. "I don't think so." He put his hand on the doorknob.

Marc's face changed from shrewd and hopeful to mean and ugly. "Then get out of here. Go back to Laura. You look like you deserve each other. You'll grow old waiting for Papa Marshall to come through. Meantime, you'll pay your dues spending time in that cold fish's bed. She's about as much fun as kissing your sister. She lays there stiff as a board, like a…"

Marc's next words were cut off by a huge fist that rammed into his chin, knocking him down, his head slamming onto the floor as he fell. Trying to sit up, he scooted back, worried the guy with the iron fist would hit him again. "Hey, back off, man. I was only telling it like it is."

Sean bent over the sniveling punk, flexing the fingers of his right hand, grabbing a handful of T-shirt with his left. "Don't you ever mention her name or talk about Laura again, not to anyone. You pack up and get out of Arizona tonight, because if you aren't gone in the morning, I'll find out and I'll go looking for you." He let go and heard Marc's head hit the worn linoleum floor again.

Unhurriedly, he left the stinking apartment and walked to his car. He got in and sat behind the wheel, taking a moment. He so seldom ever lost his temper that the fury of it startled even himself. He looked at his right hand, the knuckles red and already swelling.

He'd reacted before thinking, but he was sure Marc wouldn't be reporting him for assault. He believed he got his message across in spades. There was no reason for anyone to know about this visit, least of all Laura, if he could avoid it. She'd either be angry or upset, and she didn't need either emotion right now.

Sean sat staring at his fist. He'd reacted like a street brawler, which he'd never been. He'd reacted like a friend protecting a woman. No, not quite right. He'd reacted like a lover angry that someone had dared speak badly of his lady love.

What had he gotten himself into? Sean asked himself as he turned on the engine and left the apartment complex.

Sean checked his watch. After six in the evening. He'd started calling Laura around two, at her office, at home, even at Marshall Realty. She wasn't anywhere. He'd called every hour or so, and still hadn't reached her.

He was getting worried.

Now that he was fairly certain Marc wasn't the one who'd trashed her place or damaged her Bronco, he shifted his suspicions to this Rafe Collins character who'd sounded more sinister than desperate in the messages he'd left. A hired thug or bodyguard or whatever he was, one who'd tampered with a brake line, wouldn't hesitate to try again, and Sean had no idea where Laura was.

He'd left Marc's place, grabbed a bite of lunch, then driven to his house and worked on the back deck he was building. He'd needed the physical outlet despite his swollen hand. But even that hadn't distracted him from worrying. He'd left her all his phone numbers, and she hadn't called even once.

Where in hell was she?

If that toad, Marc Abbott, had sought her out after Sean left and harmed her in any way, he'd find him and rearrange his pretty-boy face. The thought shocked Sean.

He wasn't a violent man, yet look what he was considering. How far he'd come, the man who hadn't wanted to get involved.

Annoyed with the direction of his thoughts, he took a quick shower, got dressed and took off in his Mercedes. He had to do something; this inaction was driving him nuts. He drove to Laura's house and nearly plowed into her rental car parked in her driveway. That had to mean she was home.

Hurriedly, he rang the doorbell. He could hear the sound echo through the house, but nothing else. Damn, why hadn't she gotten a dog? He'd get her one tomorrow, and to hell with Max. If only she was all right. He pressed the button again, then walked over to the window, trying to peer inside.

Through the sheer curtain, he saw movement, someone on the couch slowly getting up. In moments, he heard the dead bolt lock slide open just before the door opened. His annoyance turned to relief.

She was wearing the same oversize white terry-cloth robe, her feet bare. Her hair was loose and mussed, her eyes still sleepy as she looked up at him. "Sean. Oh, I said I'd call you, didn't I?"

"Yeah, you did. What are you doing, opening the door before checking who's on the other side?" Anger warred with relief at finding her unharmed.

"I saw you through the window." She looked over her shoulder at the mantel clock, squinting. "What time is it?"

"Nearly seven. I've been calling you for hours."

"I'm sorry." Stepping back, she swung the door open wide, then strolled back to the couch as Sean followed her, locking the door behind them. "I had a bad morning, so I came home and took a long, hot bath. I thought I'd lie down and close my eyes for a few minutes.'' She stifled a yawn. ''I guess I fell asleep.'' She gazed up at his frowning face. ''I didn't mean to worry you.'' She was so unused to anyone worrying about her that it was hard to accept. ''Please don't be angry with me. I don't think I can handle another angry person today.'' She curled up in the corner of the couch, drawing her feet up, and used both hands to push back her hair.

Sean sat down alongside her, slipping his right arm with its injured hand along the couch back out of sight. ''Who's angry at you?'' he asked gently.

''Eleanor Hemmings. My father. And you, I guess.''

He saw that her eyes looked a little swollen, but from sleep rather than from crying, a good sign. ''Not me. I'm not angry, but I was worried.'' He decided to keep it light. ''I'm like that. If I call all your numbers and you're not anywhere, I drag out the worry beads. I worry about everyone I care about. Ask my mother. She's the one who coached me as a little kid and taught me to be this big worrywart.''

She didn't smile, but she did brighten a little.

Sean scooted closer. ''So what's with Mrs. Hemmings? Is she not going to work with you because you and Owen had a rift?''

''No, she's not mentioned my father. It's just that she's so demanding, which I'm used to with the ultrarich. However, she wants her entire home remodeled, all twenty-two rooms, removing all traces of the former owners who, in her opinion, had ghastly taste. And wants it all done yesterday.''

''That sounds impossible.'' The rest had been good for her, he decided. The bruise under her eye had all but disappeared.

''It is impossible. Apparently Dad told her I could

make the impossible possible. She's going to drive me crazy before her home's finished. And she's got a hair-trigger temper. Undoubtedly used to people saying how high when she says jump.'' She gave in to an expansive yawn. ''She wasn't very happy with me when I gave her an estimated time line for each room. I don't care who she is, I won't be rushed and wind up with a sloppy, hurried job.''

''Good for you. She'll get over it when she sees what great work you do. And what's Daddy Dearest all in a huff over?''

''Same old, same old. He called and told me to make an appointment with Ray Beaumont and I refused. He offered to double my commission and tear up my resignation letter. When I still said no, he really blew.'' Laura shook her head, remembering. ''He's going to give himself a coronary and then blame me.'' She turned to him and saw he'd moved quite close. Looking at him, his solid strength, those kind gray eyes, she wanted to just curl into his lap and stay there forever. Instead, she changed the subject. ''And what have you been up to? Delivered any future presidents?''

''Not today. I made rounds, ran a few errands.'' He reached to touch the ends of her hair, inhaling the bath powder fragrance of her, and found himself wishing he'd have been here to get in the tub with her. Never in his life had he wished such a thing. ''Then I went home and worked on my deck.''

''I'd like to see it sometime.'' Shifting, she snuggled into the crook of his arm, loving the feel of him.

''Anytime.'' He tightened his arms around her. ''Are you hungry?'' he asked, wondering if she'd bothered to eat.

''I had a banana and some cookies awhile ago.''

"Your eating habits are deplorable."

"I know." She stroked his arm, her fingers trailing down to his hand. She stopped, holding up his hand, noticing the swelling, the redness. "How did you do this?"

Sean was about to find out how good a liar he was. "Working on the deck."

Laura studied the cracked skin by each knuckle, the purplish discoloring. Suspicious, she angled to look at him, searching his eyes. "No, that's not how you got that injury, Sean. I'm not medically trained, but even I can tell that you hit something with your fist. Tell me what?"

In too deep, he improvised. "I got mad when I measured a board wrong and slammed my fist into the wall."

Funny how he wouldn't meet her eyes. "You're a terrible liar, do you know that?"

He was silent, his eyes downcast.

She waited, then decided to prod. It must have something to do with her if he was so reluctant to confess. "Tell me," she insisted.

Defeated, fresh out of lies, Sean leaned his head back against the couch. "I went to see Marc."

Laura sat up straight. "How did you know where he lives?"

He didn't want to have this conversation, but he also didn't want lies to be a part of their relationship. "This morning, when we listened to Marc's message, I made a mental note of his address. I'm sick and tired of him upsetting you, so I decided to pay him a little visit."

She wasn't entirely surprised. She'd rather suspected Sean was a take-charge person. She took his bruised fist into both her hands, noticing how swollen his knuckles were. He shouldn't have taken it upon himself to act on her behalf without discussing things with her first, but she couldn't feel anger toward him. He'd taken a big risk for her, especially since Marc was such a loose cannon. "And you hit him?"

"Not at first. We had a little chat." He looked at her finally. "Have you seen him lately?"

"No, not in at least six months."

"He lives in this crummy dump and he was already drinking before noon. I told him to lay off you, no calls and no more break-ins. Then I mentioned the Bronco."

"And he denied everything, of course."

He met her eyes, saw the worry, the suspicion. "Yes, and you know what? I believe him. Oh, he made the calls—obviously, you've got him on tape—but I don't think he broke in here or messed with the Bronco. He'd already called the insurance company and learned you'd canceled the policy. He has no reason to want you dead, or even to search your home. It's got to be someone else."

Laura leaned her head back on his shoulder, sighing. "I guess the next candidate is Rafe Collins. When he calls again, as I'm sure he will, maybe I should agree to meet with him and find out."

"Not without me you won't."

She was quiet a minute or so, thinking. "So, if you believe Marc, then why is it you hit him?"

Sean shrugged dismissively. "Oh, he said a couple of things I didn't like."

Laura could only guess what they were. "About me?"

"Yeah. But I don't think he will ever again."

She sat up, turning in his arms, gazing at his face, his wonderful face. "You hit him because he insulted me? You went to his place, not even knowing what kind of a situation you were getting into, if Marc had a gun or whatever?"

"Don't make such a big deal out of it, Laura. He needed to learn a lesson. He has. End of story."

"Oh, it's a big deal, all right. To me, it's a very big deal." She took his face between both her hands, her eyes warm and slightly damp. "No one, I mean *no one,* has ever gone to bat for me like that." Love for him overwhelmed her. With a soft sound, she pressed her lips to his.

The kiss was as soft as moonlight, as filled with wonder as a newborn child. Her heart awash with this brandnew feeling, Laura held him close, held him fast, wanting to never let him go. "I'm so glad you came back."

"I wasn't sure if, after you found out I'd been to see Marc, you'd want to see me again," Sean said, for he'd been nervous about interfering in her life the way he had.

"Make no mistake about it, mister. I want you in my life, all right." This kiss was even more meaningful, drifting toward sensual as her hands scooted beneath his cotton shirt to caress his warm skin.

Without breaking the kiss, Sean managed to stand up, scooping her into his arms and carrying her upstairs to her room. Drawing out the kiss, he slowly let her body slide down his. But he was half a foot taller than she, so Laura had to stand on her tiptoes to wrap her arms around him. And still he kept the kiss soft, gentle, lazy.

Last night, their first time, had been wildly exciting, fast and furious and wonderfully satisfying. But now, he wanted to take his time, to savor her the way she deserved to be cherished, to taste and explore every part of her. As she buried her hands in his hair, his hands inched between their bodies and fumbled with the belt of her robe, finally freeing the knot. Opening the thick material, he discovered she wore nothing beneath, and his heart began to pound, his blood to heat.

He eased back long enough to yank his shirt off over his head while her fingers opened his belt. Needing to be flesh to flesh with her, he pressed her close up against his chest, feeling the soft mound of her breasts nestle there. A shuddering sigh escaped from him—or was it her?—as he returned to her waiting mouth.

But even that wasn't close enough for either of them. Unwilling to move out of range of her hands, he removed his clothes with a great deal of maneuvering, his lips never leaving hers. Then he slipped the robe off her shoulders and let it drop to the floor. In the glowing light of the setting sun drifting through the window, his eyes feasted on her beauty.

"What do you suppose I did to deserve someone as lovely as you?" he whispered, his voice thick with desire.

There it was again, the feeling that swept over Laura when she was with him like this, where she actually *felt* desirable. There was no answer she could give him, so she sent her eyes on a journey of his magnificent body, smiling when she finally looked up. "You're not so bad yourself, Doctor."

Smiling back, he eased her onto the bed then followed her down. He kissed her again while his hands trailed down her throat, over her breasts, along her rib cage and lower. He touched her in ways no man ever had, learning all her secrets, taking her to the brink time and again, then holding back to pay homage to another area. He heard her ragged breathing, felt her restless prompting as she urged him to take her now. And still he held off, pleasuring her with lips and teeth and tongue until she was ready to beg.

Finally, because he could wait no longer, he entered her with the ease of old lovers and listened to her sweet sigh of acceptance. As the feeling built, he couldn't keep his eyes off her beautiful hair spread out on the pillow, her eyes darkening with each deliberate plunge, her mouth slightly open as her breathing grew shallow. Her hips rose with him, keeping pace, locking him inside her. Sean was certain this was one of those moments he never wanted to end.

Laura climbed with him, knowing that with this man, she'd reach the summit and feel every wondrous thing along the way. She wanted to memorize everything about this moment as her eyes stayed on him. A lock of his flaxen hair hung over his forehead, moving with each thrust. The smooth skin of his back as her hands bunched there, urging him on. His beautiful eyes that seemed to see far more than most. And his mouth that could give her so much pleasure.

Then the explosion came, catching her by surprise, and she cried out as her arms tightened around him. Behind her closed eyelids, colors of the rainbow flashed and receded, leaving her in a wondrous glow. Slowly, slowly she drifted back, knowing she was safe in his arms. Only in his arms.

Her mind and body and heart so full of the feeling, she could no longer hold the words in. "I love you," she whispered.

Chapter Twelve

Almost before the words were out of her mouth, Laura realized she'd made a mistake. A big one. The changes in Sean were small—a slight tensing, his body easing from her, his eyes closing. All that could be just the aftermath of their lovemaking.

Only she knew it wasn't.

At this point, the damage was done, Laura knew. To not have told him would mean living a lie. Whatever their relationship was—and right now she felt it slipping through her fingers like so much sand—she didn't want it based on lies.

Pulling up the sheet to cover herself, feeling exposed in more ways than one, she gathered her courage and turned to him. ''Something's changed for me, Sean, and I couldn't keep it inside any longer. I've fallen in love with you.''

Watching his face, she thought he was making a valiant

effort to keep it expressionless, his eyes remaining closed. She had to go on, to finish this now that she'd started. "Listen, I didn't want this to happen. I certainly didn't go looking for it. But there it is. And I know how you feel about…about not getting seriously involved, about commitment and marriage. I'm hesitant, too, because I've seen an awful lot of unhappy marriages, including my own."

"And mine," he said, his voice steady, even. Cool.

She was dying inside, afraid she'd shatter. Why hadn't she kept still? Why was she always falling for the wrong man? "I'm sorry," she said finally, hating the trembling way she sounded. "I thought I could control my feelings, but apparently, I can't."

Sean opened his eyes and sat up, unsure what he was feeling. There was no doubt in his mind that he cared about Laura. But the word *love* could rarely stand alone. She'd also mentioned getting seriously involved, which indicated a future together. Then there was commitment and, of course, marriage. All the things he'd told himself for the past four years that he'd steer clear of. His reasons were solid, valid, indisputable.

He turned to look at her lying with her head on the scrunched-up pillow, her face pale, hurt unmistakable in her eyes. He felt a sudden rush of need for her together with a fear of what it would be like if he lost her. He simply couldn't bear losing someone else he loved. He had to put a stop to this before it got more complicated. What could he say to her and still be true to himself?

Gently, Sean took her hand and kept his eyes downcast. "My parents had a good marriage, but they had only a dozen years together. Then he died and my mother's lived most of her life alone. She loved him so much that no one else could take his place. Awhile back, I guess I wanted what everyone else seems to want and hardly anyone

winds up with—a good marriage, a wife who was a partner, a lover, a friend, a mother to the children I hoped to
have. I wanted to be as sure of her as I am of my own
feelings for her.'' He paused, his thumb caressing her
hand, trying to find the right words, aware that she was
listening intently.

''When I met Kim, I took my time getting to know her,
and I thought she wanted all the things I did. But I found
out I didn't know her, not really. For nearly a year, I later
learned, she'd been living with me, sleeping in our bed,
caring for our child and seeing another man. She'd said
she loved me, but she didn't mean it.''

Laura could no longer be silent. ''There *are* women like
you envisioned, women who when they say I love you,
they mean it.''

At last, his eyes met hers, and she read pain and confusion in their gray depths. ''Are there? Everybody loves,
or they say they do. They write it on Christmas cards, on
notes, in letters.''

''Some of us mean it and don't say it unless we do.''

''And some of us don't.'' He let out a ragged sigh. ''I'd
give anything if I believed this would all work out, Laura.
As I've told you, from the moment I saw you, something
clicked for me. I love being with you, talking together. I
love the way you look, your wonderful laugh. I love the
intimacy we've shared. I don't want to lose all that. But I
don't feel I can offer more, at least not at this time in my
life.''

He swung his legs over the side of the bed and reached
for his clothes. ''Call me a coward, and you'd probably
be right. I'm unwilling to take a chance on being hurt
badly again.'' He stood to zip up and fix his belt, then
tugged his shirt over his head. After he slipped on his
shoes, he stood looking down at her.

"I told you I hate having you hurt, even by me. I'm sorry if I've hurt you, because I didn't mean to. I'm sorry I'm not all you want me to be. If you want to go on as we have been—as loving friends—you know where to reach me."

Thrusting a hand through his hair, he left her bedroom and hurried down the stairs. Laura listened for the closing of the door before she let the tears fall.

Her own fault, she knew as she struggled with emotions that clogged her throat. He hadn't lied to her, had warned her from the start that he was not interested in love and all that it entailed. She'd told herself she could handle that, but she'd lied to herself. A woman who lies to herself is ten kinds of fool.

Laura wasn't sure how long she stayed in bed, going over each terrible regret. But finally, she got up, slipped her robe back on, blew her nose and splashed cold water on her face. In the mirror, her red-faced, puffy-eyed image didn't please her. Determined not to cry anymore, to put this all behind her and go on, she walked downstairs.

Max uncurled himself from his nap atop the dryer and came to rub up against her legs. Animals seemed to sense when you needed affection, she thought as she picked him up, hugging him close. "Well, it looks like it's just you and me against the world, Max. At least you love me, don't you?" Burying her face in the soft fur of his neck, she listened to his purring and wondered how long it would take her to get over Sean. A great deal longer than it did to get over her disappointment over Marc.

Because she wasn't interested in "a loving friendship," as he called whatever was between them. She knew herself well enough to realize she could never settle for that, not now. Sooner or later, she'd mess things up again by saying something stupid, like the fact that she loved him. How sad that those three little words would send a man running scared. And her father felt that every man she dated wanted her money. Little did Owen realize that even with her great big stack of money, Dr. Sean Reagan didn't want her.

A full week later, Laura came home around seven after a long, busy day to hear the phone ringing. She'd been working hard because it was the only way she knew to keep her mind occupied and off her problems. Annoyed at the quick flare of hope that Sean might be calling, she dropped her briefcase and shoulder bag onto a chair and walked to the desk to answer. The voice at the other end shocked her.

"Tate! Where in the world are you? I've called everywhere trying to find you." Laura sat down in her desk chair, greatly relieved that her friend was calling her.

"Laura, I'm so sorry to worry you. I'm not going to say where I am. For all we know, your phone's tapped."

"What? Oh, Tate, I can't believe he'd go to such lengths. But that creepy Rafe Collins has been calling me, leaving all manner of scary messages, saying he has to see me, even though I've told him over and over that I don't know where you are."

Tate sounded weary as she sighed heavily. "I don't know what to do about him. I called him from a phone booth a week ago and warned him that I was going to the police if he kept this up, but he just laughed. The man's deranged."

"Wonderful. I think he broke into my house recently."

"Oh, no! You weren't home, I hope?"

"No, but I found the mess and panicked. At first, I thought Marc might have been the one, but a…a friend confronted him and we don't think he did. That leaves

Rafe. I guess he was looking for some clue to you, a letter, my address book, your phone number.''

"Probably. I just talked with Molly, and he's been harassing her, too. That's why I'm calling, to warn both of you. Rafe's ruthless, and with Josh's powerful father behind him, he thinks he can get away with almost anything.'' Tate struggled with a rush of emotion. ''God, Laura, I'm so sorry it's come to this. If it weren't for Josh, I'd...''

"It's all right. You have to protect Josh. He's somewhere safe, I take it.''

"Yes, so far. But I worry constantly. Maybe I should go back to Tucson, flush him out, get the police involved. I don't know how else to stop him.''

Laura had been debating telling her friend about the accident, had about decided not to, but she didn't want Tate hurt, either. So she told her friend about the sabotage to her Bronco and heard Tate cry out.

"Oh, Laura, you could have been killed.'' Swallowing hard, Tate Monroe squared her shoulders. ''That settles it. I'm going back to Maggie's. I'll get my old job back and somehow, I'll find a way to end this once and for all. I'm sick of running, of living in fear.''

Laura stared out her window at the darkness settling in, the shadows where anyone could be hiding. She saw a lone dark car drive by slowly, then speed up, and she felt Tate's fear. ''I don't know how you've managed to keep your sanity through all this. I want you to know that whatever you decide, I'm behind you. And I'm sure Molly is, too. If you need anything—money, a place to stay, a job, whatever—you just name it. You hear?''

Tate could no longer stop the tears. So many tears she'd shed over this. ''Yes, I hear,'' she said quietly. ''Thank you, my dear friend.''

"I love you," Laura whispered, the second person she'd said those words to recently. Only she knew that Tate loved her back.

"The same here. I'll be in touch. Take care, Laura."

Slowly, Laura hung up. It seemed as if she and Tate would never get out from under the black cloud following them around. Only Molly was at last happy.

Molly. She needed Molly tonight, her upbeat manner, her caring way. She needed Devin's quiet strength and she badly wanted to cuddle their two children, to remind herself that there was goodness in the world. Quickly, before she could change her mind, she phoned her friend.

"You sound terrible," Molly said after listening to Laura for less than a minute. She'd talked only of Tate's call, but Molly had a feeling there was more to Laura's emotional ambivalence than she was saying. "Listen, Devin's on one of his writing binges. He'll be busy for hours. I can't leave the kids, but I want you to come over here. Right now. Can you?"

She didn't want to be alone tonight, Laura thought. "Yes, thank you. I'll leave in a few minutes."

"Good. I'll put on the coffee. Or would you want tea? Or maybe some wine."

"You, Molly. I just need you. I'll be there shortly." Laura hung up, then hurried upstairs. She wasn't certain she'd be able to pour out her heart to Molly, but she badly needed to be with someone who cared deeply for her.

Having changed into a black shirt, jeans and sneakers, Laura backed her rental car out of the drive and headed north on Scottsdale Road toward Pinnacle Peak. Molly and Devin had built their large southwestern-style ranch house set on ten acres and had moved in just before Christmas. They'd designed every aspect from its circular staircase leading up from the marble foyer to the second floor with its five bedrooms and baths to its third floor where Devin's office looked out on a desert view of saguaro cacti and boulders that would dwarf the tallest man. It was country living yet within half an hour's drive of the city.

The road narrowed as Laura drove, turning on her lights as twilight darkened into evening. No street lamps up this way, and the half moon hid behind a layer of drifting clouds. Fortunately, Laura had made the trip several times, having helped Molly with the decorating during the early stages.

So she drove automatically, her mind on Tate's call. When would her friend ever be free of the jerk who'd fathered her son? How was it that three intelligent women like Tate and Molly and she had gotten involved with men who weren't worth the time of day, much less a serious commitment? Perhaps due to their backgrounds and up-bringing, each had been searching for that perfect love, and in their anxiety, had mistaken attraction for love. In this, they certainly weren't alone.

Laura glanced to the right at Reatta Pass with its large western restaurant, stores and tourist enticements, noting that their parking lot was crowded as usual. Scottsdale's winter visitors tripled the population every year, often causing traffic congestion, but not along the stretch of road leading north. Only one car's headlights could be seen in her rearview mirror.

A couple of miles beyond Reatta, Laura noticed that the car behind her had shortened the gap between them, so she edged more to the right, inviting him to pass her. Only he didn't, but rather moved closer. Squinting into the rear-view mirror, she saw that the car was dark with tinted windows, but couldn't determine the make or how many occupants there were. Suddenly aware of the lonely section of road she found herself on, with an unknown car seemingly tailing her, her heart began to pound.

Why hadn't she gotten that cell phone Sean had suggested to her? Streets out here were few and far between, houses sporadically dotting the land, miles between most of them. It wasn't as if she could pull into someone's drive and ask for help. If she had the phone, she'd call Devin, who'd come meet her, she was certain. But she hadn't gotten around to buying one.

Suddenly, Laura felt a jarring jolt as the car behind tapped her bumper. Her mouth dry, she could think of nothing to do but speed up. Undaunted, the other driver pulled alongside her, skimming the side of her car with his much heavier vehicle. Her small rental rocked as she kept a bone-crunching grip on the wheel. She braced herself as he came at her a second time. What was he trying to do, run her off the road?

Was Rafe in the car, or had she been noticed by someone else who wanted to rob her, or do worse? Laura had no way of knowing as she tried outracing him. They were coming to a curve she could see just ahead in the beam of her headlights, and a steep ditch on the right side. Pressing her lips tightly, she prayed as she tried to keep the car on the road, watching in the side mirror as he moved closer.

Revving up, the big black car came at her a third time, hitting so hard that Laura lost control, zigzagged off the road and into the ditch, the front end hitting a pile of tumbleweed. Her head hit the windshield as the seat belt was wrenched from its socket. The car rolled to a stop in the dry bed of a stream, and the engine died as Laura slumped in the seat, her head lolling back.

Steam escaping from under the hood was the only sound in the pitch-black stillness of the desert night.

The long black car backed up on the road alongside the ditch. A man dressed in black got out from behind the wheel, jumped down into the ditch and opened the driver's door. Leaning in, he felt for a pulse and found one. He returned to the car and climbed in.

"She's alive," he reported to the man in the back seat.

"Good. Now maybe she'll talk, knowing I mean business. Let's get out of here."

The black car drove off into the night.

Dr. Jonah Evans had put in a long, bruising day. He'd had two gyn surgeries in the morning, afternoon office hours and no less than three deliveries. It was after nine, and he hadn't had dinner yet. Yawning, he left the doctors' locker room at Scottsdale General Hospital and took a shortcut through the emergency section on his way to the parking lot. He was almost out the door when the ER doctor on duty snagged him.

"Hey, Jonah, you got a minute?"

Jonah turned. Douglas Green was a young-looking thirty who saw a greater variety of injuries in ER in a year than most doctors did in an entire career. Thin and already balding, he wore heavy, black-rimmed glasses and an anxious expression. Jonah liked him a lot. "What've you got, Doug?"

"Our OB consult's in surgery. I've got an accident case. Concussion, ruptured spleen and a floating clavicle. I also think she's got pelvic damage, but I can't be sure. I'm about to send her up to OR but I thought you might want to take a look. No sign of internal bleeding, but…" He shoved his glasses to the top of his nose, waiting.

"Sure." Jonah followed Doug into the curtained cubicle and saw a slender woman with black hair and very pale skin lying on the gurney. He picked up her chart. "Do you know what happened?"

"Police brought her in. Some tourists found her out near Pinnacle Peak Road. Must've lost control of her car and landed in a ditch, but the cops said there were no skid marks, like she was trying to brake. Maybe she fell asleep or…"

"Wait a minute." Jonah stared at the chart, then the ashen-faced woman lying so still. "Her name. Are you sure this is right?"

Doug peered over his shoulder. "That's what the cops said. I.D. found in her wallet. Laura Marshall. You know her?"

"No, but I know someone who does." Jonah bent down, checked her pupils. "Send her up to OR. We can do a pelvic later. I've got to make a phone call." Hurriedly, he left the cubicle.

Sean paced the corridor outside the OR, a new one for him. It occurred to him that he'd never had a loved one in surgery before where he would have to wait to hear how things went. His mother was remarkably healthy, and his father had died instantly of a massive heart attack. When Kim had been in the hospital to deliver Danny, her labor had been a mere three hours, one of the lucky ones. So worrying and wondering if someone he cared for would be all right was brand-new to Sean.

Since Jonah's call and his own hurried drive to the hospital, he'd been frantically running several scenarios through his mind, fragmented thoughts. Like, was he going to lose yet another woman he loved, this one before he'd told her how much he cared? Like, why had he held firm to the idiotic notion that by denying he cared, he'd escape the pain of loss? And, did Laura have to die in order to jolt him to his senses? Funny how nearly losing someone to death could make a man face some necessary truths.

At the end of the corridor, he dared walk into the scrub room outside the OR, but turned to leave when one of the nurses caught his eye through the window and adamantly shook her head. The hospital had a rule that no personnel could observe unauthorized, and no doctor would authorize if there was a personal connection with the patient. It was a good rule, one Sean was in favor of. Only not this time.

His strides angry, he resumed his pacing. Why had he been so pigheaded? A dozen times a day during the last week, he'd picked up the phone to call Laura because he missed her terribly, because he wanted her desperately. But his silly pride had stopped him. And now, here they were.

Where had she been heading alone on such a dark, deserted road? He'd talked with the cops downstairs and they'd told him by the looks of her car, someone had forced her off the road. It had to be Rafe Collins. He hadn't mentioned the name to the police, not before he could talk it over with Laura. Somehow he would convince her that enough was enough. The man could have killed her twice now. What was he after?

Stopping, Sean stuffed his hands into his pants pockets as he stared out the window at a dark, cloudy sky. He found himself promising God a good many things if only He'd spare Laura more hurt and pain. Kyle Bronson, the orthopedic surgeon operating on her, was a good doctor. Her injuries were not life-threatening as such, although you could never tell in lengthy surgeries. Bronson had hinted that he was surprised she hadn't awakened in ER, that the fact that she hadn't indicated a severe concussion.

This after she'd suffered a mild one as recently as a month ago. How much could she take?

His hands forming fists, Sean decided he'd find her friend, Tate Monroe, and ask her to release Laura from her promise to keep her son's father secret. Tate needed to know that her insistence on not revealing the man's identity was putting Laura in harm's way. Surely, if they were the good friends Laura claimed, Tate wouldn't want that.

"Excuse me," a woman's voice said from behind him.

Sean turned to see an attractive blonde standing there, concern clouding her blue eyes. "Yes?"

"I'm Molly Gray. Would you by any chance be Dr. Sean Reagan, Laura's friend?"

Of course, she'd have mentioned him to her close friend, Sean thought. He wondered how much Laura had told Molly. "Yes, I am."

"How is she doing?" Molly glanced toward the operating room doors. "They wouldn't tell me anything downstairs, just that she was in surgery."

"I don't know much more," he told her, leading her over to a two-seater couch in an alcove. Molly was lovely, tall and slender, wearing a pants outfit in deep blue silk. She was the smart one, Laura had told him. Yes, he could see a keen intelligence in her eyes. "They're putting a pin in her clavicle. It was broken in two places, causing a floating piece. It's the concussion that has me worried. She suffered a minor one up north, and now this."

Molly crossed her legs, frowning. "She was on her way to our house when it happened. That's two accidents in less than a month. I don't know what's happening here. Laura's always been so careful."

Sean decided to speak honestly. "I don't think they were accidents, Molly. Someone's been stalking Laura."

She drew in a quick breath. "Rafe Collins," she whispered.

"Yes, I think so. Has he been bothering you, too?"

"Not this badly. He calls the house often, even though we've got an unlisted number. I've seen the same black car Laura's mentioned. My husband went out one evening to confront him, but, of course, he drove off."

Sean let out a whoosh of air. Of course, the man would hound Laura more since she had no man on the premises. "I think it's time you two told the police what's going on. Twice now, Laura's been hurt. She could get killed over this. Do you think Tate would want that?"

"No, of course not. Tate called to warn both of us earlier tonight. That's why Laura was coming over. She was worried, nervous." Molly studied the strong, handsome face and decided to say her piece. "She was upset over whatever happened between the two of you, also, I believe."

Leaning back, Sean was thoughtful, yet unwilling to say too much. "I care about her. She knows that."

"Does she? Did you tell her that?"

"More or less."

"Then why haven't you two been seeing one another?" Crossing her legs, Molly leaned forward. "Look, I realize I'm interfering, but I love Laura like a sister and, right now, she's unable to speak for herself. She's in love with you. Did you know that?"

Steepling his fingers, he didn't look at her. "Yes."

Molly knew exactly why Sean and Laura had parted company—his unwillingness to commit because he was afraid of being hurt. She wondered if she could make him see what she'd learned the hard way, that if you're alive, if you care, you have to take chances.

Sean swung troubled gray eyes to her. "Driving over

here tonight after hearing about Laura's accident, all I could think of was I can't lose her. I tried to push her away because I was afraid of just this kind of pain. And it happened anyway.''

Molly's voice was soft, kind. ''As long as we're alive, Sean, as long as we care, we risk being hurt. But you know, going through life not allowing yourself to care puts you in far greater pain, to say nothing of the loneliness. I know, because I've been where you are.'' She felt his eyes bore into hers. ''I'd been hurt and I didn't want to feel that again. But when I met Devin, I realized I would be only half alive without him in my life.''

Half alive. Yes, that's exactly how he'd been feeling this past week. ''Thank you for sharing that with me. You're right. I've been only half alive apart from Laura.''

Molly squeezed his hands. ''Be sure to tell her that the moment she's awake.'' She checked her watch. ''I've got to go. I couldn't get a sitter at the last minute, and Devin will be worried. Will you phone me as soon as she's out and let me know how she's doing?''

''Yes, I will. And thanks again.'' He watched her walk away, thinking that he understood why Laura was so fond of Molly Gray. Hearing the double doors swing open, he turned to see Dr. Bronson, his face mask hanging from his neck, coming toward him. The gray-haired orthopedic surgeon had an excellent reputation and was well liked on staff. ''Kyle,'' Sean said, walking to meet him, ''how is she?''

''The operation went well, Sean. She lost some blood and she's weak, but we checked the pelvic area and there's no damage there. Spleen will be fine in time.'' He mopped his face with a white towel. ''The only worrisome thing is her concussion. Apparently she cracked her head so hard that the forward movement of her body pulled the seat belt out. Of course, the police said she was driving a rental car, and maybe it was loose. Best thing she's got going for her, she's young and otherwise healthy. After the recovery room, I'm ordering her to ICU so we can monitor her closely until she wakes up and we can reevaluate her overall condition.''

"Thanks, Kyle." Sean found himself swallowing a huge lump in his throat.

Bronson looked around, then frowned. "Where's Owen? I thought surely her father would be here.''

"Haven't seen him. Was he notified?''

"We called his office. They said they'd locate him." He let out a weary breath and saw by his watch that it was two in the morning. "I'll check on her one more time before I leave." With a wave, he was off.

Sean wavered between being grateful Laura was out of surgery and worry over that severe concussion. He decided to go get a cup of coffee before heading for the ICU lounge, knowing that Laura would be taken there by a different route.

An hour later, informed that Laura was settled in ICU and her vital signs taken and noted, he convinced the male nurse on duty to let him in to her glassed-in cubicle. He moved to her side, staring down at her slim frame beneath the sheet, which was only a shade lighter than her complexion. Her hair was a deep black by contrast. There was a long, wide bruise across her forehead. Her lashes were dark against the pallor of her face.

She didn't look like his Laura, Sean thought as he pulled the lone chair over close to her bed and sat down. His, indeed. What right did he have to her? He hadn't told her he returned her love twenty fold, even though he'd known it for weeks. Almost from the beginning. He had held out precious little hope to her for a future together. Yet she'd still confessed her love for him.

She'd been honest while he'd been evasive. She'd been unafraid while he'd been a coward. She'd led with her heart while he'd hidden behind his past hurt. Seeing her now looking so lovely yet so vulnerable, Sean felt ashamed.

Taking her limp hand in his, he blinked back a rush of emotion. "I'll make it up to you, Laura, I swear I will," he whispered. "Just get better. Wake up and let me look into those gorgeous eyes. Give me that smile that warms my heart. I'll let you beat me at gin and I'll even promise to love your ugly old cat. Just wake up, sweetheart, please."

His thumb caressed her hand, but she didn't move, nor did the monitors flicker. No indication that she'd heard him. Although it's not been irrefutably proven, some people believe a person in a coma can hear. Sean had never had reason to hope so until now.

He stayed awhile longer, holding her hand, whispering to her now and then, until the male nurse kicked him out of ICU, saying he'd get in trouble if he allowed Sean to stay any longer. Running a hand over the stubble of his beard, he checked his watch and saw it was nearly four in the morning. He'd go home, shower and change and come back. He'd talk to Jonah and ask him to cover for him yet again and have the office reschedule his afternoon appointments. He needed to be here, right here, when she woke up, Sean thought as he left ICU.

A tall man in a gray suit, the collar of his white shirt unbuttoned, his tie askew, rose from a chair just outside ICU as Sean walked out. He looked worried, his hair rumpled as if from anxious fingers thrusting through the dark waves, his eyes tired. He approached Sean. "You must be a doctor. I want to see my daughter, Laura, but that nurse in there tells me I can only go in for five minutes on the hour. I'm Owen Marshall. Get me in there.''

So this was the great man, Sean thought, his height giving him a three- or four-inch advantage over the older man. "I've heard about you, Mr. Marshall," he said, his voice even. "I'm Sean Reagan."

Recognition of the name had Owen nodding. "Fine. Get me in to see Laura."

"She hasn't awakened and she can't be disturbed or upset."

Owen scowled. "I'm not going to upset her. She's my daughter. My *only* daughter." His eyes narrowed as he took Sean's measure. "Do you think because you've dated her a few times you've got some authority over Laura? I know the chief of staff in this hospital. I'll get Lou down here and…"

"No one has authority over Laura. She's her own person. However, she is very vulnerable to the people she cares for. That would be you and me. We're also the people who hurt her the most and helped put her in there. I did, but so did you."

"What the hell are you talking about? You don't know me and I doubt you know Laura, from the sound of it."

"I'm the man who walked away from the love she offered me, and I deeply regret that. I plan to make it up to Laura, to marry her, if she'll have me. But you, you've had her all her life, yet you don't know her. You belittle her, intimidate her and punch holes in her self-confidence at every opportunity. Why would a father do that to a beautiful woman like Laura?"

Owen made a disparaging sound. "I get it. You want to marry her, sure you do. Like hell. You want her money. *My* money. Well, *Doctor,* you'll soon find out like the others that I control the Marshall money and Laura, too. Marry her if you must, but you'll not see a dime." His face red and furious, he marched through the swinging doors of ICU.

Sean followed close behind Owen as he approached the male nurse in charge. He spoke to the young man before Owen opened his mouth. "No one is to visit Laura Marshall unless they're cleared through me or Dr. Bronson. Is that clear?" Since Laura had not designated a personal physician on the hospital records, Sean had put himself down as primary, since he'd treated her at the cabin.

"Yes, Dr. Reagan." The nurse looked from one to the other nervously.

"You may think you're in charge, Mr. Marshall," Sean said in a low, commanding voice, "but not in this hospital. I won't have Laura upset. You can come back later, when she's awake, and then, if she wants to see you, we'll let you in." He could see the color deepen in Owen's face, and knew the man would likely go to Lou Albright, the chief of staff, and lodge a complaint, but he didn't care. The patient's needs came first.

"This isn't over, young man. You'll hear from me again." Turning, Owen Marshall left ICU.

Sean let out a ragged sigh. "I'm going home to clean up, Dave," he told the nurse, reading his name tag. "Then I'll come right back. Beep me if there're any changes, and don't let that man back in."

"No problem, Doctor."

Sean left, hurrying to his car, wondering if he'd gotten himself into hot water. Only if Owen was in fact Lou Albright's best friend.

Feeling as he had during his residency days when sleep was something he got in spurts, Sean finished making his rounds by nine that morning. After his confrontation with Laura's father, he'd gone home to shave and stand for some time under a hot shower, then put on clean clothes and grab an English muffin with his coffee on his way back to the hospital. He'd found Laura unchanged, so he'd conferred with Jonah, then heard himself paged. The Chief of Staff wanted to see him STAT.

Taking the elevator to ICU, Sean smiled as he recalled the meeting with Lou Albright, a man he'd had little to do with but had always looked up to. The gods had been with him, for Lou had reviewed Laura Marshall's case and told her controlling father to back off in the interest of his daughter's health. Sean had been concerned that Owen might be one of the hospital's large contributors, which might have changed Lou's outlook, but apparently that wasn't the case. Sean had been told, however, to keep Owen apprised of Laura's condition and to allow him to visit just as soon as she was awake and responsive, provided the patient agreed.

Sean's long strides took him to her bedside where he checked her chart and saw little change. He'd spoken with Bronson earlier, and the orthopedic surgeon had said she was coming along as well as expected. He'd also said she should be waking up any time now.

Pulling the chair over, Sean drew in a deep breath and sat down, taking her hand again. Studying her face, he thought he saw some movement behind her closed eyelids, perhaps a sign that she was beginning to come out of it, or so he hoped. Because he couldn't just sit there doing nothing, he began to talk in a low, confiding tone, words meant for her ears alone.

Sean didn't know how long he talked quietly, telling her so many things—about his childhood, the kind he'd hoped to pass on to his children, about losing his father and, more recently, about losing Danny and even the pain of his wife's betrayal. He went on to confess how foolish he'd been in refusing to acknowledge his love for her, then spoke of how he envisioned their future together, if only she'd wake up still loving him.

An hour passed, then two, and still Laura didn't respond. Head injuries were the worst to wait out, Sean knew. He also knew all her tests came back negative, indicating no brain damage. Still, he couldn't help being impatient and feeling discouraged, probably because he was so very tired.

Unable to keep his eyes open any longer, he leaned forward in the chair, laying his head onto the side of her bed, still holding her hand. In moments, he was asleep.

The thing that woke him was a hand touching his cheek and fingers fanning through his hair. Disoriented, Sean blinked, then straightened and looked into the most beautiful blue eyes he'd ever seen. "You're awake," he said, his voice rusty.

"How long have you been here?" Laura asked, her voice raspy.

"A while." He stood and smoothed the hair back from her face, careful not to touch the bruise on her forehead. "How do you feel?"

"Like I've been run over by a truck. What happened? I remember driving to Molly's and there was this big black car." She scrunched up her face, trying to recall.

"Did he force you off the road?"

"Yes. First he bumped me from behind, then came alongside and kept banging into me. I…I guess I lost control. Was it Rafe again?"

"We're going to look into who it was soon." He didn't want to go into all that with her now. Later, he'd talk with

Molly and hopefully they'd convince Tate to call in the authorities.

She lifted a hand to where a tight bandage crisscrossed her chest. "What's this?"

"It's called a figure eight, to help keep you immobile. You broke your clavicle. They had to put in a pin. It'll heal just fine in time." He sat down, smiling into her face, knowing from her clear questions and answers that her mind was lucid. "You have to take it easy for awhile. No water skiing or mountain climbing or even bowling."

She smiled. "Oh, darn." Growing serious, she laced her fingers with his. "I...I've missed you."

"I missed you more." He leaned closer. "I'm through lying to myself. I love you, Laura."

Hope flared in her eyes, but doubt moved in quickly. "Are you sure? I need to know you want me for the right reasons, Sean. Not because I had this accident and you feel sorry for me."

"I admit the accident helped clarify a few things." His hand caressed her cheek. "I almost lost you, Laura. The very thing I've been afraid of, afraid to risk. I've come to realize that loving someone is always a risk. I want to spend the rest of my life with you. Will you marry me?"

She closed her eyes a moment, then smiled. "Mmm, how I've wanted to hear you ask me that. Yes, I'll marry you."

"It might not be easy for you. Your father hates me."

"You met him?"

"Oh, yes. He wanted to muscle his way in here and I wouldn't let him. Then he tried to bully the chief of staff, but that didn't work. I imagine he's out there now, fuming away."

Laura smiled. "My, my. Someone who got the upper hand on Dad and there was nothing he could do about it.

I love it." She paused, her eyes roaming his wonderful face. "I love you." She opened for his kiss, thinking that if she had to break a few bones to get Sean to realize he loved her, it was well worth it.

"As soon as you get out of here, I want you to come stay at my place. Even if Rafe Collins wasn't on the loose still, I'd want you with me. I don't want to waste any more time. I want to take care of you, get you well. I want to hold you every night and wake up with you every morning. Think you can handle being married to a doctor?"

"Do you have your lucky coin with you?" she asked.

"I think so." He dug in his pocket, pulled out the coin.

"Okay. Heads we get married today, tails we tie the knot tomorrow."

Smiling, Sean tossed the coin in the air and didn't bother to watch how it landed, because he was too busy kissing his bride-to-be.

*   *   *   *   *

As the father of Tate's child gets closer to her, so does the man she'd always hoped to find!
Don't miss Tate's story in
THE LAWMAN AND THE LADY,
coming in August
from Silhouette Intimate Moments.

Silhouette®SPECIAL EDITION®

presents an exciting new miniseries by

PATRICIA McLINN

A PLACE CALLED HOME

WHERE WYOMING HEARTS BEAT TRUE...

On sale August 2000—
LOST-AND-FOUND GROOM
(SE#1344)

On sale September 2000—
AT THE HEART'S COMMAND
(SE#1350)

On sale October 2000—
HIDDEN IN A HEARTBEAT
(SE#1355)

Available at your favorite retail outlet.

Silhouette®
Where love comes alive™

If you enjoyed what you just read,
then we've got an offer you can't resist!

Take 2 bestselling
love stories FREE!

Plus get a FREE surprise gift!

Look Who's celebrating our 20th Anniversary:

Celebrate **20** YEARS

"In 1980, Silhouette gave a home to my first book and became my family. Happy 20th Anniversary! And may we celebrate twenty more."

—*New York Times* bestselling author
Nora Roberts

"Happy 20th birthday, Silhouette. You made the writing dream of hundreds of women a reality. You enabled us to give [women] the stories [they] wanted to read and helped us teach [them] about the power of love."

—*New York Times* bestselling author
Debbie Macomber

"I want to wish Silhouette a heartfelt congratulations on their twenty years of creative endeavors. May the next twenty years be equally successful, and if I get lucky, I'll celebrate that one with Silhouette, too."

—International bestselling author
Lindsay McKenna

Silhouette®SPECIAL EDITION®

COMING NEXT MONTH

#1339 WHEN BABY WAS BORN—Jodi O'Donnell
That's My Baby!

Sara was about to give birth—and couldn't remember anything except her name! But a twist of fate brought Cade McGivern to her in her moment of need, and she couldn't imagine letting this unforgettable cowboy go. Still, until she remembered everything, Sara and Cade's future was as uncertain as her past....

#1340 IN SEARCH OF DREAMS—Ginna Gray
A Family Bond

On a quest to find his long-lost brother, reporter J. T. Conway lost his heart to headstrong Kate Mahoney. But with her scandalous past, Kate wasn't welcoming newcomers. Could J.T. help Kate heal—and convince her his love was for real?

#1341 WHEN LOVE WALKS IN—Suzanne Carey

After seventeen years, Danny Finn came back, and Cate Anderson ached for the passion they'd shared as teenage sweethearts. But Danny never knew that Cate's teenage son was actually his child. Cate hadn't wanted to hurt Danny and her son with the truth. But now she and Danny were falling in love all over again....

#1342 BECAUSE OF THE TWINS...—Carole Halston

Graham Knight was surprised to learn that he was the father of twins! Luckily, pretty Holly Beaumont lent a hand with the rambunctious tots. But Graham was wary of the emotions Holly stirred within him. For he'd learned the hard way that he couldn't trust his instincts about women. Or could he...?

#1343 TEXAS ROYALTY—Jean Brashear

Private investigator Devlin Marlowe's case led him to Lacey DeMille, the Texas society girl this former rebel fell for and was betrayed by as a teenager. Now he had the opportunity for the perfect revenge. But he never counted on rekindling his desire for the only woman who had ever mattered.

#1344 LOST-AND-FOUND GROOM—Patricia McLinn
A Place Called Home

When Daniel Delligatti found Kendra Jenner and insisted on being a part of his son's life, Kendra was not pleased. After all, Daniel was a risk-taker and Kendra played by the rules. Could these opposites find common ground...and surrender to their irresistible attraction?

CMN0700